This month in
HIS HOLIDAY BRIDE
by Elaine Overton

Wild child Amber Lockhart had been looking for
love in all the wrong places. But then single dad
Paul Gutierrez came to her rescue like a real-life knight,
and baby sister began to believe she might have found her
Mr. Right. And when Amber finds a refuge in his home,
with the Yule-log burning and mistletoe in sight,
there is no way she can resist her sexy Latin protector,
or his cute-as-a-button infant son.

Kimani Romance is Proud to Present

THREE WEDDINGS & A REUNION

THE LOCKHARTS—
Three Weddings and a Reunion
For four sassy sisters, romance changes everything!

* * *

And don't miss the final exciting title of

FORBIDDEN TEMPTATION
by Gwynne Forster
November 2007

Available from Kimani Romance!

Books by Elaine Overton

Kimani Romance

Fever
Daring Devotion
His Holiday Bride

Kimani Arabesque

Promises of the Heart
Déjà Vu
Love's Inferno

ELAINE OVERTON

currently resides in the Detroit area with her son and dog. She attended a local business college before entering the military and serving in the Gulf War. She is an administrative assistant who currently works for an automotive-industry supplier, and is an active member of Romance Writers of America. You can contact her via e-mail at www.elaineoverton.com.

Elaine Overton

His Holiday Bride

KIMANI
ROMANCE

KIMANI PRESS™

ISBN-13: 978-0-373-86036-4
ISBN-10:   0-373-86036-6

HIS HOLIDAY BRIDE

Dear Reader,

Thank you for taking the time to read Paul and Amber's story. As you know, this is the third title in Kimani Romance's four-book continuity series, THE LOCKHARTS—Three Weddings and a Reunion. *His Holiday Bride* is probably one of the most fun projects I've done to date. This project included working in conjunction with other authors, and that was a new experience for me.

If you've ever read one of my books, you know I love to pair a spunky, slightly flawed heroine with a gorgeous, cocky alpha male. And Paul and Amber are no exception. I thoroughly enjoyed bringing my part of the story of the Lockhart family and their friends to life!

Again, thank you for reading, and I hope you enjoy the book. Also, I would love to hear what you think, so feel free to e-mail me at elaine@elaineoverton.com.

Elaine Overton

To the light of my life,

My son

Acknowledgments

First, to the creator of all, my Father, my Savior, my Comforter…thank you.

Second, to my editor, Demetria Lucas. Thank you for giving me the opportunity to work on this project, and be a part of this terrific series.

Finally, to the wonderful authors who worked with me on this project, Brenda Jackson, Jacquelin Thomas and Gwynne Forster. Thank you, ladies, for your help in understanding how the pieces fit together, and for your willingness to share what you know.

Chapter 1

"I'm not really sure what you expect me to do, Luther. I mean…how old is this girl?" Paul Gutierrez spoke into the wireless headset even while continuing to type away on the laptop braced against the steering wheel, and monitoring the activity of those leaving the back entrance of the posh L.A. nightclub across the street.

"Twenty-one." His friend, and former Navy SEAL commander, Luther Biggens, practically groaned on the other end of the phone line, already sensing defeat.

"Twenty-one? She's a legal adult. If she wants to be with this basketball player there is nothing you can do about it."

"Try explaining that to her sisters."

"Listen, man, I really wish I could help you—" Paul suddenly snapped to attention when the person he'd been looking for peeked his head around the door.

Paul sat completely still while he watched a member of

his personal protection team, Barnett Roberts, look up and down the alleyway before stepping out.

Like most of the members of his personal security force Barney was a large, muscular man. His smoothly shaven head and creamy chocolate skin made his age indeterminable at a glance. He was a former Army Special Forces soldier, and had been with G-Force Security for almost two years, which was why Paul had resisted believing the signs that led him to the most obvious conclusion.

Luther continued to plead his case. "All I'm asking is that you check out the situation. This guy is no good. If anything happens to this girl…"

"I understand." Paul watched the scene unfolding across the street with narrowed eyes. Barney was now signaling to someone at the other end of the alley. "Tell you what, I'll find her and make sure she's okay. Beyond that, there's not a lot I can do if she doesn't want to leave."

"Thanks, man. I really appreciate this."

"No thanks necessary. We're brothers." Paul spoke of the emotional bond between men-in-arms, not the genetic one, but he knew Luther would understand. There was a time he would've thought Barney understood, but not anymore.

As a van began to slowly pull toward Barney, Paul sat up in the bucket seat of the nondescript vehicle he often used for surveillance and gently placed his laptop on the passenger seat. "Luther, I gotta go." He never took his eyes off his employee.

"All right. Just give me a call as soon as you find her."

"I will." Paul pressed the end button on his cell phone, unlocked the car door and slowly began to get out. The van came to a stop several feet from the back door of the club, and a small-framed, young white male stepped out. He exchanged a few words to Barney before reaching into the side of the van.

For all the high-tech, million-dollar equipment he used in his line of work as a security consultant, Paul felt few things served him better than the fleet of Motor City subcompact cars his company routinely used. So common and ordinary, no one ever noticed people getting in and out of them. It was this blandness that allowed him to cross the alley in plain sight of both men without drawing their attention.

It wasn't until he'd almost reached them that they spotted him. He watched Barney's eyes widen in surprise as the other man turned from the van holding a small video camera.

"B-boss, what are you doing here?" Barney managed to stutter out. The sweat was already beginning to form on his forehead.

"I could ask you the same thing." Paul's deep baritone voice was intimidating under usual circumstances, but with the hint of menace lacing each word there was no mistaking the hidden threat. "Aren't you supposed to be inside watching Lacy Hill?"

The man with the camera looked from his informant to Paul and correctly surmised the situation.

He extended his hand with a bright smile. "You must be Paul Gutierrez, the mastermind behind G-Force Security Systems. Tom Stringer, *National Examiner*. What an honor to meet you, sir."

Paul had also taken inventory and fully understood the situation. He'd come here tonight based on a suspicion that had just been proven true. He glanced at the extended hand before turning his complete attention back to his employee. "What are you doing out here in the alley with a reporter when you're supposed to be inside looking after our client?"

"Um, I can explain everything." Barney's eyes darted in every direction like a cornered animal.

Just then the back door to the club opened, and rising pop star Lacy Hill spilled through the door surrounded by an entourage of colorful bodies. The top of the petite singer's curly brunette head was barely visible amongst the barrage of people whom she insisted be allowed to follow her everywhere. As a precaution, Paul had had each of the flunkies thoroughly investigated and was satisfied that beyond suffocating her no one in the group posed a serious threat. A black-clad bodyguard closed in the small gaggle of people on three sides. Barney made up the fourth man of the detail.

The three large men were each looking around their positions for overzealous fanatics and ruthless paparazzi. None commented on the fourth member of their team and their boss standing off to the side.

Paul, who believed in complete honesty amongst his team members, had already explained the situation with Barney, and what he planned to do about it.

The crowd moved along like a giant, nosy beast pushing at a snail's pace with each vying for Lacy's attention.

Apparently Tom Stringer wasn't about to let this opportunity get away. He lifted his camera for some exclusive closeups of Lacy Hill. His eyes glistened greedily as he no doubt heard the chiming of a cash register.

Suddenly, Paul collared him and held him in a vise grip. "Not so fast," he growled, holding the reporter slightly off the ground.

Two limousines stopped in front of Lacy and her group. The drivers hurried around and opened the doors. The dozen or so people tried to push their way into the car with

Lacy, but the ones who couldn't get in rushed back to the second car so as not to be left behind.

Paul couldn't help thinking the whole thing looked like some strange version of musical chairs. Within seconds, the limousines pulled away, back out onto the street, without Lacy or her friends ever knowing how close they came to being ambushed.

Once the limousines were out of sight Paul released his hostage. Tom gave him a quick, assessing glance and no doubt concluded that his life was not worth the videotape. So when Paul held out his hand for it, Tom quickly reached into his camera and pulled the cassette out.

"No hard feelings, right?" Tom swallowed and handed over the tape. Like everyone else in L.A., he'd heard the stories surrounding the owner of G-Force, the premier security company in town. But now looking into feral, dark brown eyes, he knew with certainty this was not a man he wanted to have as an enemy. "I mean, you can't blame a guy for trying." He began backing toward his van. "After all, I'm just doing my job."

"Get out of here," Paul snarled between his teeth.

Tom did not need a second warning. He hopped in the van, which was still running, and sped out of the alley, never looking back.

Once the van was out of sight, Paul turned back to his once trusted employee. His mouth twisted in disgust. "If you needed more money all you had to do was ask me for a raise." He huffed. "Up until recently you were one of my top men. So...why?"

Barney slanted his boss a dark glance. "Am I fired?"

Paul just stared at him, amazed that the question was even asked. "What do you think?"

He started to turn away, then paused, feeling the need to express his deep disappointment and regret. "This business is all about trust, Barney. Our clients depend on us to protect them from people like Tom Stringer. You not only sold Lacy out, you sold me out." Paul shook his head in disgust and started back toward his car.

"Sold you out!" Barney's angry snarl stopped him in his tracks. "You sell us out every time you take on one of these celebrity brats. You don't know what it's like out here, man! You sit in your office punching that damn computer and you think you have a beat on things?" He gave a harsh laugh. "You have no idea what it's like following someone like Lacy Hill around. She thinks we're her slaves. Always trying to order us around. She treats us like crap." He shook his head with such determination Paul was beginning to realize this wasn't just about money. "There's not enough money in the world to compensate for the way she treats us. Just a spoiled little tramp with no real talent. She uses us, so yeah, I used her back!"

Paul tilted his head and looked at the man he'd once called friend with a somewhat bemused expression. He quickly closed the distance between them. "You don't get it, do you? You didn't use Lacy Hill, Barney. You used me." With that, Paul walked away, only hoping Barney realized he'd made the mistake of a lifetime.

Amber Lockhart watched the buttons light up on the elevator of the elegant Mondrian Hotel as it climbed to the penthouse. Her heart was pounding against her chest as she envisioned the evening ahead of her. A night spent in the arms of Detroit Chargers basketball player Dashuan Kennedy.

She was feeling so good she wanted to drop the

shopping bags she carried in both hands and hug herself. Finally, she'd found Mr. Right. She glanced down at the small pink lingerie bag and smiled as she thought of the little piece of nothing she could not resist purchasing. On the charter flight from Detroit to L.A., Dashuan had revealed that green was his favorite color. *If it wasn't it soon will be,* Amber thought with a little smirk. She sighed in satisfaction, imagining the look of lust she would see on his handsome face when she came out of the bathroom wearing the slinky lingerie.

Everything was working out so wonderfully it almost seemed too good to be true. But here she was on her way to Dashuan Kennedy's penthouse suite to spend the evening with him. The first night of the rest of their lives together.

Up until now their relationship had been pretty chaste much to her dismay, just a few stolen kisses here and there. But Dashuan had explained that he hadn't felt comfortable being with her in Detroit under the nose of her close family friend, D'marcus Armstrong, who also happened to be one of the Chargers owners.

But when Dashuan called her on her cell phone late last night inviting her to fly out to L.A. with him, there was something in his voice that said he was ready to take their relationship to the next level.

She'd answered yes without hesitation and packed her bags in even less time. A half hour later Dashuan's car and driver arrived to pick her up and she was off on the adventure of a lifetime.

The elevator finally reached the penthouse level and she stepped off thinking about all the funny stories they would have to tell their children about how they came to be together against the greatest odds.

As she approached the door of the suite, she dug around in the bottom of her purse for the entry key and mentally ran through the final preparations of their special night. First she would call room service to order a romantic, candlelit dinner. Then she would slip into her new negligee and tease him by wearing it while they were eating dinner. After that, she planned to run a nice, warm bubble bath for two in the large outdoor hot tub on the penthouse balcony. Of course, by then, he should be close to crazy with lust. She smiled to herself. From there she would let Dashuan take the lead, although she was pretty sure his destination would be the bedroom.

As she entered the penthouse suite, the foyer was empty but she heard music and noise coming from the adjacent living room. She sighed in frustration, remembering the gang of hangers-on she'd been surprised to see when she'd arrived at the airfield last night. There had been a slight tinge of disappointment when she realized she and Dashuan would not be traveling alone, but she understood that was the cost of fame. The retinue included everyone from his agent, Skip Nelson, to his personal trainer, Kelvin Landy.

Dashuan had sent her on an all-expenses-paid shopping spree earlier that afternoon while he discussed a couple of endorsement deals with his agent. He'd told her that by the time she returned, all the business stuff would be out of the way and they could concentrate on cementing their relationship.

He'd promised to get rid of his friends so they could be alone, but given the noise coming from the other room, his soft heart had surrendered.

Well, Amber thought, tucking her bags in the front closet, if Dashuan did not know how to get rid of the party crashers, she did. It would be good practice for when they were married. Dashuan was much too sweet and kind to tell his friends when they were not welcome. Apparently that would be her job.

She checked her appearance in the mirror once more. She was pleased with what she saw. Her long, golden mane was just windswept enough to give her a natural sensuality, and combined with her large, golden eyes and full, pouty lips there was no denying her allure.

Her smile faded a little as she considered her belief that her beauty was her greatest asset. She had no special skills to speak of. She couldn't sing like her sister Pearl, nor was she supersmart like her sisters Opal and Ruby. But she was beautiful. She knew this with certainty because she had been told so all of her life.

She'd always felt awkward and out of place in her family of exceptional and dynamic women—until in her early teens, as a girl on the verge of womanhood, she smiled at a man and watched as his whole body reacted. There was a sense of power and euphoria that raced through her, and from that moment she was addicted. She knew being beautiful was her special skill. She didn't kid herself into believing Dashuan would've ever noticed her had it not been for her pretty face and shapely form.

Amber reached up and touched her flawless, bronze skin, looking at her reflection in the mirror. The only problem with her particular skill was that it was hers for a limited time only. As time passed she would grow old and her beauty would fade away.

And so will I...

Shaking off the melancholy mood that sometimes struck out of the blue, she pasted on a smile and prepared to get rid of Dashuan's unwanted guests. From the sound of drunken revelry that became clearer and clearer, she knew it would not be an easy task.

But like it or not, they had to go. She had a basketball player to seduce.

As she rounded the corner leading into the living room, she heard something that sent a chill up her spine. It sounded like a woman moaning in sexual pleasure. Amber slowed her steps upon hearing the noise, which was followed by a deep, satisfied, masculine groan. She paused, feeling the hair on the back of her neck stand up. Every instinct in her was telling her to turn around and flee.

Instead, Amber forced one foot in front of the other and continued until she was standing in plain view of the large living room. Then she felt the blood drain from her pretty face.

Chapter 2

With Paul's connections, finding Amber Lockhart had been a matter of a couple of phone calls. Of course, the fact that she was staying in the penthouse of a five-star hotel with a famous athlete who was recognizable on sight didn't hurt matters.

Paul entered the lobby of the Mondrian Hotel and headed in the direction of the check-in counter. Although he had no desire to disappoint Luther, Paul was pretty sure he already knew how this was going to play out. After all, the girl was twenty-one and, from what Luther told him, something of a wild child. He doubted seriously if she would willingly leave Dashuan Kennedy's penthouse.

Paul's plan was simple. He would find the guest phone, call the penthouse and ask Amber to come down and meet him. If she agreed, he would express the concerns of her family and friends. She would probably tell him to mind his own business and return to the penthouse suite.

Then Paul could tell Luther she was okay but refused to leave, and that would be that. Paul sighed in exasperation, thinking that between Lacy Hill and Amber Lockhart he'd had his fill of spoiled brats for one night.

After the desk clerk pointed him in the direction of the guest phones across from the elevators, he glanced at his watch, surprised to realize it was after midnight, not that that meant much in a town like L.A. He decided he would catch a late dinner once he finished up here and head home. He picked up the guest phone and dialed the extension the clerk had given him for the penthouse. He leaned against the counter and listened to the ringing.

The elevator doors parted in front of him and there stood an angel. Paul tilted his head to the side as if considering what his eyes were seeing. She wiped at her nose with the balled-up tissue in her hand, and blew loudly into it. The uncouth gesture was enough to make her real.

Paul watched as she stepped forward out of the elevator with slumped shoulders and fresh tears in her eyes, and he wanted nothing more than to drop the phone and take her into his arms. She looked around the large lobby as if surprised to find herself there.

Her golden eyes settled on him and ran the length of his long body in quick assessment, before returning to his face and moving away. She sniffed again, and Paul frowned, wondering what kind of monster would make an angel cry.

She just stood there holding shopping bags in each hand and looking so lost and forlorn, it touched his heart. The penthouse phone had rung several times. Paul was tempted to hang it up and go offer his assistance to the angel. But he'd promised Luther he would find Amber, and that had to come first.

Seeming to finally get her bearings, she began moving away from the elevators. Just then, the doors on another elevator opened, and out stepped Dashuan Kennedy. Paul only recognized him from sports clips on ESPN and newspaper write-ups. Paul himself wasn't exactly a Chargers fan.

Dashuan raced across the lobby and headed straight for the angel. Paul twisted his mouth. Of course the angel would be with the pro athlete. He slammed the phone down on the receiver and followed Dashuan Kennedy. By the time he reached them, Dashuan had the woman's arm in a vise grip and they were arguing loudly enough that people were beginning to stare.

"Just come back upstairs and let's talk about this!" Dashuan was hissing at her.

The woman's golden eyes were wide with anger and some other unreadable emotion. "Let me go! There is nothing to talk about. I saw what I saw!"

"What do you think you saw, Amber? What are you going to tell people?" Dashuan was holding both her arms so tightly, he was slowly lifting her off the ground.

"Let her go." Paul's deep baritone seemed to ripple on the air.

Still holding Amber tight, Dashuan spun around to confront whoever would dare to get in his business. "Keep walking, man. This doesn't have anything to do with you."

Ignoring Dashuan, Paul looked directly into Amber's startled eyes. "If that's Amber Lockhart you're holding, then I'm afraid you're wrong."

Her thin sandy brown eyebrows crinkled and she tilted

her head. Paul realized that a confused angel was as adorable as a sad one.

"Do I know you?" she asked. Her soft voice cracked on the tears that continued to form no matter how she wiped them away.

"I'm a friend of Luther Biggens." Paul paused, realizing this was going to play out a lot differently than he had first assumed. "He sent me to get you. That is…if you are ready to leave."

She nodded her head frantically.

It was all the authorization Paul needed. His attention swiveled back to Dashuan. "I'm only going to say this once more. Let her go."

"I don't give a damn who sent you. This has nothing to do with you." He turned his attention back to Amber. "We need to talk about this."

"There is nothing to talk about, Dashuan. It's over! You've made your preference perfectly clear!" Her mouth twisted in disgust. "And to think…I thought you were the one."

Something like hope came into Dashuan's light brown eyes. "Baby, don't you see? Now that you know the truth, I *can* be the one. We can give each other just what we need. I'll take care of you, Amber, I swear—"

Dashuan's oath was cut short when Paul karate-chopped him on the shoulder. He released Amber and turned on Paul.

Paul stood in a battle stance, his muscular legs solidly placed. Even as his hand reached out for Amber, his eyes narrowed on Dashuan's face.

Amber saw the large hand being lifted toward her and apparently needed no further coaxing. She rushed past Dashuan right into the arms of the stranger.

Paul's strong arm closed around her waist as he pulled

her close to his chest. He watched Dashuan Kennedy transform into some mad animal right before his eyes.

Dashuan reached behind him and pulled out a small handgun from the waistband of his slacks.

Paul huffed, looking at the small cap gun. *Someone's been watching too many movies.* Still holding Amber against his side and trying to ignore how good her soft body felt nestled against his own, Paul lifted his jacket to reveal the long-barreled Magnum tucked neatly at his side. There was no mistaking the message. *My gun could eat your gun for breakfast.*

He glanced around at all the people who'd stopped to watch the confrontation, including several of the hotel staff. He wondered if 911 had been called yet. Probably so.

Paul quickly regretted letting his temper get the better of him and striking Dashuan. Now he realized this thing could get real ugly. He had to try and reason with the man before someone got shot. Given the way Dashuan was shaking, he hadn't ever used the weapon. Probably just a showpiece, Paul thought.

"Now come on, Kennedy. Think about it. Do you really want to get into a shootout in a hotel lobby? Your face will be on the cover of every gossip rag in L.A. by morning. From what I hear your career is struggling as it is. Is this really the kind of publicity you want?"

Dashuan looked around, as if noticing for the first time that they had drawn a crowd. He quickly tucked the gun back in his pants but it was too late. Everyone had already seen him with it.

"Amber, please!" Dashuan pleaded. "Stay and talk to me. It's not what you think."

Seeing the desperation in his eyes, Paul could almost

feel sorry for the guy. He looked down at the top of the golden head of the woman in his arms, feeling her soft breasts rise and fall with every heartbeat. Okay, he did feel sorry for the guy.

"I know what I saw, Dashuan. No amount of conversation is going to change that."

Paul saw the elevator doors open again and a group of burly men step out. They came up behind Dashuan, and Paul took them for the basketball player's bodyguards.

He looked into the faces of the men, sizing them up and knowing he might have to fight his way out of here. "We're leaving. If you try to stop us this could get ugly, Kennedy. Just let us go."

Dashuan was glaring at Amber. "Keep your mouth shut, bitch," he said under his breath, but he never moved.

Paul felt Amber's small, fisted hand dig deeper into his shirt. *Don't worry, I won't let you go.* He resisted the urge to kiss the top of her head in reassurance. Taking her hand, he turned and headed toward the door.

Halfway there he felt the hairs on the back of his neck stand up. With lightning fast reflexes, he pushed Amber to the side. Paul swung around and saw Dashuan charging toward him. He was holding the small gun backward with the butt extended high over his head.

Paul heard someone scream "Look out." He went in low tackling Dashuan right in his midsection. The ball player let out a whiff of air and collapsed on his side. In a second, Paul was back on his feet in a defensive posture as he watched Dashuan's boys slowly moving in, determined to finish what he'd started.

He reached in his pocket and tossed Amber the car keys. "Get in the blue Focus parked out front."

"What about you?"

"Don't worry about me. Just go!" Paul watched the guys closing in on each side. There were six of them and one of him. He would have to take out the ones standing between him and the door first. Then…

The six men stopped moving. Their attention had been drawn to something over his shoulder.

"Is there a problem here, Paul?"

Paul recognized the voice of his friend, LAPD detective Keith Montfield. He glanced back to see Keith and the four uniformed officers who had quietly come up behind him.

"Nothing I can't handle, Keith." He relaxed his stance.

Keith chuckled. "I know, but how about you let us lend a hand anyway?"

Paul stepped back, and gestured in front of him. "Help yourself."

The officers closed in on the six bodyguards, and one stopped to pick Dashuan up off the floor.

Paul patted Keith on the shoulder before he turned to leave. "Can I give you a call tomorrow to explain?"

Keith nodded and looked his friend over. "Sure you're okay?"

"Yeah. I'll fill you in tomorrow."

As Paul headed toward the exit he heard one of the bodyguards ask, "Why does he get to go?"

He heard Keith's laughter. "Who, that guy? He's harmless."

Paul couldn't help smiling. He turned and winked at Keith, seeing the humor in the detective's eyes. Everyone in L.A. knew that statement was the furthest thing from the truth.

* * *

Paul hurried out to the car he'd double-parked in the luggage loading area. Try as he may he could not stem the growing excitement he felt remembering the beautiful woman who would be there waiting for him.

Feeling ridiculous even as he did it, he checked to make sure his shirt was tucked neatly in his slacks. He ran his hand over his short, curly hair. *What the hell am I doing?*

He should be thinking about reassuring the girl. He wasn't sure what had happened between her and Kennedy, but whatever it was apparently upset her a great deal.

He reached the car and stopped short realizing the passenger seat was empty except for the small key ring lying in plain sight. He looked in both directions but did not see her. His mind quickly calculated the possibilities that one of Dashuan's guys had gotten by him when he wasn't looking. But no, he was fairly certain there were only six of them and they were all accounted for inside.

A young valet was standing not far from where he was parked. Paul approached him with a description of Amber and asked if he'd seen her.

"Yeah, she went walking that way." He gestured toward West Sunset Boulevard. "I offered to get her a cab, but she said no thanks."

Paul quickly tipped the guy for his help before climbing into his car. Taking the keys from the passenger side, he started the engine. Amber was distraught, Paul thought. In her current state of mind who knew what she might do.

He caught up with her within three blocks. "Amber! Amber!" He rolled along slowly, ignoring the horns blaring behind him and the foul language of those that managed to get by him. "Amber, get in the car!"

She glanced at him. The golden eyes that had pleaded for help in the hotel were now glaring with cold intensity. She was an angry angel, Paul thought, unable to stop himself from making the comparison.

"Where are you going?" he called out the passenger-side window.

"Somewhere away from you and my meddling family!"

Paul forced his way out of traffic and pulled into the parking lot of the grocery store several feet in front of her. He hopped out of the car and came around to wait for her to catch up.

Amber just ignored him and continued to walk right past, as if she didn't even see him.

Paul fell into step beside her. "Correct me if I'm wrong, but when I asked you if you wanted to leave did you not nod your head?"

"Don't be ridiculous. Of course I did. But that doesn't mean I wanted to leave with you." She gave him a sidelong glance. "What is your name anyway?"

Paul closed his eyes and shook his head, realizing in the mist of all the confusion he'd never introduced himself. "Paul Gutierrez." He extended his hand but she ignored it.

"Look, Amber, I know you've been through a lot tonight, but if you would just—"

She stopped dead in her tracks and slowly swiveled around to face him. Her golden eyes were dark with some unidentifiable emotion. "You have no idea what I've been through this evening. So don't even stand there and pretend like you understand!"

Paul frowned, seeing the tears begin to form in her eyes again. *What did Kennedy do to you?* He knew he could not ask the question no matter how it ate at him. As far as she was concerned he was just a meddlesome friend of a friend.

"Fair enough," he said softly. "So, where are you heading?"

Amber looked at the endless sidewalk ahead of her and realized she really didn't know. When she'd left the hotel all she wanted to do was get away from Dashuan, the handsome stranger whose name she now knew was Paul, her family and anyone else who knew her. She wanted to go off by herself and cry into a pillow. She felt like a complete fool and that was not something she wanted to share with anyone.

How could he? It was the question she'd been asking herself repeatedly for the past hour. How could Dashuan betray her like that? He was supposed to be the one. Mr. Right. When, in fact, he was Mr. Incredibly Wrong.

She sighed. "I'm just going to check in to another hotel." She glanced up into his concerned brown eyes. "Don't worry. I'll call my family as soon as I check in and let them know I'm okay."

"What hotel? I'll give you a ride."

She frowned, getting a little irritated by the man's insistence to help where none was wanted. "Really, it's okay. I'll be fine."

"You're kidding, right? Two o'clock on a Saturday morning and you're out walking the streets of downtown L.A. You're lucky if you don't get picked up for prostitution."

"You son of a—" Without a thought of the consequences, Amber took a swing at the man and it felt good. She put into it all the anger and frustration she was feeling and still missed by a mile as he ducked neatly out of the way of her arm.

"I'm sorry. That came out wrong." He grabbed her arms to hold her still. "I didn't mean that the way it sounded."

She struggled for a few moments more, before realizing it was getting her nowhere.

He whispered her name close to her ear and she felt her whole body melt. "Let me help you."

"You can help me by taking me to a nearby hotel."

Paul was sure Luther would not appreciate him dumping the girl at some anonymous hotel and abandoning her to her fate. But if she was determined, there was nothing he could do to stop her. "All right." Reluctantly he released her. "I'm parked right over here."

He led her back to the car and watched her pretty little nose twitch as if she suddenly smelled something bad.

She studied the modest car as if seeking some secret message. "What exactly do you do for a living?" she asked. Accepting the open door he offered, she climbed into the passenger seat.

Paul quirked an eyebrow, suddenly remembering that this was a girl who chased a wealthy basketball player all the way from Detroit. *Just another gold digger.*

"I'm in security," he answered vaguely, having no desire to replace Dashuan Kennedy's checkbook with his own. She was beautiful, there was no denying that. And probably as shallow as a saucer, he thought, as he pulled away from the curb.

"So, where do you want me to take you?" he asked, pulling back out into traffic.

"I don't care, just somewhere nice and…reasonably priced." She yawned, relaxing back into the seat of the small car.

Paul headed in the direction of the airport, thinking to drop her someplace that had shuttle service to the airport terminals, so she wouldn't have far to go later that morning. He still didn't like the idea of leaving her alone in a hotel, but he didn't want to stay in her line of vision too long, either.

He'd met women like Amber Lockhart many times. Women who used their pretty faces to manipulate men. He glanced at her again and wondered what man would be strong enough to resist an angel. Certainly not himself. No, it was best to leave her at an airport hotel and wish her a safe flight home.

He glanced at the shopping bags and purse she'd tossed in the backseat and wondered where her luggage was. She'd probably left it behind at Kennedy's penthouse. What had upset her so badly that she would leave without her luggage?

"I know it's not my business, but what exactly happened between you and Kennedy?"

She snuggled into the car seat and yawned again. "I caught him in bed with someone else," she said drowsily.

Paul knew the confession was a sign of just how exhausted she really was. The woman he'd met earlier would've never revealed that embarrassing information. Paul knew she was too tired to edit out what she was saying, and he ruthlessly took advantage of it.

Of course, finding her boyfriend in bed with another woman would be devastating to a woman like Amber, a woman so sure of her appeal. But something about the whole thing just felt more intense than a casual one-night stand. "Did you know her?" he asked.

"Yes." She yawned and he could tell she was fading away.

"Was she a close friend of yours?" he asked, sure he was on the right track. Nothing hurt worse than a close friend sleeping with your mate.

"No." She yawned one final time. "It was his personal trainer, Kelvin Landy."

Kelvin? Paul's eyes widened, realizing the implications of the statement. *Dashuan Kennedy, the famous basketball player, caught in bed with another man!* His mind quickly sifted through everything that happened earlier. It explained the fear Paul had seen in Kennedy's eyes. Something like this would ruin the guy's reputation and possibly his career.

Keep your mouth shut, bitch. Dashuan's last words to Amber kept replaying in his head. He glanced over at his passenger, who was now asleep. She was so helpless, alone in an unfamiliar city, and yet her pride refused to accept his help.

With one final glance at the vulnerable form, he made his decision. He pulled all the way over into the right lane and took the next exit. They were no longer headed toward the airport. Plans had changed. He wondered briefly what she would say when she woke up and realized what he'd done. He was not looking forward to it.

Chapter 3

Why, Amber thought, did the greatest revelations in life come too late to be useful?

She sat curled in a ball in the car with her eyes pressed tightly closed. She wanted to continue to appear asleep even though she'd been awake for several minutes now. Soon, she thought, they should arrive at a hotel and she would be free of Paul Gutierrez, the handsome stranger who'd appeared out of nowhere to rescue her.

She made a mental note to thank him when they parted company. Looking back on the situation she wasn't sure she would've been able to get away from Dashuan so easily without his help. And all she'd given him in return was attitude, which was strange considering men like him usually brought out only the best in her.

A flirtatious smile, the wink of an eye—that was how she would typically greet gorgeous men. Not with tear-filled eyes and a flippant tongue. She could still see the concern shining in the depths of those soft brown eyes. As nice as he was to look at, Amber could only hope never to see him again after tonight.

She would check into an anonymous room tonight and be on a flight to…somewhere tomorrow. Not home. The humiliation of returning to her family under these circumstances would just be too great.

No, she needed some time alone, maybe on a tropical beach somewhere far from Opal's self-righteous "I told you so." Far away from Ruby's temper, and Pearl's sympathetic eyes. In other words, far, far away from her sisters.

The image of what she'd seen earlier that night was not only seared on her brain, it seemed to be on some kind of auto replay that she could not stop.

The look of horrific surprise on Dashuan's face when she'd thrown open the bedroom door to find his naked body kneeling over another. The look of shock on the face of his lover. And she could only imagine her own frightful expression as her brain tried to reason out exactly what her eyes were seeing. It wasn't real. It couldn't be real. It was like a magic trick, she thought. When the mind knows that what it is seeing cannot be and yet there it is…right in front of you.

She felt her whole body stiffening, remembering the vision that had greeted her as she rounded the corner and come to a halt in the entrance to the living room. It was a scene straight out of a graphic porn movie. Clothes were strewn all over the floor as naked bodies twisted and contorted in every imaginable way. Men and women coupled, and in groups having sex all over the large room. Women with men, women with women, men with men—she simply could not believe it. The air was pungent with the smell of sex and Amber felt herself getting sick.

No one seemed to even notice her standing in the doorway too stupefied to move. Or if they did notice they didn't seem to care. She forced herself to look into each and every face, recognizing many of them as friends of Dashuan's, but there was no sign of Dashuan in the midst of the orgy. Amber remembered feeling overwhelming relief when she first discovered he was not among the bodies.

Her eyes fell on Skip, Dashuan's agent, the man he was supposed to be spending the evening with discussing business. But the only business Skip seemed interested in was what the two young female groupies were doing to his genitals.

His eyes met hers over the tops of their heads and there was something dark and sinister in the way he looked at her that told her she had to get out of there in a hurry, or she could become an unwilling part of this whole disaster.

She had to find Dashuan and let him know what was going on. He would put a stop to this. Of that she was certain. She made her feet move in the direction of the bedrooms lining the back hall of the suite, hoping that Dashuan had fallen asleep in one of them and was unaware of what was going on in the other rooms. She threw open the double doors of the master bedroom and surprisingly it was empty, as were the next two bedrooms. She was almost convinced that Dashuan was nowhere in the suite when she came to the fourth bedroom.

She heard the muffled groan too late, because by the time the noise registered she had already thrown open the door and surprised the two men coupling on the bed.

Amber knew she would never forget the look of intense pleasure on Dashuan's face, or the sight of his strong, muscular arms bracing his body over his trainer. She knew she would never forget because he looked exactly as she'd always imagined he would look. Only in her imaginings, she had been the one beneath him.

She felt the car make a turn, and the shifting movement brought her back to the present. Slowly, the car came to a halt. Amber felt her heart pounding as she remembered the man sitting next to her. They had finally reached the hotel. Now all she had to do was get away from him with what was left of her dignity intact.

"I know you're awake, so you might as well open your eyes." A gentle voice broke the silence.

So much for dignity. Amber opened her eyes and found herself staring into a pair of soft brown ones again. The man really was beautiful, she thought. Too bad they had not met under different circumstances. Looking out the driver's side window beyond him, she realized they were in some sort of neighborhood. She sat up and realized they were sitting in the driveway of a large, newly built home. She continued to look all around. A subdivision? she thought. What happened to the hotel?

"Where are we?" Amber felt the first stirring of unease since Paul Gutierrez had appeared, reminding her that she did not know this man.

"I thought you would be more comfortable here than in a hotel."

She narrowed her eyes and studied his face, trying to see any signs of deceit or ill intentions. "I asked you a question. Where are we? Whose house is this?"

Paul arched an eyebrow, realizing she did not assume it

was his. Of course not. He reminded himself of her reaction to his little compact car. *What exactly do you do for a living?* He could still see the slightly contemptuous expression on her pretty face. *Gold digger.*

"A friend of mine. I'm house-sitting."

She scooted back against the door of the car. "I asked you to take me to a hotel. Why did you bring me here?"

"I just told you. I thought you would be more—"

Suddenly she threw open the door and stood. Paul matched her step for step.

"Amber!" he called to her realizing she was now trembling. "Calm down, I should have told you what I—"

"Do you really know Luther?"

"Of course. How else would I have found you?"

"How do you know him?"

"We were in the Navy together. Look, I know you've been through a lot tonight but you're going to have to trust me."

"I don't know anything about you! All I asked was that you take me to a hotel and you brought me here. Where are we, anyway?!"

He sighed. "Moreno Valley, about an hour southeast of L.A."

"We've been driving for over an hour?" Her eyes widened, and she glanced at the small gold watch on her wrist for the first time since she'd climbed into the car. It was almost 3:00 a.m. "Oh, my God!" She grabbed her head with both hands. "What was I thinking? Getting in a car with a *total stranger?*"

"Amber, calm down. You are perfectly safe here." Realizing she was about to bolt, Paul held up his hand. "Stop and think for a minute. How else would I have known where to find you? Your name? Think about it."

She did, but she did not draw the conclusions he wanted. "For all I know you could just be some creep who hangs around hotel lobbies trying to pick up women. As for my name, you heard Dashuan call me."

His mouth twisted in frustration. "You name is Amber Lockhart. You are twenty-one and you grew up in Detroit. From what Luther told me, your family is worried about you right now. So, why don't we go into the house and give them a call to let them know you're safe and sound."

Her heart slowed considerably as he recited information that could've only come from someone who knew her. "Okay, I believe Luther sent you."

"Thank you!" He threw up his hands in relief, believing the battle had been won.

"But that doesn't change the fact that you took me an hour outside of town without my permission when all I asked is that you drop me off at a hotel."

"Stop obsessing about the damn hotel. You'll be much more comfortable here, all the same amenities and more. This is for your own good."

"How would you know what's good for me?" She shook her head in defeat. "You know what— Never mind. I'll find a hotel on my own." She quickly opened the rear door of the car and grabbed her bags and her purse. Slamming the door shut, she turned and headed down the driveway back toward the street.

"Where are you going?" Paul asked, wondering if his friendship with Luther was really worth this headache.

"I told you. I'll find my own hotel," she called over her shoulder.

"You don't even know where you are!" he shouted and

instantly regretted it when he noticed the front room curtains moving on the house across the street. Apparently they had an audience.

Amber did not even bother responding. She just kept walking. The plan was simple. She would hail a cab. Cab drivers always knew hotels and restaurants in their areas. In the morning she would find some way back to L.A., and from there on to…wherever. *I'll worry about that tomorrow.* Right now all she wanted was a bed, and sweet, sweet sleep.

Paul stood and watched her leave and was determined not to follow. He knew she would be safe enough inside the large subdivision, but what if she did manage to find her way out onto the main street? What if the dizzy broad got herself run down or mugged? Of course, Luther would hold him responsible.

He rested his head on top of the small car, wondering what crazed compulsion told him to bring her back to his home. The girl was nothing but trouble. Look at the situation he had to bail her out of tonight.

She wasn't the only one with troubles, he thought, remembering that only a few hours ago he'd been forced to fire a man he had considered a friend.

He shook his head and decided to let her go for now. Maybe she would be more reasonable after she cooled off. A couple of hours on the hard concrete in those heels she was wearing, and she would regard his compact car like the finest of limousines.

Paul opened the front door of the house as quietly as possible, not wanting to awaken Rosalie, the sixty-seven-year-old Hispanic woman who took care of his eight-month-old son, Joachim, during the day. But that proved pointless as he entered the large kitchen and found her sitting at the table.

Rosalie often volunteered to spend the night when Paul needed to do late-night surveillance, such as tonight. Being that all of her children were adults, there was only Rosalie and her elderly husband, Enrique, at home. Paul knew that taking care of Joachim was more than just a job for Rosalie, and he was grateful for whatever intuition had led him to hire her.

The older woman was usually never without a smile or kind word for anyone. But now a worried expression marred her light brown face. Her worn, wrinkled hands were closed around a mug and Paul knew instinctively this night was about to get even worse.

"Paul!" Hearing him enter the room she sprung to her feet with the agility of a woman half her age and ran to wrap her robust arms around his lean form. "I was so worried about you. I know you said you would be late tonight, but it's almost morning, and I was so afraid. And Enrique, my Enrique has to have emergency surgery—"

"Shhh, shhh." Paul stroked her back, trying to calm her. "Now, slowly, tell me."

"My Enrique has to have emergency heart bypass surgery in the morning." She began wringing her hands in agitation. "Oh, Paul, I am so worried. What am I going to do?"

Paul guided her back to the table. "First, you are going to slow down before you have to join Enrique in the hospital," he said, in a poor attempt to lighten the mood.

Rosalie smiled, grateful for the effort. "You're right. He's always been such a strong, healthy man. I don't under-stand how this could've happened to him."

"What hospital is he in?"

"Riverside County," she managed to say before the tears began to flow. "Oh, Paul, I am so scared." Her eyes widened as she remembered the important conversation she needed to have with him. "I have to go be with him, Paul. But I don't know what to do about Joachim."

"Don't worry about Joachim. I'll just work from home for the next few days. You go be with your husband."

She leaned across the table and hugged him again, and Paul knew in some way she needed the affection more than he did. She stood and hurried toward the hall. "Thank you so much," she called over her shoulder.

She paused in the entryway and returned to the table to take one of his large hands between hers. "Please say a prayer for us." She smiled and touched his lean cheek. "Your prayers will be heard. You are touched by the angels."

Paul forced a smile and regretted the many mornings he'd sat sharing his war stories with her over a pot of coffee. But during those early days when she'd first come to work for him he had needed someone to talk to, and Rosalie had been a kind and compassionate listener.

She was also a deeply religious, yet superstitious woman. After hearing how many times he'd barely escaped being captured by the Taliban, she'd concluded that he had "special favor." An opinion he'd yet been unable to change.

He looked into her eyes, trying to determine how to pose his question without offending her. "Rosalie, Enrique's hospital stay…is it going to pose a hardship for you? Because I can—"

She quickly covered his lips with her finger, and much to his dismay her eyes once again filled with tears. "Such a generous offer, but we are fine. Enrique has insurance and thanks to you, so do I. With our savings, we'll be just fine."

She glanced at the clock on the wall. "It's time for Joachim's feeding. I'll leave right after that."

"You don't have to—"

"No, no, I want to." She crossed the room to where a bottle sat cooling on the stove. "I'm going to miss him so much. I just want to spend a little time with him before I have to leave." She hurried out of the room and a few minutes later Paul heard the door to the nursery gently open and close.

Paul rose tiredly and picked up the cordless phone. Running through the numbers on the speed dial he finally found the one he wanted. He dialed and leaned against the counter, waiting for an answer and wondering if he should describe the mission as accomplished or failed.

"Hello?" The drowsy voice of Luther Biggens answered on the other end.

"I got her." Paul decided to cut straight to the chase. He rubbed the bridge of his nose feeling the pressure of recent events coming down on him.

"Thanks, man. Can I talk to her?"

"Um, let me rephrase that. I don't exactly *have her* have her."

"What's that supposed to mean?"

"She's in the neighborhood, but not in the house."

"What?"

Paul sighed. "It's a long story. Out here it's almost three in the morning and neither of us has slept all night. Can I have her call you back when she wakes up?"

Luther paused for a long moment as if attempting to understand his old friend. "All right, I guess. And when you wake up, I'd be interested to hear this long story."

"You got it." He yawned, unable to hold back his exhaustion any longer.

A few minutes later he grabbed his keys off the foyer table in preparation to go search for Amber. He needed to find her and talk some sense into her quickly. Now that Rosalie was leaving he couldn't stay away long.

Just as he opened the door, he saw a dragging, drunken figure weighted down with shopping bags wandering up the driveway. He shook his head, amazed that she was still on her feet. He wanted to rush toward her and help her, but knew the help would be rejected.

She stopped just outside the doorway. "What the hell kind of freakish community is this? There's no way out!" She glared at him as if it were his fault she'd spent the last thirty minutes wandering in circles.

He bit his lip to keep from laughing and waited. She looked so disgruntled he almost felt sorry for her.

Finally she placed one foot inside the door and paused. "I'll stay tonight, but first thing in the morning you're taking me to the airport." She wagged a finger in his face that told Paul that, despite her ranting about strangers, she was not the slightest bit afraid of him.

He stepped aside to allow her inside. Amber entered looking around at the bare walls and the staircase leading to the second level. The only light was the foyer table lamp, so she couldn't see much.

"So? Where do I sleep?"

"The second bedroom at the top of the stairs."

Without another word she turned and, weaving back and forth, finally made her way to the top of the stairs. Paul just shook his head, realizing the only thing keeping her exhausted body upright was pure determination. From where he stood at the bottom, he could just see her shadow as she entered the room and closed the door.

He was sitting at the kitchen table fifteen minutes later when Rosalię came back down. "Okay, his bottom is dry and his belly is full." She smiled. "He should sleep until around seven now. There are several bottles already prepared on the refrigerator door and the directions for mixing his formula are on the tack board over there." She made a gesture over her left shoulder.

After watching her drive away, Paul quickly locked the door and set the alarm. Happiness began to grow as he came closer and closer to the master bedroom. He threw open the double doors and without even undressing just stretched out across his large four-poster bed. He sighed heavily, yawned once and quickly faded away.

Ten minutes later, a baby's angry howl brought him back to his feet once more.

Chapter 4

Amber glanced at the clock on the side of the bed and decided she couldn't wait any longer. She had to go in search of a bathroom. She cracked the door open and crept out into the hall. Even with just two hours of sleep she was feeling much better and could see things much clearer. She realized the house was even bigger than she'd originally thought. The entire second level was almost circular in design. In the center of the opening there hung a large chandelier.

It was a beautiful house, Amber realized, despite the boring white walls and lack of decorative creativity. Paul had said he was house-sitting for a friend of his and Amber knew immediately the friend was a man. The house had that kind of sterile "place of residence" feel to it that men seemed to favor instead of the hominess that women tended to create in even the smallest of places.

Her body reminded her of why she'd come out of her room and she continued the search for the bathroom. She found it down the hall.

When she came out a few minutes later, she stood completely still, hearing what sounded like voices coming from downstairs. Telling herself that she needed to know as much as possible about this man who'd basically kidnapped her, she decided to investigate.

At the bottom of the stairs she leaned around the corner and saw a light coming from the living room. Stealthily, she moved along the wall until she was almost standing outside the entryway. Her lips twisted in disappointment when she recognized the voices of Roseanne Barr and John Goodman, and realized the voices were coming from the television.

Looking around the corner, she could see someone on the couch. Edging away from the wall, Amber tiptoed across the floor until she was standing just behind the end of it.

Paul's head was resting against the back of the couch and his mouth was wide open. He was sound asleep.

Perfect. She leaned against the end of the couch and did what she'd wanted to do since the moment the hotel elevator doors opened. She looked at him. Really, really looked at him, soaking up that gorgeous face and slightly muscular body. She decided her initial assessment had been correct; it wasn't just a trick of the light. He was beautiful.

His perfectly chiseled features defined every inch of his flawless olive skin. At first glance she'd thought he was maybe mulatto, but now she could clearly see he was of Hispanic decent. His soft brown, almond-shaped eyes were now shielded by long, thick lashes. As she visually outlined his full, pink lips, she subconsciously licked her own. Feeling bold, she stood and edged around in front of the couch to see if the muscles she remembered from earlier were real or imagined. She tiptoed closer and closer and stopped suddenly, seeing the small bundle that was cradled tightly against his chest.

All she could see above the blanket was a crop of dark curls, but there was no mistaking he was holding a baby. Her mouth fell open and she stood there in stunned silence for several minutes just…staring.

Not knowing what to think, she quietly returned to her bedroom and crawled back between the cool covers. She lay there for a long while before beginning to feel sleepy again. She had had enough surprises in this one night to last a lifetime.

Amber had always considered herself the more adventurous and daring member of her family, a title which up until now she'd worn proudly. She knew that after this night she would definitely have to reconsider her opinions on the matter.

Amber awoke to the wonderful smell of bacon the next morning. She turned over in the comfortable bed, surprised by how well she'd slept in it. Normally, she did not fare well in strange beds.

She lay staring at the white ceiling overhead, trying to get her bearing on her surroundings. Slowly, she sat up in the bed, holding the covers close to her chest.

Because she had torn out of Dashuan's penthouse so quickly, she'd left her luggage in one of the guest bedrooms. All she had to sleep in was the negligee she bought during her shopping spree for their special night.

She huffed to herself, deciding that the three hundred dollars she'd spent on it had been a big, fat waste of money.

"Could've spent that on the cost of a ticket home," she muttered, turning to put her feet on the floor.

She stretched and yawned as her feet sunk into the plush carpeting. She heard a low voice talking, and the image of Paul Gutierrez instantly came to mind. Luther's friend, and now her personal hero.

She remembered what she'd seen last night, and the desire to solve that mystery brought her to her feet. She quickly slipped back into the slacks and blouse of the previous day. She pulled her hair back and finger-brushed it, finishing it up with a loose, french braid that fell midway down her back.

She started to leave the room and paused when she noticed a partially opened door on the other side of the room. Her head tilted in confusion, she crossed the room and pushed the door open.

"I'll be damned." She frowned, and then chuckled at her own foolishness. She'd stumbled around the large house looking for a bathroom, when there was one in the bedroom all along.

She shook her head, and started to turn away before catching her own image in the mirror. Although she was undoubtedly thrown together, she was still lovely. If Paul Gutierrez was like any other man, he would find no fault in her haphazard appearance. Well, any man except Dashuan Kennedy, she thought, and felt her confidence fading.

She headed toward the bedroom door and stopped again with a frown when she remembered that all of her personal hygiene items were in her suitcase in Dashuan's suite. She briefly considered not going downstairs, until the wonderful smell of bacon once again filled the air.

When she reached the large kitchen, the image that

greeted her was that of Paul's broad shoulders as he leaned against the island counter in the middle of the room. He was on the phone, but speaking low. Amber paused in the doorway when she realized the conversation was about her.

"Yeah, Luther, she's okay, just worn out, but given everything she's been through that's understandable."

Amber's mouth fell open and her heart accelerated as she imagined her worst fear. *He's telling Luther about Dashuan and Kelvin!*

She came into the room, intentionally bumping into a chair at the round dining table, hoping to halt the conversation. As expected Paul turned at the sound, and their eyes locked.

Amber was surprised to see her memory had failed her. She'd remembered him as being good-looking, when he was in fact exquisite.

She smiled, but it felt strained and artificial on her face. She needed to get him off that phone, on the off chance that he had not said anything yet.

"Here's the lady of the hour now." Paul never took his eyes off her. "Hang on." He extended the cordless phone receiver to her. "It's Luther. Want to talk to him?"

Amber quickly crossed the room and took the cordless phone, covering the receiver with her hand. "Um, did you…tell him about, um…"

Paul shook his head slowly. "Just told him about what happened in the lobby, and that I brought you back here."

Amber felt relief course through every vein in her body. She wanted to wrap her arms around Paul and thank him, but that would be pathetic.

Instead, she just nodded in acknowledgement, and took a deep breath before speaking into the phone. "Hi, Luther."

"Amber! What the hell were you thinking running off with someone like Dashuan Kennedy? Your sisters went crazy wondering if you were okay."

"I'm sorry. I never meant to worry anyone. Tell them I'm okay."

Luther paused. "*Are* you okay?"

Amber smiled at the subdued tone. She and Luther usually went head to head, and she knew her easy surrender had caught him off guard.

"Yes." She smiled at Paul standing nearby. "Thanks to your friend here."

"Paul's a good guy. I told your sisters that you were safe and sound with him. But of course, they want to hear from you themselves."

"I know." She turned her back to Paul just slightly, feeling tears forming in her eyes and not certain why. "I will, just...I'll call them later."

"When are you coming home?"

"I don't know."

"Amber..."

Amber felt a tear slide down her face, at the same time she felt a hand press against the small of her back as Paul lifted the receiver out of her hand. The small gesture seemed to be some kind of signal to her body, because as soon as Paul had the phone again, the tears began to run down her face in a steady stream.

"Luther, it's still really early here, and Amber is just waking up. Let her get some breakfast and we'll call you back."

Amber pulled a couple of paper towels off a nearby roll and went to look out the window into the backyard. She quickly wiped her face and blew her nose. She only caught snippets of the conversation after that, but by the time she pulled herself together Paul had hung up the phone and returned to cooking the bacon.

"I hope you like bacon," Paul said, while flipping the partially cooked meat. "It's the only breakfast food I know how to cook."

Amber chuckled. Just then she heard the clanking of something plastic. Turning toward the sound, she noticed the playpen in the corner for the first time. She crossed the room and looked down at the most adorable little face she'd ever seen.

The chubby baby boy lying on his back was dressed comfortably in a light blue onesie. His small head was covered with large, fluffy curls, and he seemed to be completely absorbed in the plastic key rings trapped between his tiny toes. That was, until Amber's face appeared over his playpen. His perfect round face spread in a wide grin at the sight of the visitor, as if he had been fully expecting her.

Unable to resist, Amber reached down and lifted him up. "Well, hello there, aren't you the sweetest little thing."

The baby looked back and forth between Amber and his plastic toy, which fell off his feet when he was lifted. He was obviously torn.

Deciding his toy could wait, he focused his complete attention on Amber, his large brown eyes running over every detail of her face in complete concentration.

"He's beautiful. Is he yours?" Amber asked Paul, who was scooping bacon out of the skillet.

Paul gave the pair a cursory glance. "Yes. His name is Joachim."

"Hello, Joachim." Amber wiggled her fingers, as the baby playfully tugged at them.

Joachim's eyes widened in surprise, and his pink, heart-shaped mouth fell open in fascination as Amber laughed.

"Oh, he is a darling." Without really thinking about what she was doing, Amber wandered over to the table and sat down with the baby in her arms. "How old is he?"

Paul tilted his head, considering the question. "He'll be eight months exactly, in two days."

Amber bounced the baby on her lap. "Happy birthday, Joachim," she said cheerfully, and Joachim smiled and gurgled in return.

"I think he likes me," Amber said proudly. She frowned as she saw the smirk flash across Paul's face. "What?" she asked suspiciously.

"My son's no fool," he said, dishing several perfect strips of bacon on two plates. "If a beautiful woman coddled me and bounced me on her lap, I'd be happy, too."

Amber made a face, and turned the baby away from the heat of the skillet. "Um, look, Paul, about last night."

"Yeah, what about it?" Paul placed the skillet in the sink.

"I just wanted to say thanks."

"No thanks necessary." He gently took the baby from her arms.

Joachim quickly protested until his father began to lower him into the playpen and he spotted his plastic key ring. Sitting on his diapered bottom, he reached over and grabbed the toy with his chubby hand and immediately put it to his mouth.

"I'll be out of your house as soon as I can." Amber glanced around the room as a thought occurred to her. "Nice digs for a security guard," she said absently.

"Look, Amber." He grabbed a piece of bacon, and looked directly at her. "What you told me last night is between you and me. Your family will only know what you tell them. They won't hear anything more from me."

Embarrassed at how easily he'd read her thoughts, she quickly returned her attention to the plate. "I'll be out of your way by noon. Can you tell me where the closest airport is?"

"There's no one here but me and Joachim. You're perfectly welcome to stay as long as you like."

She bit her bottom lip, refusing to accept the tempting offer. Staying here with her hero and his sweet baby would mean not having to face her family, or Dashuan. "That's a generous offer, but I couldn't—"

"Just think about it. If you still want to leave later, I'll take you to the airport. Deal?"

She nodded, and glanced around the large kitchen. "You said there's no one here but you and Joachim?"

"Mmm-hmm." He took another bite of bacon.

"What about Joachim's mother?" she asked with the lift of an eyebrow.

Paul's dark eyes honed in on her face like a predator. He slowly wiped his mouth with a paper towel and stood. "We're not together." Paul grumbled as he went to scrape the crumbs into the garbage before putting his plate and the skillet in the dishwasher. Then without any warning, he walked over and picked the baby up from the playpen.

"There's some guest towels and washcloths in the hall closet, also a new toothbrush and toothpaste in the guest bathroom," he called over his shoulder, as he headed for the doorway.

Amber frowned down at her plate, wondering if her breath was worse than she thought. "Thank you," she muttered.

No longer hungry, she pushed her bacon around on the plate, and listened to Paul and Joachim climb the stairs. The room temperature had gone from comfortable to freezing cold in a matter of seconds. What had she said wrong?

About an hour later, after she'd taken a shower, Amber finally mustered the nerve to call her sisters.

She sat down on the side of the bed and picked up the phone. She decided to call Pearl first. They had always been close, and she was pretty sure Pearl was the least likely to judge her.

Pearl answered on the first ring. "Hello?"

"Pearl?"

"Amber! Where are you? We've been worried sick about you. Are you all right?"

Suddenly, Amber heard the sound of Opal on the other end. "Amber, is that you?"

Amber covered her face. So much for approaching Pearl first.

"Really, I'm okay." She heard Ruby in the background, trying to get the phone from one of her sisters.

"What were you thinking?" Opal said with frustration. "Running off with someone like Dashuan Kennedy?"

"I know. It was a stupid thing to do."

"Are you coming home today?" Pearl asked, before the phone was taken out of her hand.

"Amber, are you okay? Did that man hurt you?" Ruby said.

"Really, everybody, I'm fine."

"Where are you?" Opal asked.

"I'm with Paul, Luther's friend, somewhere outside of L.A."

"Somewhere outside of L.A.? You don't know where you are?" Ruby asked in alarm.

"Ruby, I'm perfectly safe. Paul's a really nice guy, and he has this adorable baby boy."

"Yes, Luther told us all about him. He's a security consultant, that's why it was so easy for him to find you." Pearl was back on the line again.

Amber snickered. "A security *consultant,* huh? That's a nice fancy title for it. Anyway, he's house-sitting for a friend, and we're staying there."

Suddenly, the line went silent, and Amber wondered if they had somehow gotten disconnected. "Hello?"

"House-sitting for a friend?" Opal said in confusion.

"Do you have money to come home today?" Pearl interrupted. "I can wire you some again, if you need me to."

Amber shook her head as if they could see. Once again she had to fight back tears. It seemed as if her sisters were always bailing her out of one mess or another. Dashuan was supposed to be her new beginning, her fresh start, and instead he turned out to be a same old-same old.

"I have money." The first tear slid down her face and she wiped it away. "Look, guys, I have to go, but I'll let you know as soon as I'm headed home. Okay?"

Amber knew her sisters all took that to mean she'd be calling later that day. With that, Amber hung up the phone and stretched out across the bed.

In truth, it really shouldn't have been that hard for her to pack up and return to Detroit with her tail between her legs. Goodness knows, she'd returned to the bosom of her family after worse disasters than this. There was that time last spring break when she and some of her college friends pooled their money for a Caribbean cruise. She'd met a gorgeous Jamaican guy in the ship's bar. Mason, he'd said his name was.

Even now that night was fuzzy. All Amber remembered

was waking up in her stateroom without her purse, which contained all her money and credit cards. That was the *again* Pearl referred to when she spoke of wiring her money.

She spent the rest of the cruise trying to find Mason, and some kind of redemption, without luck. It was as if he'd disappeared into thin air. It wasn't until she'd returned home that she found out about the con man that took advantage of tourists on such cruises.

Then there was the incident in Mexico with the local police, but Amber was convinced that that could've been taken care of much quicker, and she would not have had to spend a night in their prison if it wasn't for the language barrier problem.

And the ill-fated affair with her statistics professor two semesters ago. The man wore no wedding band, nor was there a line on his ring finger to indicate he was married. Although, his wife had no doubts whatsoever about his marital status when she came after Amber that night in the hotel.

The list went on and on. Unfortunately, her family was well-versed in the art of bailing her out of trouble. Why should this be any different? But for some reason, she was finding the idea of going home distasteful.

She heard a quick knock on the door.

"Just a minute." Using her hands, she wiped away the tears and sat up in the bed. "Come in."

Paul cracked the door and came in with the baby in his arms. "I was about to put him down for his nap, but wanted to check on you first. Everything okay?"

Amber was pretty sure he knew she'd just talked to her sisters, but he said nothing about it.

She smiled. "Yes, I'm fine." *Humiliated beyond belief, but fine.*

"Well, okay." He started to close the door. "Just let me know if you need anything."

"Paul!"

He opened the door wider, and waited.

"Is that offer to stay for a while still open?"

His dark brown eyes searched hers. "Yes."

She nodded. "I'd like to take you up on it, if you don't think your friend will mind."

Paul smiled with such understanding, Amber wanted to climb into his arms with Joachim. Instead, she sat holding herself still on the bed.

"He won't mind. You're welcome to stay as long as you like."

"Thank you."

He smiled and winked. "Enough already with the thank-you's." With that, he closed the door.

Amber stretched back out on the bed, wondering if she was doing the smart thing by accepting an offer of hospitality from a man who was little more than a stranger to her. She decided, with her track record, she had nothing to lose.

Chapter 5

Paul stood at the window overlooking the majestic mountainous Moreno Valley waiting for Vanessa, his receptionist, to answer the phone at his office.

After three rings a familiar voice answered.

"G-Force Security, the only name you need to know for all your personal protection needs. Vanessa speaking, how may I assist you?"

"Vanessa, it's me." Paul braced his long body against the windowsill.

"Hey, boss, where are you? I checked your calendar and didn't see any appointments. Karen's been going crazy getting the home system prototypes tested and keeping up with her cold calls, and with Ryan on vacation and you out of the office she's swamped. And Matt's crazy girlfriend stole his car again."

"Vanessa—"

"I swear, boss, Karen may be a wonderful salesperson, but—"

"Vanessa!" Paul regretted the harsh tone when the line went silent.

Vanessa Willis was a sweet teenager who'd come to work for him almost a year ago. She had no previous work experience, but five minutes into the interview Paul knew everything there was to know about the unexpected pregnancy that resulted in the birth of her little baby girl, Anna. And how her mother had given her the ultimatum to find a job or get out.

Although her story had tugged at his heart, Paul had decided to give the girl a chance, not because of her hard luck story, but because of her enthusiasm. He figured anyone who could be bubbly and upbeat while reciting such an account of her life would be described as an optimist.

As it turned out, hiring Vanessa was the right decision. She had energy and enthusiasm to spare, she was also bright and eager to do a good job and, most important, the customers loved her. But she did have one fatal flaw that Paul had not figured out how to handle. Vanessa loved nothing better than a few tidbits of juicy gossip. She was also sensitive to criticism.

"I'm sorry," he said on a sigh.

"It's okay," she muttered. "I know I talk too much. Where are you, anyway?"

"I'm working from home today. Where's Karen? I tried her cell phone, but she isn't answering." Paul knew in her current depressed state, it was too soon to abandon Amber. Which meant he would have to rely on his lead salesperson, Karen Grable, to keep things moving forward in his absence.

"It's Saturday, remember? She's out doing cold calls. She probably turned her cell phone off."

"Damn, I forgot all about that."

"Why are you working from home?"

Paul knew better than to answer that. News of his house-guest would be all over the office within the hour. "If Karen calls in, tell her to call me here."

"All right. Is Joachim okay?"

"Yes, I've got to go." With that, Paul pressed the button to hang up.

He sighed. Amber Lockhart could not have shown up at a worse time. He was right in the middle of developing a line of home security products to market to the public—in fact, his own home security system was a prototype for the line—and the commitment date to have it on the shelves was coming fast. The prototypes Vanessa mentioned were the second batch to be tested so far. And there had been countless other complications. There was so much to do, and so few hours in a day.

He tossed the cordless phone on the desk, braced his arms on the windowsill and continued to stare out the window, wondering what the hell he was thinking telling Amber Lockhart she could stay as long as she liked.

You were thinking that she would never take you up on the offer. That's what! Now he was stuck with an unwanted houseguest. He let his head drop and his shoulders sag. His sanctuary had been invaded. But there was nothing to be done about it now; the offer had been extended and accepted and now he had to live with the consequences of his actions. Hopefully, she would not want to stay too long. He shook his head, before sinking down into his black leather office chair.

About an hour later, Paul was on the phone with one of his manufacturers when the soft whimpering of Joachim's cry came through the door. By the time Paul ended the conversation and hung up, the whimper had become a fullfledged cry. Paul shot up out of the chair and headed toward the door. When he reached it, the crying had stopped, which alarmed him even more.

Taking the stairs two at a time, he reached the top landing in no time and hurried down the hall to Joachim's room. The image that greeted him was a complete surprise.

Amber was bent over the diaper-changing table, where Joachim lay with his feet in the air, playing with his toes.

Paul stood in the doorway, listening as Amber hummed a song. It took a couple of bars for him to recognize "Amazing Grace." With precision, she removed the soiled diaper and had another on his little bottom in a flash.

Joachim was so occupied with his feet, he barely noticed what she was doing. But the instant smile he gave her when she picked him up again told Paul that his bottom not only recognized the difference, but he was glad for it.

He stood silent as she rocked the baby in her arms and continued to hum. Turning in a slow circle, Amber froze when she turned toward the door and found Paul standing there.

"Oh, I hope you don't mind. His little bottom was wet, and he was crying so, and you were in your office. I figured, why bother you for something I can do myself."

"I'm sure Joachim is as grateful for your quick response as I am. Diaper-changing is not something he and I have mastered yet." He came toward them, but stopped a few feet away when he realized Amber was not going to hand the baby off to him.

"It's easy. You just have to stay out of the way of the waterfall." She laughed, and Paul felt the sensual sound from the tip of his toes to the top of his curly head.

"The waterfall?" he asked, picking up a nearby stuffed giraffe. He needed to do something with his hands. For some reason they were itching to wrap around Amber and Joachim.

"Oh, yes, the waterfall. Every baby boy's secret weapon."

Paul chuckled. "Ahh, the waterfall." He nodded. "I am well aware of the danger."

Amber walked across the room, still holding the baby in her arms, and Joachim seemed to be content to stay there, even as she lowered herself into the large rocking chair.

"You have to be careful when removing a dirty diaper as soon as you lift the second flap and the air hits his little wee-wee." She snapped her fingers.

Paul smiled. "Waterfall."

"Exactly!"

Amber bounced the baby, and Joachim giggled.

"You're a natural nurturer," Paul said.

"Not really," she answered. "It's just that babies are easy. They have a few basic desires—food, clean bottoms, toys and love." She turned the baby, prying his fingers off the thin, gold chain she wore around her neck. "It's adults I have a problem understanding," she said.

Paul watched the conflicted emotions run over her face. He knew that she was thinking of Dashuan Kennedy, but was unsure whether he should say something to her about it. Should he offer some kind of reassurance or would she rather he pretend not to understand?

"You know, Amber, you're not the only woman that something like that has happened to."

Her golden eyes narrowed on his face, and Paul knew he'd made the wrong decision. He'd gone too far to stop. "I mean, there are a lot of gay men out there dating straight women."

"Oh?"

There was something so vulnerable in her expression, Paul felt his heart twist inside his chest. All her insecurities, all her uncertainty was right there, exposed in her eyes. Paul felt her need for reassurance reaching out to him across the room. Her need to be desired, to be made to feel like a woman, was so strong it was almost tangible, and Paul felt it pulling him across the room. As if being drawn by a giant magnet, Paul found himself walking until he stood right in front of her.

He sank down on his knees before the rocking chair, looking up at her. "You are a beautiful, desirable woman, and Dashuan Kennedy is a fool."

Amber's eyes dropped as her lush brown lashes shielded her eyes. "Considering some of the decisions I've made in my life, I have to wonder if Dashuan is the fool."

Paul rested both his large hands on her warm thighs, and felt a jolt of desire course through his whole body. The way Amber sat straight up in her chair, he knew she felt it, too. His fingers tingled with the sensation of warm flesh, and he fought the urge to squeeze her soft flesh in his hands.

She lifted her lids until her tawny lioness eyes were looking into his. So lost in them, he didn't even feel his son's hand reaching out to touch his face.

Paul felt like a helpless animal trapped by her mesmerizing gaze. Like lightning to a rod, he sought her, powerless to resist.

Amber was a beautiful woman, but that wasn't what was making her so damn attractive. In his business, beautiful women, celebrities and socialites surrounded him. And more than a few had made a play for him. But being a single father was hard enough without trying to juggle a social life, so Paul declined invitation after invitation. But beauty and availability were not the things that had his whole body wired right this moment.

No, the something special about Amber Lockhart, the thing that had him breathing hard and growing harder, was something else. It was his one weakness when it came to women. The thing that drew him to Michelle, and tore them apart.

Paul had always been a sucker for a passionate, hot-blooded woman. And looking into her eyes, he could see that Amber Lockhart was burning with passion. It was straining, aching to be set free, and the man in him wanted nothing more than to open the floodgate.

He knew he shouldn't have, but he could not help himself. Paul leaned forward, wanting to taste her lips. At that moment, he honestly wanted a taste of Amber more than air to breathe.

Sensing his intent, Amber stood. "Isn't it time for Joachim's feeding?"

Paul, still kneeling, still hungry, his eyes level with the crotch of her slacks, was unable to comprehend her words.

"Paul?"

He took several deep breaths through his nose, and stood. Taking the baby from her arms, he licked his lips and tried to speak. "Yes. I'll do it."

He knew Amber did the right thing by standing; he knew it was for the best. The way he was feeling, who knew where even the smallest little kiss could've led?

Yes, denying the attraction was the smart thing to do, but somehow knowing that didn't make the acceptance of it any easier.

Paul paused in the doorway. "Thanks again for changing his diaper. I appreciate the help."

"That was my pleasure. He is such a sweet baby."

Paul tried to force a half smile before walking out of the room.

When she heard his footsteps on the carpeted stairs, Amber sank back down into the rocking chair. She could still feel Paul's large, warm hands on her thighs. For a moment there, she was almost certain he was going to pull her legs apart and come between them. Truth is, if he'd tried, Amber wasn't at all certain she would've stopped him.

She laid her head back against the hard, wooden chair and released a deep sigh. Amber wanted to stay with Paul another day or so, just long enough to get the courage to face her family and their guaranteed criticism. But now, there was no denying the sexual attraction she felt pass between her and Paul. Staying with him meant running the risk that those feelings would crop up again, and next time…there was no saying what might happen.

She could not let herself forget that this man was a friend of Luther's, who was like a brother to her. If she slept with him, even on the rebound, it could change her relationship with Luther forever.

She nodded, deciding on a plan. She would just have to make sure she stayed as far away from Paul Gutierrez as possible—if possible. *Lord, when will I learn to stay away from pretty men?*

Chapter 6

Later that same evening, as he chopped onions for the pot of chili that was boiling on the nearby stove, Paul glanced at the clock hanging on the wall over the dinner table and realized it was almost seven o'clock. He had not seen his houseguest in almost seven hours.

He looked at Joachim, who was bouncing in his swing, trying to grab the overhanging mobile that was just out of reach.

Paul's mind replayed the image of walking into the nursery and finding Amber huddled over the dressing table. She'd looked so natural there, so comfortable with the task, a person would think she changed dirty diapers on a regular basis. Of course, for all he knew about her she well may have. But from what Luther had told him about her, and what he'd seen himself, she did not strike him as the nurturing type. Then again, there was the indisputable proof of how well she handled Joachim. Maybe some women were just natural mothers. Give them a baby and they just knew what to do.

Then there were those who should never be mothers. His mind conjured the image of another beautiful woman, and the most horrific experience of his life.

The day he found Joachim's mother, Michelle, dead from a drug overdose. His infant son sat strapped in his car seat wailing from a combination of a soiled diaper and an empty stomach.

Paul was no innocent to scenes of death, having served on the front lines of a war zone. He'd seen his fair share of dead men, some of whom had been killed by his own hands. But nothing in his experience had prepared him for the traumatic experience of finding his former lover, the mother of his child, prone on a motel bed, her cold, dead body already beginning to stiffen.

Shaking off the melancholy image, he scooped the onions and hot peppers he'd chopped earlier into the boiling pot. Wiping his hands on the dish towel, he glanced back at his son once more before he turned and headed up the stairs to the guest room.

He stopped outside the door and lifted his hand to knock, but paused. *Maybe I should just leave her alone,* he thought. He knew the impact of what she had experienced had taken its toll. Paul could not even imagine how a woman would begin to get over finding her boyfriend in bed with another man. He could almost see her sitting on the side of the bed, replaying the image over and over again in her head.

He knocked, and heard movement in the room.

"Just a moment."

He listened to the sound of a nose being blown into a tissue. A few muffled sniffles, and then some more shuffling around. Paul assumed she was getting rid of the evidence of her misery.

"Come in."

When Paul opened the door, it took a moment for his eyes to adjust to the darkness. The only light was coming from the moon outside the large picture window.

Instead of the bed, Amber was perched on the pillows of the window seat, staring out over the large wooded area behind the house.

Paul came to stand beside her.

"Is this real?" She spoke in almost a whisper.

Since he had been wondering pretty much the same thing all day, Paul had no answer for her.

"Are you real?" She glanced up at him before returning her attention out the window. "Because if you are, and if this house is real, that means that everything that happened, the trip to L.A., Dashuan…that means that all of that is real, too."

It was just as he suspected. She was sitting in the dark room, feeling sorry for herself. Paul sat down on the seat beside her. "Sorry, angel, I'm afraid it is all too real."

She slanted her head just the slightest bit, and it revealed the single tear flowing down her face. Paul lifted his hand, and let it fall. Although every ounce of blood in his body wanted to console her, he knew if he took her into his arms, in her vulnerable state, things could easily get out of hand.

He folded his hands together. "So, is this what you plan to do all evening?"

She swiped at the tear. "Pretty much. Except, I thought maybe later, I'd let loose and cry myself to sleep."

He shook his head and made a ticking noise with his mouth. "I'm afraid that's not acceptable."

"Oh?"

She quirked an eyebrow in indignation, and Paul hid the smile that came to his lips. She may be a little battered, Paul thought, but she wasn't broken.

"See, there's a house rule that all houseguests have to do their fair share of the chores."

The other eyebrow went up. "Chores?"

He nodded. "I'm cooking dinner, even as we speak, which leaves the cleanup for you."

She folded her arms across her chest, and Paul took it as the clear sign of rebellion that it was.

"And if I don't?"

Paul stood. "Then you don't eat."

He walked across the room without ever looking back. He had started to pull the door closed behind him when he felt a pillow hit the side of his head.

"You know, I was wondering when the tyrant I met last night would resurface. This whole Mr. Mom thing you've got working here is just a front. In a way, I'm grateful you're showing your true colors. It's comforting to know I was at least right about *you*."

Paul glanced back over his shoulder with a wolfish smile. "Glad I could help. We're having chili for dinner, and it will be ready in about thirty minutes. And don't worry. I have rubber gloves to protect your delicate fingers." He quickly exited, and chuckled to himself as he heard the thump of another pillow hitting the door.

"No, sweet angel," he muttered under his breath, "you're not even close to being broken."

At seven-thirty, Amber appeared in the doorway of the

kitchen. Paul felt her presence as soon as she arrived, but continued to stir the pot without acknowledging her. Out the corner of his eye, he watched as his normally easy-tempered son began to squirm and wiggle in his walker.

Joachim became frustrated with his inability to make the walker go where he wanted. He began bouncing up and down and whimpering in earnest, his short chubby arms reaching for Amber.

Amber crossed the room and picked up the baby and he settled down, having gotten what he wanted. He tugged at a lock of long, golden brown hair that had come loose, and chatted in baby gibberish. It was obvious he'd missed his new friend and wanted to fill her in on the hours they'd been apart.

Paul glanced over his shoulder at the pair. "You're spoiling him."

"It's the other way around. I can't remember the last time any man greeted me with this much honest enthusiasm."

Paul smiled to himself and continued to stir the pot. "The chili is not quite ready, but there are dishes in the sink…if you want to get started now."

"No thanks, I'll wait." She gave him a smug smile as she passed by the stove and headed toward the dinner table. Amber sat down and began playing with the baby on her lap. She glanced around the large kitchen.

The room was large enough to fit thirty people comfortably. The walls were all covered in lacquered wood overlay and, combined with the stainless-steel appliances and the redbrick tiled floor, the effect was stunning. "Your friend has a nice house. What does he do for a living?"

Paul's mouth twisted. "Why do you ask?"

She shrugged. "Just wondering."

Satisfied that the chili was coming along okay, Paul

wiped his hands on a nearby dishtowel. He folded his arms across his chest and leaned a hip against the counter. "Can I ask you something?"

Amber shrugged, her attention focused on the laughing baby in her arms.

"How did you end up in L.A. with someone like Dashuan Kennedy?"

She glanced at his face, then looked away. "I thought Luther would've filled you in."

"No, he was too concerned with your safety to worry about details."

"So, now you want all the gory details?"

Paul stood straight and began to put away his seasonings and spices. "Look, it's your business, if you don't want to talk about it, that's okay."

"No…it's no big deal. Hell, thanks to Dashuan's entourage, most of Detroit probably already knows the story, anyway."

She crossed the room and put the baby down in the playpen. Joachim started to protest, until he realized all his toys surrounded him. He rolled over on his tummy, and then up on his knees like a pro, crawling toward his favorite.

Amber wrapped her arms around her body and walked to the large window that looked out on the night, framing the mountains silhouetted in the background.

Paul just stood watching her, giving her time to decide if she wanted to share what was obviously an embarrassing memory.

"My sister Opal works for the Chargers owner D'marcus Armstrong. He gives me tickets to the games. The seats are so close to the team I could smell their sweat."

Paul's eyes widened at the blatant sexual expression on

her face. He was beginning to understand what Luther meant about a wild child.

Amber glanced over at Paul and cleared her throat. "Anyway, Dashuan and I noticed each other right away, but he was so focused on the game, and I could respect that so we didn't say anything to one another. Until about three weeks ago, after the game Dashuan invited me and my friends to an after party."

Paul stirred the chili once more before turning the burner off. "I'm assuming you went."

"Well, me and my girlfriends went to the party, but not long after we got there we all got separated, and Dashuan was nowhere to be found." She nodded. "But the party was jumping. You name it, some of *everybody* was there. They had this live reggae band that was phenomenal, and the food…" She closed her eyes as if drifting away to a better place. "Delicious."

Paul smiled as he watched her blissful expression. "I take it you had a good time."

"Wonderful." Her smile faded.

"What's wrong?" Paul asked, pouring chili into a bowl.

"There were things about that night that just didn't click, if you know what I mean. But now, knowing what I know, everything is clicking into place."

Paul put the two bowls on the table and pulled a box of crackers out of a nearby cabinet. "Like what?"

"Like the first time I saw Dashuan all night was several hours after we arrived, and he was coming from the direction of the pool house…with Kelvin."

"Oh." Paul didn't know what else to say. He pulled a chair away from the table and stood behind it with a hand extended toward Amber.

She smiled, before coming to take the seat. "What a gentleman," she said continuing to smile up at him.

"Thank you." Paul returned the smile. "But you're still washing dishes."

She made a face, and stuck out her tongue, before scooting her chair closer to the table.

He grinned in return. Despite her spoiled-princess persona, Amber Lockhart was a fighter, Paul decided.

"Hey, this chili is pretty good," she said, having swallowed her first spoonful.

"Thanks."

"I have to admit, I'm a little impressed."

"Don't be too impressed. Chili is all I do."

"Hmm…a man who does not know how to cook for himself means that you are either an only child or the only male in a family full of women."

"Neither." Paul's whole demeanor changed as his body tensed.

Amber sensed that this was not a subject she should pursue. So, she chose something she thought would be easier. "Where is Joachim's mother?"

Paul froze with the spoon of chili halfway to his mouth. He lowered his eyes, and despite the tension permeating the dinner table, Amber could not help admiring his lush black lashes. The man really was sinfully gorgeous—everything from his chiseled features to his muscular frame.

Amber found she was more curious than she should've been for the answer to the last question. She had to know what woman would leave him alone to care for a stranger in the home of a friend. Looking at it, the whole situation stretched the imagination.

As if released from a spell, Paul took a spoonful. "She's dead."

Amber fought the urge to cover her mouth in horror. *When will I learn to keep my big mouth shut?* "Oh, Paul, I'm sorry to hear that."

"You never did finish telling me about how you met Dashuan."

Paul changed the subject, and Amber found that she was grateful for the conversational shift.

"Well, Dashuan and I spent an hour or so talking that night, then I had to get going home, because I had an exam the next day. When I got ready to leave, I found out my friends had left without me. Dashuan was nice enough to offer me a ride home. After that, we started going out once or twice a week." She shrugged and toyed with her chili, twirling it around her spoon. "A couple of nights ago, he called and asked if I wanted to come to L.A. with him, and here I am."

"Just like that?"

"Just like that."

"Hmm." Paul's thick, dark eyebrows crinkled.

"What?" She glanced at his face.

"Nothing. It's just— No offense, but if he wasn't interested in you—"

"Why invite me in the first place? Believe me, I've been asking myself that question all day. I hate to admit it, but Pearl tried to warn me about him."

"Who's Pearl?"

"My sister." She smiled. "I have three. There's Ruby, she's the oldest, and Opal and then Pearl. Sometimes I think she's the only one who gets me."

Paul was certain he could hear a little sadness in her

voice. Were her sisters the reason she didn't want to go home? "Have you decided what's next?"

"Not really." She glanced at his face and looked away, wondering if that was his less than subtle way of telling her not to overstay her welcome. "Where's your friend?"

"What friend?"

"The one you're house-sitting for."

Paul choked.

"Are you okay?"

He nodded, wiping his mouth with a paper napkin. "I'm fine. He's away on business."

Amber looked around the kitchen. "Must be some business to afford a place like this. When will he be back?"

Paul's eyes narrowed on her face, wondering if she was deciding to set her sights on his wealthy *friend*. "Why do you ask?"

She shrugged. "Just wondering how long we could stay here."

"Indefinitely. Now eat up. Those dishes are not going to wash themselves, you know."

She frowned, but it was more like a pout. "Tyrant."

The tyrant across the table just smiled in response.

Chapter 7

Amber felt her heart pounding against her chest, as a warm, masculine hand slid across her calf. She held her eyes closed. She did not need to see his face to know who it was. The large hand crept up her leg, gliding over her outer thigh, moving toward the inside, toward that place that begged to be touched.

Her legs fell apart, and her knees bent as her body shaped itself around the intruder. Her arms lifted, and as she knew they would, they landed on hard, muscular shoulders. She let out a deep sigh of relief, as his heavy weight settled on top of her.

Wrapping her legs around his slender hips, she felt his warm breath on her face. "Kiss me," she begged, lifting her lips to his, but the kiss never came. She knew he was still there, she could feel his throbbing penis against her stomach. He wanted her almost as much as she wanted him. "Please, Paul, kiss me."

Unable to bear the agony any longer, she opened her eyes, and they widened in surprise and horror to realize she was staring up into the sneering face of Dashuan Kennedy. Amber pushed with all her strength, and felt a sharp sting of pain as her bottom landed on the carpeted floor.

She glanced around, desperately trying to get her bearings, then covered her face in relief to discover she was alone in the dark guestroom. It was a dream. No, a nightmare.

Looking down at her body, she realized she'd somehow gotten wrapped in the bed linen and was now sitting mummified on the floor. She managed to disentangle herself and get to her feet.

Her mind was still trying to come to grips with the bizarre images when she heard another noise. She glanced at the glow-in-the-dark clock on the nightstand and realized it was two in the morning.

She stumbled out into the hallway and listened again. The noise was coming from the kitchen. She wiped at her eyes and wandered down the stairs, wondering what Paul would be doing up at such an hour.

As she rounded the corner and came into the kitchen, she covered her face when the bright lights hit her in the eyes. She could see a blurry outline standing with his back to her, near the stove. "What are you doing?" she asked.

"Sorry, to disturb you," Paul answered. "I was just fixing Joachim's formu—"

Amber jumped at the loud clatter of the pot being dropped. She shielded her eyes from the light in a desperate attempt to see what was going on. "What was that?"

What she saw was Paul standing in the middle of the room, a spilled pot of milk at his feet. He was staring at her with his mouth hanging open, and a look in his eyes that Amber knew too well.

As things began to come into focus, so did her thoughts. That was when it occurred to her what she was wearing. The only thing she had to sleep in—the slinky negligee she'd bought for her special night with Dashuan.

She let out a strangled screech and attempted to cover herself with her hands. Her own mortification and anger found a misplaced outlet in Paul. "What the hell are you staring at?"

Paul never took his eyes away from her. "Perfection."

Embarrassed beyond belief, Amber turned and rushed back up the stairs. She slammed the bedroom door shut and threw herself across the bed.

She pounded the pillow with both hands. In truth, she couldn't explain the intense feeling of humiliation. After all, it wasn't as if she was naked—okay, not *exactly* like she was naked. And it was not as if she had never been naked, or almost naked in the presence of a man before. It was just…why this man?

This man who already knew far too many humiliating things about her. It just seemed so unfair that he got to keep his dignity while hers was being stripped away piece by piece.

At a hard knock on the door, Amber shot straight up on the bed. "Go away!" She waited for the apology that was certain to come, which explained why her eyes widened when he threw open the door and stormed in without any warning.

Paul stopped a few inches from the bed, his roving eyes picking up right where they left off.

Amber was in no mood to provide a peep show. She crawled under the covers, pulling them up to her neck. "I said go away!"

"Why are you so mad at me? I'm not the one scampering through the house in my birthday suit. And by the way, if you wanted to get my attention all you had to do was ask!"

Her eyes widened in indignation. "What!"

"You heard me!" A wicked sneer twisted his pretty mouth. "I understand a woman like you needs attention, and I would be more than happy to provide you with some."

"A woman like me? What's that supposed to mean?" Angered beyond reason, she shot up on her knees in the bed, letting the covers fall to her waist.

His dark eyes raked over her form once more before returning to her face. "Some women get lonely faster than others."

"I'll never be that lonely. Now get out!"

His dark eyes narrowed, and Amber could feel the anger radiating off him. He turned and stormed out of the room, slamming the door shut behind him.

Paul gripped the balcony railing, bracing his heavy weight against it while he waited for his blood to stop pounding and his temper to cool. His strong hands balled into fists. She had done it on purpose. Flaunting her beautiful body in his face like he was made of steel.

His lips thinned. *I could show her what steel feels like.* His eyes widened, shocked by his own crude thoughts. He ran a trembling hand through his curly hair, trying to steady his nerves. Whether she'd deliberately come into the kitchen wearing barely nothing, Paul could not deny one thing. She was incredible, perfectly made, as if she were formed from his most secret dreams. And he wanted her more than he'd wanted a woman in a long time.

From the moment he took her out of that hotel in L.A.,

Paul had known this could happen if he did not keep his guard up. But how could any man possibly keep his guard up when she was strutting around in that outfit?

Just then, he heard Joachim whimpering as he began to wake up for his late-night feeding. In short time that whimper would become a full-fledged cry, and the only thing he had to offer was a pot of spilled formula.

His thoughts still scrambled, Paul debated between going to the baby and rushing downstairs to clean up the mess and prepare a new bottle. He decided there was no reason to go into the nursery empty-handed. So, he hurried down the stairs. Just as he entered the kitchen, Joachim let go of a howl that brought the hairs up on the back of his neck.

Amber lay on the bed listening to the baby cry, certain that his father would be there to stop the mournful pleas. But as the seconds ticked by, Joachim continued to wail at the top of his lungs.

Unable to bear the heartbreaking noise, Amber slipped off the bed, taking the time to slip into the slacks and blouse she'd worn for the past two days now. She went down the hall to the nursery.

When she entered the room, Joachim was attempting to stand on the side of the crib, but because he had not yet mastered balance, his little legs kept giving way and he kept landing back on his diapered bottom, which added to the frustration of his empty stomach.

She crossed the room, and when he spotted her, his chubby arms reached forward, grasping at air. Amber scooped him up in her arms, pressing him against her chest. "Shh, little one, shhh. It's okay, Daddy's coming."

Just happy to have someone acknowledging his plight,

Joachim seemed to settle down at the soft cooing, although he continued to cry in earnest hunger.

Amber rocked him back and forth, hoping that Paul was on the way with a bottle. Then she remembered the pot of spilled milk on the kitchen floor, and knew what was taking so long. She was still deciding if she was brave enough to face him in the kitchen once again, when he appeared at the nursery door with a bottle.

When Joachim spotted the bottle, he practically jumped out of Amber's arms reaching for his father. Amber handed the baby over without a word, and stood watching as Paul settled down in the rocking chair to feed his son.

"Sorry I took so long, little man." Paul apologized to the baby, but Amber couldn't help feeling as if the apology was for her.

Joachim wasn't interested in any apologies, as he settled in the crook of his father's arm, sucking on the bottle. After four or five huge gulps, he took a deep, fortifying breath, and then continued drinking at a slower rate.

Amber stood in the middle of the room for several awkward seconds before it became apparent that Paul was not going to say anything to her. She turned and headed toward the door, wondering if she should attempt to find somewhere else to stay. She was almost to the door when she heard Paul speak.

"I appreciate you putting on some clothes in front of my son, but you don't have to be so formal."

Amber turned, fire blazing in her eyes. She'd had just about all the smart remarks she could stand. "Unfortunately, I *do* have to be formal. If you'll remember when you found me at the hotel I was leaving in somewhat of a hurry and forgot my suitcases!"

Paul's eye's widened as the rocking chair came to a slow stop. He felt as if it would swallow his shrinking form. He had forgotten all about the fact that she did not have any clothes, other than the ones she'd arrived in.

So, where did the little slinky, sexy thing come from? He remembered the shopping bags she'd been carrying that night. Obviously the outfit had been purchased for the pleasure of Dashuan Kennedy, he realized with jealousy.

Still, the girl had no clothes, and he'd not offered to help her in any way. He'd just criticized her for wearing the only thing she had to wear.

He'd let his hormones take control of his brain, and that situation hardly ever worked out. Hardly ever. He looked down at the bundle in his arms, remembering the one time in his life when hormones had ruled over intellect and created something wonderful.

Realizing no argument would ensue, Amber turned to walk out of the nursery.

"Amber," Paul called her once more before she'd walked through the door.

She turned, paused, but his next words seemed a long time coming.

"Thanks for checking on Joachim for me."

Amber knew it was an apology of sorts, but it just wasn't enough. After the way he'd talked to her, she was still stinging from the blow to her pride. "Don't thank me. I didn't do it for you."

Paul watched as she walked out of the room with a stiff spine and her head held high. He'd hurt her. In that moment, he knew there was nothing more heartbreaking than a wounded angel.

Chapter 8

When Amber awoke the next morning, she turned over and looked at the clock on the nightstand. She was surprised to see it was almost nine. It was much later than she normally slept, but given her busy night, it was understandable.

As she pulled her tired body upright, she also accepted that it was time to leave Casa Gutierrez. Although, it wasn't even Casa Gutierrez, was it? she thought, looking around at the scarcely furnished room. Her eyebrows crinkled as she considered just how comfortable Paul seemed in his friend's house.

She stood and pulled the scarf off her head, running her hands through her relaxed hair with a large yawn. She was halfway to the bathroom, when her eyes landed on the set of clothes folded on the dresser.

She couldn't help smiling as she picked up the folded

jeans and the plain red T-shirt. It was a truce, an apology. And, she hoped, an invitation to stay.

The truth was, although she was prepared to leave and return home to her family with her tail tucked between her legs, she would much rather stay here with this interesting man and his adorable baby boy a little longer.

After a quick shower, she dressed in the jeans that ended up needing to be folded at both the top and the bottom in order to make them fit. When she pulled the large T-shirt over her head, she ended up looking like a five-year-old dressed for a day at the beach. But that didn't matter. She was feeling better than she had in days.

She bounded down the stairs with renewed energy, and was surprised to find the kitchen empty. She wandered from room to room, trying to find Paul to thank him for his temporary donation to her scarce wardrobe.

As she came to the study door, she could hear talking coming from the other side. She knocked, and waited.

"Come in," Paul's gruff voice answered.

She reared back, looking at the door in indignation. But she still had enough of the good vibe thing going to ignore his tone. She cracked the door open and saw Paul sitting behind a large mahogany desk, his attention focused on the laptop in front of him.

"What do you need, Amber?" he asked, never taking his eyes off the screen.

"Just wanted to say thanks." Her eyes scanned the room, and when she saw no sign of Joachim, she assumed he was still napping.

Paul's dark eyes glanced at her before returning to the screen. "No problem. If you want, later I'll take you to the mall."

He did want her to stay. "Thanks, that would be great." Her attention was drawn to a picture on a small side table near the window. She looked at Paul, still engrossed in whatever he was doing, and decided to inspect the picture for herself instead of asking him a bunch of questions.

Out of curiosity, she crossed to the table and picked up the picture, but frowned in confusion when she saw it was a picture of Joachim when he was much smaller. Her eyes begin to scan the room, and she went from table to bookshelf, pausing to look at the pictures.

She realized this was the coziest room in the whole house. It was personalized and well-used. She gave a short gasp as the truth hit her in the face. It was extremely personalized and well-used…by the *homeowner.*

A few minutes later, Paul finished the quote for the six guards to transport some precious artifacts to New York for the Metropolitan Museum. He stretched, taking his eyes off the laptop, and only then did he notice Amber was still in the room. She had taken up position in one of the wing chairs on the other side of the desk and, considering the folded arms across her chest and the intense frown on her face, she had something on her mind.

Could she still be angry about the night before? No, if that were the case, she would've been angry when she entered the room.

He titled his head in concern and was just about to ask, when she exploded.

"House-sitting for a friend, huh?"

Paul's frantic eyes quickly scanned the room, as he realized his mistake. He'd been so involved in writing the report he hadn't stopped to think about what she would see when she entered the room. Signs of his life before and after Joachim were everywhere.

Paul stood. Given the fire raging in her eyes, something told him not to make any sudden moves. "I can explain."

She huffed. "This should be good. By all means, explain, Paul. Tell me why you would bring me out here to the middle of nowhere and then claim the house belongs to a friend."

"I thought you were—"

"What? You thought I was what?"

"I didn't know you, and—"

"Are you even a security guard?" She glanced around once more, and then burst into laughter. "Of course not!" She shook her head and stood. "What have I gotten myself in to?"

"Amber, I just didn't know you well. And after Luther told me how you followed Kennedy here, I thought…"

"Oooohhh, I get it now." She stood and moved away from the chair. "Okay, I get it. Didn't want the little basketball groupie getting the wrong idea, right?"

"That's not what I meant."

"Of course, it is. After all, we know how women like me are." She pressed both hands to her chest in an exaggerated gesture. "The kind that gets lonely faster than others. I see some hotshot in his big fancy house, and who knows what I might do, right?" She went to the end of the desk and leaned forward, her eyes narrowing on his face. "Afraid I might crawl into your bed one night and force myself on you, Paul? Afraid I might get attached to your beautiful home and your sweet baby, and you'll never get rid of me. Is that it?"

Paul listened in silence. She finally seemed to run out of steam, though the fire in her eyes had not even dimmed. "Are you done?"

She just continued to glare in silence.

He gestured to the chair on the other side of the desk. "Sit."

Amber folded her arms across her chest and stood still.

He hunched his shoulder and flopped down in his chair. "All right, suit yourself. Before you get too high up on that soap box, you need to consider the fact that you are to blame."

She opened her mouth to protest and he put up a hand to silence her. "No! You've had your say, now it's my turn."

With a deep breath, she conceded and sat down.

"When I picked you up at the hotel, do you remember the look you gave my car? You turned your pretty little nose up like it was some kind of diseased monster."

"Well, it's ugly!"

"See?" He pointed one long, elegant finger at her. "That attitude right there is the reason I did not tell you."

"That does not explain why you lied about the house and your occupation."

"I didn't lie about my occupation. I told you I was in security, which I am. You assumed that meant I was a security guard. Truth is, I own a security consulting company called G-Force."

Her mouth thinned again. "And the house?"

"Okay, I can admit that was just my own bad reaction to your behavior earlier that night. When we pulled up, and you asked whose house it was, you had already assumed it could not be mine. So, I let you go on believing that. But that was two days ago. I apologize, but you have to admit that you are partially responsible."

"I will admit no such thing." She stood again, and without another word headed for the door.

"Where are you going?" Paul called to her.

"To get my stuff together. It seems I've overstayed my welcome. I'll be heading back to Detroit today."

"Sure you want to do that?"

"No!" she shouted in frustration. "But what choice do I have? Dashuan doesn't want me, you don't want me, no one wants me!" The tears began to pour down her face in earnest.

Paul was unable to resist the dejected figure standing before him, with her proud shoulders slumped in defeat. He crossed the room and took her in his arms.

"You're welcome to stay. I'm sorry, I've been such a jerk. I'm not normally this much of a pain in the ass." He propped his chin on the top of her head. "It seems you bring out the best in me."

She chuckled against his shirt. "If this is your best, you're in trouble."

"I know, so see? You have to stay, to help me improve my behavior and learn the proper way to treat a houseguest."

Even though Amber wanted to stay cuddled in his strong arms, she was even more afraid of living up to his lowest expectation—a kind of femme fatale that preyed on wealthy men.

She stepped back out of his arms. "No, I appreciate the offer, but I better get going."

"I tell you what, give it twenty-four hours. If you still want to leave this time tomorrow, I'll take you to the airport. It's only been a couple of days. Give yourself some more time."

Amber knew she should've declined the offer. The problem was that most of her wanted what he was offering too much to turn it down. "Twenty-four hours?"

"Just one more day out of your life to be sure you're making the right decision." *And one more day for me to convince you not to leave.* Paul did not examine the reasons he wanted her to stay.

"All right," she said. "I'll stay another day, and thank you for offering."

"Hey, why don't we pack up Joachim and go shopping now?" Even as he said the words, Paul glanced back at his laptop. He hadn't done any work in two days. This woman was wreaking havoc on his schedule.

Amber saw his eyes dart to the laptop. "No, it's okay, we can go later."

Paul wrapped his arm around her waist and guided her to the door. "No, I insist." As they left the office, Paul pulled the door closed behind him. He justified his behavior by deciding that even the boss deserved some time off now and then.

Chapter 9

Almost three hours later, the couple found themselves pushing a baby stroller down a crowded avenue. They had been returning from the mall in creeping traffic, when Paul commented that the congested roads were due to the Avenue Art Fair that was going on that weekend.

Amber had lit up in delight at the prospect of seeing some local artisans' work, and Paul had been too mystified by her excitement to discourage her. And now, here they were.

"Oh, look at this, Paul." Amber stopped beside a covered booth that had two shelves lined with hand-blown jars in various shapes and sizes. She picked up a small oblong-shaped cylinder, turning it this way and that, studying the detailed engravings that surrounded the bottle.

"You have good taste, miss." The booth operator spotted the couple and made his way toward them. "This is one of my personal favorites."

"Do you do the glass yourself?" Amber asked, still studying the jar.

"Each and every one. I start with a detailed drawing, images that come to me in my dreams. And even with so much preparation, the glass still manages to take on a life of its own."

"How much?" she asked. Being an experienced barterer, Amber knew a line when she heard one. He was setting her up.

"That one took almost three weeks, from—"

"How much?"

The man frowned. "Four hundred dollars."

"Four hundred?" Amber's eyes widened and she turned the vase upside down.

"What are you doing?" the booth owner asked.

"Looking for the Waterford symbol on the bottom. I assume it must be *Waterford* crystal for that price!"

"What about you, sir?" The booth owner turned his attention to Paul. "Is four hundred dollars too much to pay to bring a smile to your wife's face?"

Paul and Amber exchanged nervous glances.

"I'm not his—"

"She's not my—"

They began and stopped in the same instance, giving each other a strange look neither had the nerve to question.

The booth operator pointed at the baby snuggled in the stroller. "Sorry, I just assumed."

"I'll give you one hundred for it," Amber offered.

"One hundred? That's just a fraction of its worth. Two fifty."

"Never mind."

"Two hundred."

"One fifty."

"Fine!" the man huffed, then went to wrap the glass in paper.

Amber felt Paul's eyes on her and turned to see him smiling at her. "What?"

"Nothing. It's just…you didn't strike me as the bargaining type." His smile widened, and Amber felt those stupid butterflies taking flight inside her belly once more.

"I watched the way you shopped today," he continued. "You were actually looking at tags."

"I'm a full-time student, and even with my grants, between tuition and books, there isn't a lot left over for the little extras. So, you learn to become careful about what you splurge on."

"And you thought that vase was worth one hundred and fifty dollars?"

"It was worth two, but I'm not telling him that. Did you see that detailing? He's right—it probably took him several hours to get that kind of intricate design in place." She shrugged her shoulders. "What can I say, I like unique things."

"You *are* a unique thing." Paul said, his dark eyes looking into hers.

Amber wasn't sure what to say in response to such an odd compliment, if it even was a compliment.

"Paul?" A tall blond woman came up beside Paul and touched his arm. "I thought that was you. Harold, I told you that was Paul."

"Hey, buddy," A dark-haired man came up, taking Paul's hand in a vigorous shake. Something in his eyes cried apology, and it didn't take Paul long to find out why.

"Aren't you going to introduce us?" The woman smiled at Amber.

Paul rolled his eyes. "Brenda and Harry Michelson, meet Amber Lockhart. Amber's a friend of mine, visiting from out of town. Amber, the Michelsons are neighbors of mine."

Amber smiled and offered greetings to the couple.

"You know when I saw you two pull into the parking lot ahead of us, I said, 'Harold that looks like Paul with that pretty young lady.'" Brenda bent forward to play with the baby. "So, are you Joachim's mother?" Brenda asked.

Paul's eyes narrowed on her back. "If you want to know something about Joachim, Brenda, talk to me. Got me?"

Realizing she'd overstepped her bounds, Brenda stood straight. "I'm sorry, I meant no offense, it's just—" She turned pleading eyes on her husband, and Harry stepped forward, shaking his head.

"Excuse my wife." Harry smiled at Amber. "Sometimes she can be a bit overzealous when she meets new people."

Brenda's worried eyes roamed over Paul's face. "Paul, you know I meant no harm. It's just so rare we see you with anyone." She looked to Amber. "I apologize if I—"

Amber took pity on the woman, and raised her hand to still the apology. "You didn't."

"Well, we'd better be going," Harry said, taking his wife's elbow and leading her away.

Once they were alone again, Amber waited for Paul to regain control of his temper before she spoke. "She meant no harm, you know."

Before Paul could respond, the booth owner handed Paul the wrapped package as Amber paid for it.

He accepted the package, cradling it in his arm like he would his son. "I know. For the most part Brenda's a sweet lady. She's just so damn nosy, it drives me crazy."

Amber was tempted to blurt out that just like Brenda,

she, too, was curious about Joachim's mother. But she still remembered the way he tensed up the last time she'd asked. She was having such an enjoyable time, she didn't want to say anything that might ruin it.

As they continued along the avenue, Paul seemed lost in his own thoughts. He was trying not to think too much about the woman at his side. That morning, she'd been ready to leave, he could see it in her eyes. And a part of him knew that was for the best. The last thing he needed to bring into his son's life was another Michelle. He'd been around enough to know that women like Amber Lockhart were all the same. And as certain as he was about that, he was even more convinced that if she continued to scamper around his house in next to nothing, she would scamper right into his bed and he would do nothing to stop her. He should've let her go while he had the chance. But for reasons he did not want to examine, he'd been unable to just stand by and let her leave.

Although, he'd known her a short while, living in such close proximity had sped up the familiarizing process, and a part of him had gotten used to her being there. Most of the time it was just him and Joachim, and during the day Rosalie. And now there was this vibrant presence in his home twenty-four hours a day. He just wasn't ready to go back to the silence.

Feeling a tug on his arm, he looked down to see Amber, her arm looped through his. "Did I tell you thank you for taking me shopping?"

"You're welcome. Although I do question your choice of sleeping attire," he said with a frown.

Amber laughed, knowing he was referring to the one pair of pajamas she'd bought. In truth, the abstract design, colored in with olive green and hot pink, was indeed ugly, but the plush material was so soft against her cheek she could not resist buying them. "I don't know what you're talking about," she teased. "I think my new pj's are quite stylish."

He huffed with pure skepticism. Noticing that the sun was high in the sky, Paul bent forward and pulled the stroller visor down over Joachim. In doing so, he noticed they were being followed. "Don't look now, but I think we're being tailed."

Of course, being told not to look, Amber looked over her shoulder, and laughed to see the staunch little seagull waddling along behind. "Where did he come from?"

"We're not too far from the ocean, you know. Orange County has over forty miles of coastline, and some of the best beaches in the world." He gestured to the tall, stately trees that lined both sides of the avenue. "Haven't you noticed how green everything is around here?"

"Not really." Amber bit her lip. "Just how…*suburban* everything is."

Paul chuckled, and shook his head.

Amber had a feeling that his humor was at her expense. "What?"

"You say *suburban* like it's something foul."

"No, it's just not my thing, I'm a city girl. And granted, I know little about you, but you just don't seem like the picket fence type. I would think a man like you would be bored to death living out here."

"After living in a war zone, I'm satisfied with boredom."

Amber tilted her head and gave him a strange look. She had almost forgotten that Paul and Luther had served together in the military. "What was it like?" she asked, needing to know what could bring such a melancholy expression over his handsome face.

Paul smiled. "It's nothing I would ever want to share with a beautiful young woman." Just then, their forgotten feathery escort balked and flapped his wings, almost as if to regain their attention.

Amber, unsure if the bird was becoming violent, moved to position her body between the animal and the stroller. "Why do you think he's following us?" she asked, baffled by the bird's strange behavior.

As Paul shooed at it with his hands, the bird scurried out of reach, and then caught up with them again. This continued for several feet, and Paul was becoming more and more frustrated by the minute…and Amber's taunting laughter was not helping.

"Paul, you're frightening him." She laughed.

Paul glanced around at the people who'd stopped to watched the show of man versus bird. "Get out of here!" He fanned his arms, but the bird continued to follow.

Remembering something, Amber stopped the stroller and dug in to her purse. She came out with a little bag that said Cookie Factory on the front. In the bag was the remains of a half-eaten, oversized chocolate chip cookie she'd bought at the mall. She crumbled it up and sprinkled the crumbs on the ground between them and the bird.

When they begin to walk away, this time the bird did not follow, as he was too intent on his treasure. Almost instantly, the little seagull was joined by at least a dozen other birds, everything from pigeons to sparrows fighting to devour the crumbs.

Paul glanced back over his shoulder. "There's your answer."

"My answer to what?" Amber glanced back, surprised by the number of birds that had appeared out of nowhere.

"Why he was following us. He knows a soft touch when he sees one."

A short while later, they pulled into the middle slot of Paul's three-car garage.

"Thank you for today," Amber said, before yawning and stretching. She'd fallen asleep on the way back from the street fair.

"Will you stop thanking me?" Paul said, turning the engine off. "I enjoyed it as much as you. Between work and Joachim, I don't get a lot of time for street fairs and window-shopping."

Amber ran her hand over the leather interior of the SUV. "Now, this is more like it. Much better than your other little mutt of a car."

Paul frowned. "You know, Amber, that attitude is the reason you've found yourself stranded here. You're too caught up in what a man has and not who he is. You follow someone like Dashuan Kennedy across the country because you're impressed by his money and fame, and look what that got you."

Amber sat straight up in the seat, the feeling of contentment she'd been experiencing all day gone. "Who the hell do you think you are? You don't know enough about me to make any kind of judgments. Not that I owe you any explanation, but for your information, I couldn't care less about Dashuan's money or fame. I came here with him because I thought he cared about me."

She leaned forward across the console, her eyes narrowing on his face. As ticked off as he was, it still took Paul's full concentration to ignore the fact that her movement had parted her blouse, exposing a small glimpse of tempting cleavage.

"And before you get too high and mighty, let me remind you of that look in your eyes last night when you burst into my room. You think I don't know what men see when they look at me?" She sneered, seeing the slight doubt that flashed across his face. "Tell me something, Paul, while your eyes were taking in every inch of my body, were you thinking about a deep and meaningful relationship?"

Unable to resist her provocative smell, Paul reacted without thought. Reaching across the seat he grabbed her collar and pulled her closer. "No, beautiful girl, I was thinking about this." His mouth descended on hers, devouring her with such intensity he took her breath away.

Amber struggled to get free, not because his soft lips weren't wonderful, as this kiss was the sweetest thing she had ever tasted, but because of the sheer power of his hold, she couldn't breathe.

Feeling her resistance, Paul tilted his mouth at a different angle, and although he still wouldn't release her or allow her to break their connection, she could breathe once again.

Finally, he began to pull away from her. Then, as if having second thoughts, he pulled her close once more and kissed her again. His warm tongue feathering over her bottom lip was pure torture. Then he released her.

Amber blew out long, slow breath.

Paul balled his fist, as he struggled to slow his racing heartbeat. "I'm sorry. I shouldn't have done that." He glanced at her. "I guess I just confirmed everything you said."

A stiff silence fell over the pair. A few minutes passed before Amber broke it.

"I truly thought Dashuan cared for me."

Paul could hear the sadness and disappointment in her words.

"I had even hoped he would learn to love me. Not because I wanted his money." She smiled. "Don't get me wrong. The fact that he was rich and famous wasn't a bad thing. It's just I thought I had found a man I could have something solid with. Know what I mean?"

Paul's mouth twisted as Michelle's pretty face flashed before his eyes. "Yes, I know what you mean." He reached across the seat and took her hand in his. He needed to touch her. The kiss had awakened his desire and in no way satisfied the craving to feel every part of her. "But, Amber, you had to know what kind of man he is."

She arched her eyebrow in surprise, and Paul laughed.

"Okay, maybe not *exactly* what kind of man he is. What I mean is, the celebrity type. You deserve to be more than some basketball player's piece of—"

"Hold it right there!" She shook her finger in his face. "I'm not some kind of sports groupie. You make it sound like I go chasing after every man who winks at me."

Paul stared at her, a glint of humor appearing in his eyes, and a slow smile came across his face. "Look at us. Why can't we be together for more than five minutes without going for each other's throats?"

Her mouth twisted. "That's because you're irksome."

His eyes widened in surprise. "Well, thank you for clearing up that little mystery."

Amber was unable to stop the smile that came across her face.

He started to open his door to get out, and noticed a car passing on the street. He stood and watched as a black Mustang went to the end of the block and then turned the corner. He wouldn't have noticed the car, except that he was certain he'd seen that exact same car pass two other times, just while they'd been sitting there in the driveway.

Amber opened the back door and was unbuckling Joachim's car seat when she noticed Paul's intense expression. She looked toward the now empty street. "What's wrong?"

He frowned. "Probably, nothing." He glanced at Amber and noticed how she was scrutinizing his face. He forced his features to relax and even tried to smile. There was no use alarming her. After all, for all he knew it could just be someone who was lost. But in his gut, he felt it was something more. The rental car company sticker on the bumper increased his concern.

It could just be a lost tourist. Or an angry basketball player looking for the one person who could ruin his career. Either way, Paul made a mental note to be more watchful.

Chapter 10

As they entered the house, Paul could hear the phone ringing. He went into the kitchen and grabbed the cordless phone off the counter.

"Paul? It's Rosalie."

"Hi, Rosalie, is everything okay with Enrique?" He leaned a shoulder against the wall, watching as Amber removed Joachim's hat and jacket.

"Oh, yes, he is recovering well. In fact, I feel confident I can leave him for a few hours every day now."

He watched as Amber lifted the baby over her head. Joachim squealed in delight, reaching for her face as he was brought closer to her. She kissed his soft cheek and settled him in his playpen.

"There's no hurry to return, Rosalie. Joachim and I are doing just fine. You take as long as you like. Besides, it's not safe leaving Enrique alone for hours every day."

Just then Amber stretched her slender body, giving Paul a perfect silhouette view of her shapely outline. No wonder she was sleepy, he thought, remembering her appearance in the kitchen in the early morning hours. He never did find out what she was doing up at that time of the night.

She yawned and pointed toward her bedroom, before waving and heading up the stairs. Paul watched her go.

"Are you sure, Paul? I know Joachim can be a handful, especially with you trying to work from home."

"No, really, Rosalie. It's fine. In fact, I'm enjoying our time together."

"Well, okay, then, and thank you, Paul."

After he hung up the phone, he walked over to the playpen and found his son curled on his side sleeping soundly. He'd fallen asleep as soon as Amber put him down. He noticed the soft blue blanket across him and titled his head in confusion.

When did she do that? he wondered.

While you were lusting over her body, his libido answered.

He scratched his chin, amazed that he could be so distracted. Then he chuckled to himself when he remembered that he was *supposed* to be a surveillance expert.

He headed to his office, deciding that with both members of his household asleep, there was no better time to get some work done.

Amber couldn't asleep. She was lying across the bed, staring at the ceiling remembering the kiss Paul had given her in the car.

She smiled to herself as she recounted how he'd tried to release her and then pulled her back. Her smile turned to a full grin. *He couldn't have stopped himself if he wanted to!*

There was something so savagely satisfying in knowing that she could have that effect on a man as controlled as Paul Gutierrez. It was redeeming, it was validating. And she now knew with absolute certainty that Dashuan Kennedy was the exception—not the rule.

She still had all of her feminine allure, and she wanted to turn every ounce of that charm loose on Paul. But there were a couple of complications to that plan. The first and greatest being that he already thought she was the kind of woman who used her sexuality to manipulate men. Which was probably true, but Paul was not a man who would be easily manipulated. The second complication was Amber's uncertainty as to what she wanted. She was wise enough to understand that she was swimming in new depths.

At the most, all she could offer Paul was a fling, considering she only planned to stay a few days. But would that be enough? She knew in her heart that there was no way she could treat Paul like every other man she'd ever dated, because Paul was not like any man she'd ever known.

And what about little Joachim? She already adored him. If she got involved with his father would she be able to just pack up and leave them both when the time came?

She turned on her side and released a defeated sigh. Who was she kidding? Paul Gutierrez would never agree to a casual fling. He was controlling and possessive to his core. Not to mention, stuffy and uptight. And she was just not cut out for the role of wife and mother. No, she decided, it was better to just leave things as they were.

Later than evening, Amber was just pulling her roast from the oven, when Paul appeared in the kitchen doorway.

"Hmm, something smells wonderful." He let his nose lead him to the stove.

"Since chili is all you do, I thought I better take control of the situation."

"Hey, I don't just do chili. I do *great* chili," he said, lifting the lid off one of the pots on the stove top to find seasoned pasta inside.

"You won't get any argument from me, but I like variety." She tilted her head and smiled. "What about you?"

Paul studied her pretty face, realizing there was some kind of hidden meaning in her words, but was unsure as to what it was. "No, I can be happy being served the same dish every night, as long as it's something I love."

"But don't you think it might be fun to mix it up now and again, try something new?" Her eyes slid over his long form. "A sample. You know, just to see what it tastes like."

Paul twisted his mouth, her vague references becoming clearer. "But what if I like what I…*sample?*" His dark eyes bore into hers. "What if I decide to make that my everyday meal?"

Her eyes widened. "Well, you can't!" Amber felt like a hare caught in a trap. The man was too intelligent by far. She'd hoped to learn a little of his attitude about life in general, by asking the most innocuous questions imaginable, but he'd already figured out what she wanted to know, and was giving the exact answer she'd expected. "I mean, a sample is just that, a sample. You can't make it an everyday dish."

Paul leaned against the counter, folding his arms across his chest. "Why not?"

Amber turned away from the stove, unable to take the scrutiny of those eyes. What could she tell him? That she could never be an everyday dish, that all she'd ever been was a lifetime of samples?

Just then, the baby swing Joachim was in stopped moving, and he begin to squirm and whimper. Amber went to him and rewound the swing. Once it was back in motion, Joachim turned his attention back to the tray of toys in front of him.

"Answer me, Amber." Paul spoke from behind her. "Why? How do you know what it can be until you try it?"

Feeling cornered, and regretting that she was the one who started this conversation, she turned her frustration on Paul. She swung around to face him. "Because! That's just the way it is with some foods!"

Paul smiled and ran the back of his hand along her cheek. "Angel, we stopped talking about food a long time ago."

She brushed his hand aside. "Just forget it. I'm sorry I even brought it up." She moved around him and returned to the stove. "Dinner will be ready in a moment."

He walked up to the other side of the counter to face her. "I'm not sorry you brought it up. I'm not good at games, Amber, so I'll just be blunt. I want you. And I think you want me. But I don't do casual, and you don't do long-term. So where does that leave us?"

"Nowhere." She turned off the pasta.

He leaned forward. "You sell yourself short, Amber. You're a beautiful young woman, and you deserve to be treated better than a late night…*snack*."

"Maybe that is all I want."

He made a huffing noise. "Right. You think I don't see how you look at Joachim? Some part of you wants more whether you realize it or not."

"Just forget I said anything. Let's eat."

Paul studied her face a few seconds more, before

circling the counter to take plates out of an overhead cabinet. When he turned back around, Amber was standing in front of him. She reached up, standing on her tiptoes to place her arms around his neck.

When her soft mouth covered his, Paul felt the fire take hold of his insides. He almost dropped the plates trying to find the countertop to set them on.

Wrapping his arms around her slender body, he pressed her against his form, reveling in every inch of her soft, willing body.

Without warning, she released his neck and stepped back from him. "Make love to me, Paul," she whispered.

In that moment, he almost hated her. The witch was trying to use his own lust against him. His dark eyes narrowed to slits of coal. "You're welcome to come into my bed anytime, Amber. But when you do—" he cupped her chin in his hand "—plan on staying."

"And if I don't want to?"

"That's not an option."

He released her and picked up the plates again. After placing them on the table, he came back for the food.

Amber stood by and watched him prepare the dinner table. She could feel the anger radiating off of him in waves. And she did not know him well enough to gauge how far he could be pushed before he began to push back.

She bit her lip, watching the muscles in his upper body flex with each movement. She wanted him so badly, she could almost feel his hands on her body. Touching her, exploring her. She shook off the dangerous thoughts before she did something stupid—like agreed to his terms.

She glanced at Joachim playing in the swing. He was

such a good baby. He hardly ever cried, and loved to laugh. And he needed a mother, didn't he?

She covered her face. *What am I thinking? I'm too young for this kind of commitment. I'm still in school, for goodness sake.*

"Do you plan to eat tonight?" Paul grumbled from his seat at the table. The vicious way he was cutting in to the roast made her wonder if he was seeing her face on it.

She walked over to the table and stared down at the top of his curly head. He never looked up. It took every ounce of restraint not to reach out and touch his silky locks.

She sat down across from him, but other than a quick, disinterested glance, he never even acknowledged her presence as he continued to torture the roast. She knew he was more sexually frustrated than angry. She also knew he didn't have to be. They could both get what they wanted.

She lifted her plate and waited while he placed a few shredded slices of beef on it. *You're right. I do want you. And I will have you.*

Chapter 11

By the next morning, Paul was certain the woman was trying to drive him insane. It started the night before, after he'd spurned her tempting invitation. And it seemed as if the war began as soon as she sat down at the dinner table.

She reached for the pasta. Her arm brushed his. He thought nothing of it.

She reached for the rolls. Her breast brushed against his shoulder. He swallowed hard and pretended to ignore it.

After dinner, as they were clearing away the dishes, she found a need to squeeze between him and the table, her bottom brushing against the crotch of his pants.

He gasped. She smiled and continued on to the sink with an armful of dishes. The gauntlet had been thrown down.

Which was why Paul thought it odd when she decided to turn in after eight. Amber did not strike him as the kind that would retreat in the middle of a battle.

So, deciding he'd won by default, he shrugged off the whole incident and went into the living room to watch some television while feeding Joachim his bottle.

Fifteen minutes later, she reappeared in the entryway announcing that she couldn't sleep and asking if she could watch some television with him. Paul thought nothing of it, until she crossed in front of the television wearing that little bit of nothing that had started everything.

Paul was so shocked, he shot up off the couch and almost dropped his son in the process. Joachim wasted no time in letting him know his displeasure at having his feeding disturbed.

Amber sauntered over and took the baby from his arms, giving him an appealing view of her backside in the sheer teddy when she turned away from him. His suspicions were confirmed. She was indeed perfect from all angles.

His traitorous son didn't help matters by quieting down as soon as she wrapped her arms around him. As far as Paul was concerned, he was siding with the enemy.

He wanted to explode. To tell her that her dirty little tricks wouldn't work. That he was a stronger man than she could ever imagine.

But he also wanted to tell her that she'd won, that he would give her whatever she wanted so long as she would come into his arms at that moment. He wanted to describe in vivid detail all the things he would do with that lovely body. He wanted to beg her to touch him.

He decided neither response would do, so he sat back down, as if nothing had occurred, picked up the remote and began to channel surf.

He knew he'd made the right choice when her eyes widened and her mouth fell open. She looked back and forth between him and the television as if deciding what to do next. He was nervous for the safety of his fifty-four-inch plasma screen.

He had enough experience to know a thwarted woman was pretty much capable of anything. Including the complete destruction of expensive electronics.

She stood there for several seconds more, trying to ignore the Chargers game, before turning and stomping out of the room. Not that it had the desired effect, considering her sexy legs were bare, right down to the tips of her pretty little feet. He smiled to himself, realizing she was so angry, she apparently forgot she was holding a baby.

Later that night, unable to sleep—for the most obvious reasons—Paul wandered into the nursery and found Joachim sound asleep in his crib.

He stood beside the crib looking down on his innocent son. Still after all these months it amazed him how something so perfect could come out of such a disastrous relationship.

Paul had first met Joachim's mother, Michelle Valens, during his first year of active duty. She was a communications specialist in his unit, and the most beautiful woman he'd ever seen. Her exotic, Polynesian looks had a mesmerizing effect on men, and Paul was no exception.

They became friends and that relationship quickly escalated into something more intimate. Paul fell in love almost instantly, but it didn't take him long to realize Michelle did not feel the same. She enjoyed her effect on men and continued to flirt. Although Paul's jealousy caused them to fight constantly, he still couldn't give her up.

Michelle was wild, uncontrollable and unpredictable. She loved to party, more than life itself, and that attitude eventually earned her a dishonorable discharge.

Afraid he would lose her, Paul talked her in to getting an apartment with him off base, but that only lasted a short while. When he came home one day, she was gone. She'd packed her things and disappeared, and Paul thought he'd lost her forever.

Heartbroken, and looking for a way to forget, Paul signed up for the SEAL program. He dedicated himself to the training with a frightening zealousness, and felt he had found his calling. Until 9/11, and the war that followed.

Paul had been in many combat situations, but nothing had prepared him to fight an enemy like this. In his last tour of duty, Paul had seen and experienced things he knew would haunt him for the rest of his life. He wanted out. His soul wanted rest. Two years ago, he accepted an honorable discharge.

When his military buddies threw him a going home party, Michelle had shown up out of the blue, and Paul knew that he still had deep feelings for her. He was also encouraged by her new attitude. She seemed gentler, calmer in some ways. Paul was hoping that they could build a new life together.

Paul took her home with him back to Los Angeles. He took out a small business loan and started G-Force, hiring as many ex-military men as he could find to run the small security company. But he was so occupied with building his business, he didn't notice Michelle's rapid decline. She had returned to her old ways, hanging out and partying, sometimes not coming home until close to dawn. They were constantly bickering, and when they did, Michelle would disappear for days. So, Paul stopped saying anything, hoping that whatever demons were riding her would burn out of her system.

It never happened. In fact it got worse.

She began to criticize their modest lifestyle. He explained to her that starting a business took time, and patience, and that G-Force would grow and they would have enough money to get married. She didn't want to wait.

She began to openly flaunt other men in his face—wealthy men. She would leave wearing one thing, and come home wearing an outfit that cost much more.

And she would be high. Not just a mild high off the marijuana he knew she smoked. No, she would be on some kind of super high, and sometimes it seemed to last for days. Discovering Michelle's drug of choice was Paul's first encounter with the methamphetamine drug known as crank.

Paul thought if he could keep her clean and sober, everything would work out. But he soon realized that trying to keep a meth addict from her drug was like trying to cage a wild animal. And there were days when Paul was certain that was what he saw looking back at him from her beautiful eyes. A wild animal.

By the time Paul had given up and decided he had enough, he found out she was pregnant. But given her behavior, he had good reason to doubt the child was his.

He wanted it to be.

He desperately wanted it to be. Despite everything that had happened he still loved Michelle, and he hoped the baby could do what he could not—settle her down.

When Joachim was born, Paul thought God had heard his prayers, for his infant son was his very image. There was no doubt as to his paternity, even though Michelle tried to deny that in future arguments. And miraculously, he was born drug-free.

The birth of Joachim was like an awakening for Paul. It changed everything in his life. He doubled his efforts to build his business, working ridiculously long hours. He found a terrific day-care center that took infants, since he did not know where Michelle was during the day, and he did not want his child with her.

Despite Joachim's birth, Michelle did not change. Paul reached a point where he was fed up with her behavior. In his anger, he made a critical error. He announced to Michelle his intentions to file for sole parental guardianship of Joachim.

The next day he came home and Michelle was gone, and she'd taken Joachim with her. Paul was able to use his G-Force connections, and within two days he found them at a seedy motel in Hollywood. But by the time he got there it was too late. Michelle was stretched out across the bed… dead. On the dresser was the setup for a mini-meth kitchen. Sitting on the floor, near the bathroom door, was his son still strapped in his car seat, letting out the most bloodcurling howls Paul had ever heard.

Brought back to the present by Joachim's fidgeting, Paul reached into the crib and touched his son's soft cheek. If he had not experienced it, he would not believe that starving, miserable baby was the one sleeping soundly in the crib.

He'd managed to build a decent life for Joachim in these months following Michelle's death. He bought this house and hired Rosalie to care for him full-time, and G-Force was thriving.

And now another temptress had entered his life…and he was distraught to realize he wanted Amber Lockhart ten times more than he ever wanted Michelle.

Despite his intense feelings for her, he was certain now that he couldn't get involved with her. Not even for the casual fling she wanted. Women like that destroyed the men who desired them. He couldn't go through that hell again, and he certainly couldn't expose his son to it.

Amber frowned at the doorknob and then tried to turn it. It was locked. Her frown intensified. *So this is how he plans to avoid me.*

She folded her arms across her chest, as she considered a way to get past the locked door. Seducing Paul Gutierrez was proving to be more of a challenge that she'd thought it would be.

She knocked. "Paul?"

The acute silence that followed was unnatural in its stillness, and a dead giveaway. She knew he was considering not responding at all.

"What is it, Amber?"

"You haven't eaten all day. Do you want me to fix you a sandwich?"

"No thanks. I've got a lot of work to get caught up on."

She tilted her head, wondering if that accusing tone was imagined. Was he blaming her?

"All right. Let me know if you change your mind."

Another silence fell, and she had turned to walk away when he responded.

"I *won't* change my mind, Amber."

Just like the night before, food had become a symbol for a much more sensitive issue. She knew he was not just rejecting a sandwich.

That afternoon, Amber cradled the phone in the crook of her neck, while she attached the second elastic tab on Joachim's diaper. "That's wonderful! Oh, Pearl, I'm so happy for you. I leave home for a few days and you're engaged and have an audition for a record deal! And in Nashville!"

Pearl chuckled. "Well, the record thing is too far out for me to accept as a reality, but, Amber, please just keep this to yourself for now, okay?"

"Why? This is wonderful news!"

"Well, not everyone may think so," Pearl mumbled.

Amber knew she was referring to her conservative minister fiancé, Wade Kendrick.

Amber picked up the baby and carried him over to his crib. Sensing what she planned, Joachim grabbed the collar of her shirt in his tiny fists and held on.

Amber surrendered. Joachim was dry and content and she wanted to keep him that way. She carried him back to her bedroom with her. "So, when is the big event?"

"Everything has been happening so fast, Wade and I haven't talked about it. Amber...when are you coming home?"

Amber sat down on the side of the bed. "I don't know." She huffed. "I'm just so tired of being the family screwup."

"Don't say that! You're not a screwup! You just made a bad choice, that's all."

"And the beat goes on."

"What's that supposed to mean?"

"Just that I don't seem to learn from my mistakes like other people."

"Sure you do. I don't think you would *ever* follow a man you barely know across country again, will you?"

"No. But I might be tempted to move in with a total stranger, who was kind enough to rescue me from a bad situation, and then proceed to try to seduce him."

"Amber! You can't be serious! Do you realize this man

is a close friend of Luther's? How could you even consider doing something like that?"

"Spoken like a woman who has never set eyes on Paul Gutierrez. Trust me, if you had, you would not be asking that question."

"So, he's fine?"

"*Super* fine."

"Still, you would create some seriously bad blood if you go to bed with a friend of Luther's. Luther is the closest thing we have to a brother. If it ends badly, he may feel obligated to defend you."

Amber sighed. "I know. Believe me, I've considered all that. But this man— Oh, Pearl, I just can't explain it. He's like something out of another time. He's handsome, and chivalrous, and protective…and addictive."

"Well, you better find a cure because this is a worse idea than the whole Dashuan Kennedy fiasco. At least, everyone agrees that guy is a creep. But this guy…this is Luther's friend."

"I get it, Pearl!" Amber snapped.

"Look. You know I am the last person in the world to criticize you. But, Amber, think *real* careful about this before you actually *do* anything. I mean this could have repercussions you can't even imagine."

Amber smiled at the little baby, lying on his back staring up at her with adoring eyes. "It already has."

"What do you mean?"

Amber was considering telling Pearl about the deeper emotions Paul had awakened in her, but decided if Pearl couldn't handle the idea of a meaningless seduction, she certainly couldn't handle the thought that she may be falling in love with Paul.

"Never mind. So, fill me in. What's going on back there?"

Pearl proceeded to tell her of all the happenings in Detroit, everything from the arrangements of their sister Opal's upcoming wedding to millionaire D'marcus Armstrong, planned for the day after Christmas, to the latest on Pearl's roommate, their cousin Paige Richards.

Almost an hour later, Amber hung up the phone feeling much better. Talking to any one of her sisters about her troubles always made her feel better. But there was no denying that Pearl was her favorite. Being the closest to her in both age and temperament, Pearl had always been her advocate with their other two sisters, the older and more mature Lockharts.

Ruby, Opal, Pearl and Amber had always been close. But when they lost their mother five years ago, the bond had been strengthened ten times.

Amber barely remembered their father, Raymond Lockhart, a police officer who was killed in the line of duty when she was only four, whereas her sisters had solid, fond memories of him.

So, although they all grieved for their beloved mother, for sixteen-year-old Amber, losing the woman who'd been both mother and father to her was devastating. Especially considering how it had occurred. The cancer came out of nowhere, and Emerald Lockhart was gone from the world within three months of the diagnosis. If it had not been for the love and support she found in her sisters, Amber was unsure she would've survived.

After the death of her mother, Amber had gone a little wild. But no matter what she did, nothing seemed to stop the intense pain she felt whenever she remembered her mother's smiling face. And even as crazy as things got, they could've been much worse had it not been for the intervention of her sisters. And when the Lockhart sisters intervened...*they intervened!*

Anyone who knew their family could tell you that one Lockhart woman was enough challenge for anyone, but all of them together were unbeatable. Amber never stood a chance against her sisters' undying faith in her. They honestly, truly believed their little sister would become the woman they all believed she could be. Strong and confident like them. But Amber knew better.

Still, her neverending cycle of disastrous relationships and spectacularly poor judgment never shook their unified loyalty. No matter how many times she metaphorically fell down, her sisters were there to pick her up.

It was that ridiculously misplaced confidence in her that always kept her from going too far in her pursuit of the wild life. And it was that same confidence in her that kept her hiding out in Paul's home. She'd disappointed her sisters once again, and she had no desire to face those three pairs of understanding, sympathetic eyes.

But staying in Paul's home held its own potential for disaster. It meant staying in close proximity to a man who made her *want* in every imaginable way. His home had become her sanctuary. His child had become her comfort. And the man, himself, well...he had become her heart's desire.

Chapter 12

Paul glanced at the clock on the wall. It was almost seven in the evening. He'd done it. He'd managed to keep his resident beauty at arm's length for a full day. Of course, there was a touch of guilt in leaving her to care for Joachim all day. But he knew if there had been a problem she would've told him. As it was, she'd only come to the door once, to offer him a sandwich. But he knew she was tempting him with more than just two slices of bread and some deli cuts.

Amber was a woman used to getting her way, and with that face and body, he could understand why. He doubted that many men could say no to her. A few years ago he might have been one of those men. But now there was more than just himself to think about. Now there was Joachim's heart on the line. He already knew his son was becoming attached to their houseguest. He'd accepted her from the first time she picked him up. Of course, there was always the obvious answer....

He could make it clear to Amber that it was time for her to leave. Even if she wanted to stay, her pride would force her to go. But the truth was, he didn't want her to go. Although she made him feel all the wrong things, the point was, she did make him feel. It had been so long since he'd felt anything other than anger and jealousy where a woman was concerned.

So, if he wasn't going to ask her to leave, the only other alternative was exactly what he was doing. He was pretty sure he could keep his hands to himself—even if it killed him. But would he be strong enough to resist if she touched him first?

Maybe, just maybe, if he could keep his distance, she would give up, and they could go back to the way it was before he saw her—all of her—in that sexy little thing.

Stop it! He shook his head in a desperate attempt to get rid of the visual image. He stood and wiped his damp hands on his jeans. He'd sequestered himself all day, but now it was time to face the music.

He headed toward the door, hoping Amber had cooked again. Her roast the night before was delicious, even after he'd mauled it with the knife in frustration.

Don't think about her gorgeous smile, or those golden bedroom eyes. And whatever you do, don't think about the way her cute little bottom looked in that negligee! He reached the door, put his hand on the knob and his mind was overwhelmed with a dozen images of Amber, most of which were erotic.

Amber in his bed. Amber standing at his stove cooking dinner. Amber on the kitchen table. Amber shopping in the mall. Amber against the glass store window, with her long legs wrapped around his waist. Amber, Amber, Amber.

Paul braced his head against the door. *I'm doomed.*

He went from room to room, looking for Amber and Joachim with no luck. The kitchen was quiet, not a single pot on the stove. He climbed the stairs to the second floor and found Joachim sleeping in his crib. But no Amber.

He went down the hall to her bedroom and knocked, but there was no answer. He wondered if maybe she was napping, too. He felt a chill run down his spine, as another thought occurred to him. What if she had been so discouraged by his rejection, she'd decided to leave? But she wouldn't have left without saying something, right? Would she? He decided she would've never left Joachim alone. Somehow, he just knew this.

He was about to go back downstairs and check outside when he noticed the crawl space ladder at the other end of the hall. He looked up and saw that the door was open.

Paul went to the bottom of the ladder and called, "Amber?"

"I'm up here!" she called.

Paul frowned in confusion and started up the ladder. At the top, he found an open invitation. Amber was bent all the way over in a large cardboard box. He stopped, his eyes widening as he took in the little bottom pointing at him. Paul moaned.

"Did you say something?" she asked, never lifting her head from the box.

"What are you doing?"

With a flip and a turn, her tempting bottom disappeared beneath her as she sat with her legs crossed, glaring at him. "Do you realize Christmas is less than a month away?"

Paul had not thought about it. Not that it would've made a difference. He'd hadn't really celebrated Christmas since he was a little boy in his parents' home.

"Um, no, I hadn't noticed."

The frown on her face said that was not the right answer. "Not noticed? How do you not notice the birth of Jesus?" Her eyes widened in sudden realization. "Unless you're not Christian."

He smiled. "Yes, born and raised a good Catholic, but let's just say it's been awhile since I visited the confessional."

Her pretty face relaxed. "Then, as I was saying, how can you not notice the birth of Christ? And this being your son's first Christmas!"

Now it was Paul's turn to frown. "He's an infant."

"He's *still* a child, and this is *still* Christmas. Anyway, I found a few boxes of lights and ornaments."

"Those aren't mine," Paul said, pulling the box over to examine the contents.

"They're not?"

He shook his head in answer, surprised to see that some of the lights were still in new boxes. "No, I've been here less than a year, and I've never bought Christmas decorations. The previous owners must have left them."

"See? It's a Christmas miracle!"

He gave her an odd look, but said nothing.

"Well, we have enough lights for the windows, and we'll need more ornaments, but the most important thing is the tree. We *really* need a tree." She arched an eyebrow.

"What?"

"You have to go out and get a tree."

"Oh, no." He shook his head. "I'm not going anywhere tonight. I just spent the whole day catching up on case files. I'm tired, I'm hungry."

She flashed her brilliant smile. "Great, me, too. Why don't you pick up some burgers on the way back?"

"No, you're not hearing me, Amber. I'm not going any-where."

Her playful grin turned seductive as she began to move across the floor.

Her golden eyes locked on his face, and Paul felt as if he were trapped in the gaze of a hungry tigress. "What are you doing?"

"Please, Paul," she begged in a near whisper.

He felt his iron will dissolve into vapor in a matter of seconds. Even after spending a full day fortifying himself against her charms.

"Don't do this to me."

She was almost on him before he gave in.

"Okay, I'll go get the tree! Just please, please don't touch me."

Anyone else hearing those words might have been offended. But Amber only smiled, because looking in his eyes she understood what was terrifying him. It wasn't her touch, but his own reaction to it. Amber couldn't help finding a certain satisfaction in knowing that he was suffering as much as she was.

Three hours later, the couple was in the living room, moving furniture around and trying to accommodate Paul's trophy tree.

Exhausted, Amber sat down on the sofa, looking at the monstrosity he had dragged into the house a few minutes ago. "What *were* you thinking?"

The live tree was over eight feet tall and at least four feet wide, and had it not been for Paul's double door entryway and cathedral ceilings, it would never have fit in the house.

Paul lifted the glass coffee table out of the way. "You said get a tree, so I got a tree."

"Where did you go to find that thing? The redwood forest?"

"Very funny. Look in that bag—" he nodded over his shoulder "—and hand me the base."

Paul was not about to tell her that he'd driven over fifty miles to find a tree he thought would impress her. It wasn't until the tree lot workers began to load it onto his SUV that he began to have his doubts. The tree dwarfed his vehicle, and his was no small vehicle.

The strange looks he got from other drivers on the way back intensified those doubts, but there was no turning around. He tried to convince himself that he was doing it for Joachim, but in his heart he knew why he'd gone to such lengths.

Christmas was a time when people wanted to be with their families. But it was almost a month away. A month was a long time. Time enough for Amber to work up the courage to face her family, and time enough for him to convince her to spend Christmas with them.

Some part of him hoped that maybe, just maybe, if he could give her an incentive to stay…maybe he could have a Christmas like the ones of his early childhood. A fun-filled time with the people he loved.

Paul frowned to himself as he assembled the base. *Love?* Where did that come from? No, he decided, love had nothing to do with it. It was just with everything that had occurred that year, he didn't want to be alone this Christmas.

"Do you think you need all this?" Amber asked, holding a doll-sized dancing Santa on the palm of her hand. She pressed a button and he began to shift his hips back and forth. She chuckled. "Kinda provocative for Santa, don't you think?"

Paul smiled, and shook his head. Just then, Joachim's mournful cry came through the baby monitor.

Paul went to get up, and Amber put up a hand. "Don't bother, I'll get him."

He watched her leave the room. He loved the sassy way she moved. There was even energy in her walk.

It took him a few minutes to assemble the tree base. Afterward, he sat back looking at the mountains of bags spread in every direction.

Okay, so maybe he'd gone a *little* overboard. He just wanted to make sure he had all the making of a winter wonderland—California style. So, there would be no snow like a Detroit Christmas, but who missed freezing temperatures?

Amber came into the room, carrying a smiling Joachim in one arm and dragging his walker behind her.

Paul gave his son a wistful smile. Joachim's little arms were wrapped around Amber's neck. He looked so peaceful. Paul knew it was already too late for both of them. In a matter of days, she'd managed to wrap them around her little finger.

Amber settled Joachim in his walker, and he began to protest until his big brown eyes fell on the tree. They widened and widened, and his little mouth opened to form a perfect *O*.

Paul's smile widened. How could he have almost missed this? Of course, Joachim needed a tree and decorations for Christmas. But he knew that if Amber had not mentioned it, he would've never thought of it.

Deciding he'd had enough rest, Paul went over and attempted to lift the heavy tree. He'd had a hell of a time getting it into the house, before remembering that it had taken two of the tree lot workers to wrestle it up onto his SUV. Now all he had to do was get it into the base, and it would stand on its own.

With sheer determination, Paul dragged the tree several inches and stopped to catch his breath, before dragging it a few more feet. He noticed Amber standing nearby. Her top row of teeth was biting into her bottom lip, and she had a strange look on her face. It didn't take him long to realize she was holding back laughter.

"Think you can do better?" he asked.

Amber exploded in laughter, unable to hold back any longer. "No, no, you're doing a wonderful job. Keep up the good work." She gave the thumbs up, and he wanted nothing more than to wipe that smug expression off her face.

He dragged the tree some more until he reached the base, where he wanted to position it.

Amber cleared her throat. "Um, Paul, can I ask a question?"

"What?" he asked, standing upright and rubbing the sweat off his forehead with the bottom of his T-shirt.

Amber was temporarily distracted by the muscular expanse of smooth, olive skin exposed to her.

"What's your question?" Paul asked, still annoyed by her humor.

"What?" Her guilty eyes shot to his.

"Your question. What's your question?"

"Oh, um, why didn't you just take the base to the tree, instead of bringing the tree to the base?"

Paul's eyes narrowed on her face, but he felt his mouth tugging up at the end. "*Now* you tell me."

"I would've suggested it sooner, but I was so enjoying watching you play the big, strong lumberjack."

"You're a brat, you know that?"

"So I've been told."

"Okay, I'm going to set it on the base, but I need you to hold the tree steady while I maneuver it in."

Paul lifted the tree onto the base, and Amber came over to take his position while he got down on his belly to check the alignment. "No, not quite."

He stood again, and came up behind her. "Here, like this." He put his arms around her and knew that he'd made a mistake. With her soft bottom pressed against his crotch, she felt so good, so damn right. Just like he knew she would.

Unable to stop himself, he leaned forward and pressed his lips against the soft, sweet-smelling skin of her neck, and Amber tilted her head to the side, giving him full access.

Paul felt as if his hands had taken on a life of their own as they snaked around her waist, pulling her back hard against him.

Amber released a sigh of satisfaction as she settled back against his chest.

The slight movement served as a trigger, and Paul's whole body tensed as he realized what he was doing.

"Don't fight it, Paul. Why shouldn't we have this time together?"

His strong hands flexed and released over her flat stomach several times, as he tried to build enough strength to let her go. He had to let her go, if not tonight, some other night in the not so distant future. He wouldn't lie to himself, he knew it would be much harder later than sooner.

Amber reached up and wrapped her arms around his head, pulling his lips down to hers. Her golden eyes were half-lidded, and he could almost read her hunger in them.

He just wasn't strong enough.

He took what she offered, pressing his warm lips to hers until her lips parted beneath his, and her tongue came out to meet his with eagerness.

Paul twisted her body, needing to feel her pressed against him. Neither noticed the loud *swoosh* of the tree falling to the floor.

He pressed her body to his, shoulder to hip, noting that she was even the perfect height for his hands to rest comfortably on her small waist.

Paul devoured her mouth, reveling in her intoxicating taste. She smelled like a rose garden in the summer time, with skin softer than the softest rose petal.

Amber placed her arms over his shoulders. Her head lolled back as he ran his hands over her face and neck, following every inch of explored skin with a soft kiss.

His whole body was aching, and knowing there was a couch a few feet away made it worse. Wrapping his hands around her bottom, he pressed her up against the rising bulge of his pants.

She rubbed against him, and he felt the tremor through his whole body. Without another thought he bent, scooped her up in his arms and with five long strides reached the couch.

Laying her on the cushions, he came down on top of her, bearing his weight on his braced arms. He could've lifted himself some more, but he wanted to feel every inch, every shapely curve, every part of her. His mouth continued the exploration of her face and neck, even as his fingers worked to undo the buttons of her blouse.

Amber had no objections to anything he was doing. She wound her fingers through his loose curls and held tight, hoping she would last long enough to enjoy the entire experience. She already felt so alive, so vibrantly ready, so on the edge, one kiss in the right place would send her over the top.

Wrapping her slender legs around his waist, she felt him sink farther into her body. Even the coarse feel of the denim fabric could not disturb her euphoria, as her mind raced ahead and imagined the feel of him inside her. Every part of her body was ready for him.

Paul managed to get the blouse open, and wanted to thank the heavens when he realized she was wearing a front-latching bra. He smiled. He laughed out loud. And then with one flick of his hand, the bra fell apart revealing bronze mounds tipped in caramel.

His eyes came up to her face, and she returned his smile. It was all the go-ahead he needed. Paul swooped in, taking one full breast into his mouth. Amber gasped and arched her back, caught unaware by his intense passion.

Bracing her back with both hands, Paul held her to his mouth, feasting like a starving man. She was like warm honey on his tongue.

Without conscious thought, his hips gyrated against her, simulating what was to come. He released her breast, licking up his own juices around the outer edges and down into the valley between.

He pressed his nose to her skin, breathing in the scent of roses everywhere. Paul felt as if his heart were bursting with joy, and all he wanted to do was hold her. He wrapped both arms around her waist and squeezed her tight, wordlessly expressing his longings, his need, his fear.

Amber understood him. As much as she hated what she must do, she knew if she did not speak up, she would be a liar and a hypocrite. She wasn't sure what pain was in

Paul's past, but she would not add to it. Forcing herself to break the spell, she pulled back from him.

The sudden space between them felt cold and Paul started to pull her back to him, wanting her body against his.

But she put her palm against his chest to hold him. "Nothing is changed, Paul. You know what I want." Her soft eyes asked the question before her lips. "Can you accept that?"

In the distance, on the outer edges of his lust, Paul could hear Joachim making happy, musical noises as be bounced up and down while playing with the toys attached to the tray of the walker. He didn't seem the slightest bit interested in the grown-ups' activities.

Paul looked into Amber's eyes and read the truth of her words. She was right, nothing had changed. Regardless of whatever happened between them tonight, she would see it as nothing more than a holiday fling. When the time came she would leave without the slightest regret, and he would be left to the silence once more.

And what about Joachim? He'd already accepted her as a permanent part of his world. How could his young son understand when her sweet-smelling warmth abruptly vanished forever?

It was too much, too soon, but Paul could not stop the words from tumbling from his lips.

"Stay with me, Amber. I promise you will never want for anything."

"Paul, I'm still in school—"

"You can go to school here! California has some of the best colleges and universities in the country, and there are annexes all over Orange County."

"I hardly know you."

His lips formed a thin line. "Hardly know me?" His dark eyes mercilessly examined her bare chest, and Amber became conscious of her vulnerability.

The silent insult was unmistakable. "Let me up."

His cold eyes stared into hers. "And if I don't? What are you going to do? Like you said, you hardly know me."

Amber felt her heart racing. He was trying to intimidate her. She would not give him the satisfaction of knowing just how frightened she was.

She pushed hard against his chest. "Get off me right now!"

Her shout startled Joachim. He dropped his toy and began to cry.

Paul made a sound that sounded like a growl, and then pushed himself up. He glanced at the beautiful, half-naked woman on his couch before cursing and going to his son.

He picked Joachim up from the walker, but the little outstretched arms reached past his father's shoulder.

"Shh, shh." Paul tried to console his angry baby. "He's hungry. I'm going to go fix him a bottle." He spoke to Amber without looking back, then walked out of the living room, heading to the kitchen.

The farther away from Amber he walked, the louder his son's wails became. He continued to try to comfort him, but never turned around. It was time for Joachim to accept what he already knew. Amber Lockhart could never be a part of their lives.

KIMANI PRESS™

An Important Message from the Publisher

Dear Reader,

Because you've chosen to read one of our fine novels, I'd like to say "thank you"! And, as a special way to say thank you, I'm offering to send you two Kimani Romance™ novels and two surprise gifts — absolutely FREE! These books will keep it real with true-to-life African-American characters that turn up the heat and sizzle with passion.

Please enjoy the free books and gifts with our compliments...

Linda Gill

Publisher, Kimani Press

...off Seal and Place Inside...

FREE GIFTS
PUBLISHER'S SEAL
THANK YOU

Two NEW Kimani Romance™ Novels
Two exciting surprise gifts

I have placed my
Editor's "Thank You" Free Gifts
seal in the space provided at
right. Please send me 2 FREE
books, and my 2 FREE Mystery
Gifts. I understand that I am
under no obligation to purchase
anything further, as explained on
the back of this card.

PLACE
FREE GIFTS
SEAL
HERE

168 XDL ELWZ   **368 XDL ELXZ**

FIRST NAME   LAST NAME

ADDRESS

APT.#   CITY

STATE/PROV.   ZIP/POSTAL CODE

Thank You!

BUSINESS REPLY MAIL
FIRST-CLASS MAIL   PERMIT NO. 717-003   BUFFALO, NY

POSTAGE WILL BE PAID BY ADDRESSEE

THE READER SERVICE
3010 WALDEN AVE
PO BOX 1867
BUFFALO NY 14240-9952

NO POSTAGE
NECESSARY
IF MAILED
IN THE
UNITED STATES

Chapter 13

As soon as Paul was gone from the room, Amber sat up on the couch. She took a deep breath, before relatching her bra and buttoning up her shirt. It took several minutes for her heart to slow its rapid pace.

She had the eerie feeling of having just escaped potential danger. She didn't seriously believe Paul would've done the unthinkable. But there was a hard edge about him that terrified her. She knew she'd wounded him...deeply.

Her confession had had the opposite effect of her intent. She'd told him the truth to avoid any misunderstanding, and all it did was complicate matters further.

She stood and balled her fists, still feeling the effects of unfulfilled arousal. She just did not understand Paul Gutierrez. Most men would've taken what she was offering without a moment's hesitation. Why was he trying to make it more than it could be?

She'd known him for less than a week. What the hell did he want? A declaration of undying love? *Stay with me, Amber. I promise you will never want for anything.* Her mouth twisted in frustration.

When Paul returned a half hour later with Joachim cradled in his arm, he seemed surprised to find her still there. The tree lay on its side, and Amber was sitting on the floor, struggling to push the base onto the bottom.

Hearing Paul come into the room, she looked up. "It won't fit. The tree is too big for the base."

Paul looked at her, but she felt he was looking through her instead. Without a word, he handed her the baby and began to struggle with the base.

After several attempts, he gave up and sighed. "I'm going to have to cut it down some. I have a saw out in the garage. I'll be right back."

He was almost to the door, before she called to him. "Paul?"

"What?" he snapped, turning to face her.

Amber's heart twisted to see the hurt in his eyes. This was just what she didn't want to do. To create this unbearable tension between them. For a moment, she regretted every kiss they'd shared. "I just wanted to say— I mean I didn't—"

"I think it's time for you to go."

There was such finality to his simple words, Amber could not believe what she was hearing. "Go?"

"Not tonight, but in the morning, I'll take you to the airport to get your ticket. I'll pay for it if you don't have enough. I'm sure your family is—"

"What? You're kicking me out? Why? Because I won't vow to love you forever? This is *crazy!*" She pointed an accusing finger. "*You're* crazy!"

She glanced at the baby in her arms and could see that her screaming was beginning to upset him. As outraged as she was, Amber still worked to control her tone.

She took a deep breath. "Fine, Paul. I'll leave in the morning." And she watched him walk out of the room.

Amber looked at little Joachim and found those big, brown eyes looking back at her in bewilderment. It was obvious he sensed something was wrong. Amber hugged him and fought back the tears she felt forming in her eyes.

"I'm going to miss you so much, precious one." She kissed the top of his curly head, so much like his father's, just trying to absorb his wonderful baby smell and store it in her memory forever.

Out in the garage, Paul was slamming the trimmer against the wall. At that moment, he wanted to jump outside his body, so that he could punch himself in the nose for being such an idiot. Amber was right, he was indeed crazy—and he had no idea how to stop being crazy.

He leaned against the SUV, holding his face in his hands. Why did he always fall so hard, and so fast? They had only known each other a few days, so why did he feel the overwhelming need to get some kind of commitment from her before they made love? *What is wrong with me?*

He thought about the scene that had just played out in the living room. He was hurting, and he'd lashed out the only way he knew how. And now…he was stuck with his decision. She'd agreed to go home.

Given his growing obsession with her, maybe it was for the best.

After putting Joachim to bed for the night, Amber tried to follow suit but ended up staring at the ceiling for what seemed like an eternity. Giving up, she padded down the stairs for a late-night snack. Halfway down, it occurred to her just how comfortable she had become in this house in a few days. Far too comfortable. It was beginning to feel like home.

At the bottom of the stairs, she turned to go into the kitchen when she noticed a blinking light reflecting off the opposite wall. It was coming from the living room. She rounded the corner, and a wide grin came across her face at the sight that greeted her.

The monster tree was standing tall in its base and was covered in tiny, colorful, flashing lights. She felt like a kid on Christmas morning, waking to find the evidence that Santa had visited the night before.

She spotted Paul on the other side of the room, pulling boxes of ornaments out of bags. "Wow, it's coming together." When she saw his back stiffen, she realized she'd startled him.

He glanced at her over his shoulder. She almost laughed at the disappointment in his eyes as they ran over her completely concealing pajamas.

He stood and dusted his hands. "I still may not have enough ornaments to cover the whole thing."

"Can I help?"

He hesitated, and Amber thought he was going to say no. "Sure." He held out a box of shiny balls.

Amber crossed the room, and with one glance at his face knew that the box represented a truce of sorts. She also knew that he was regretting what happened earlier as much as she was.

Together they worked to cover the tree with dozens of ornaments, and the end result was a festive and cheery Christmas tree. They sat together on the couch, watching the lights glow and shimmer against the glittery balls.

"Thanks for this," Paul said.

"For what?"

"I would've never thought to put up a tree, or any decorations for that matter had you not suggested it."

She shrugged. "You probably would've eventua—"

"No, I would not have." He leaned forward, resting his elbows on his knees. "These last few years...life with Michelle was not exactly filled with joyous celebrations."

Amber bit her bottom lip, trying to hold back the urge to ask. She couldn't. "Is Michelle Joachim's mother?"

He sighed, and much to her surprise answered. "Yes."

Amber felt as if she had just jumped some major hurdle. She knew she should stop there.

"Where is she?"

She watched his shoulders droop, and regretted asking the question.

"She died six months ago."

Amber reached forward and wrapped her arms around his neck. "Oh, Paul, I'm so sorry."

"I'm not."

Hearing the harsh statement, Amber jumped back away from him. "How can you say that?"

"I know it sounds terrible, Amber. But you don't understand how it was. You don't know how many dope houses I had to drag her out of. You don't know what it's like waiting to hear a doctor tell you whether your infant son was born with a drug addiction or worse! You don't know what it feels like knowing the woman you love will give herself to any man with a fat wallet. Or having her run away with your son, wondering if she'll sell him to the first dealer she meets for a fix, wondering if he's being abused. And through it all...I still loved her. Can you believe that?"

He turned to look at her, and she could see the tears forming in his beautiful eyes. "Can you believe that through all that, I still loved her?"

She reached up and ran her fingers down his cheek. "Love is powerful, Paul."

He blinked and a single tear slid down his cheek and over her fingers. His eyes ran over every inch of her face. "And unpredictable." He sniffed and sat straight up as if attempting to regain his composure. "It's a damn nuisance, if you ask me."

Amber smiled. She'd never thought of love as a nuisance.

"Anyway, that's my sob story," he said with more than a little sarcasm. "It may sound cruel, but these past six months, I've had more peace than I've known in quite some time."

Amber didn't know what to say to that. She'd always been taught not to speak ill of the dead, but considering the pain this woman had put her family through, Amber wasn't so sure she could say anything good about her, either. She came up with something. "But you have Joachim."

He smiled, and she felt her heart swell to bursting, knowing she'd caused it.

"Yes, I have Joachim, don't I?"

"He's such a wonderful baby," she continued, wanting to increase his good feeling. She smiled. "And he looks just like you, which isn't a bad thing."

"Think so?"

She watched his eyes change right before her. They went from reflective to predatory in a matter of seconds, and even seemed to darken, if that was possible.

Fighting her own instinct, she scooted back on the couch away from him. But a part of her wanted to go to him and finish what they started earlier. She knew better. Amber had no intention of getting into a serious relationship, and with a man like Paul it couldn't be anything else.

"I guess we better clean up this mess." She stood and felt Paul's strong fingers wrap around her wrist.

"Sit down. I'm not going to jump you. No matter how much I still want you." He chuckled and glanced over her body. "You'd think those ugly pajamas would've turned me off, but surprisingly enough…" He shrugged. "Anyway, you were right earlier. We don't know each other well enough for what I want, and I'm not able to give you the kind of casual relationship you're used to. It's just not in me."

He released her arm and offered his hand. "So, I guess the only thing left is…friends?"

"Friends." She accepted the handshake. "Does that mean I can stay?"

"Oh, no, you still have to go."

"Why?" She couldn't have hid her disappointment if she tried.

He shook his head. "Sorry, angel, you are just too much temptation." He turned pleading eyes on her. "You can only ask so much of a man."

Amber wanted to argue, but she held her tongue. After all, it was his house, and therefore, his decision.

After putting up the rest of the decorations around the house, they spent the early-morning hours clearing away the empty boxes and cleaning up the living room. Amber got her late-night snack, when Paul made a few minisandwiches.

They curled on the couch, sitting at opposite ends, and shared stories of their childhood Christmases. Amber told Paul about the joys of growing up in a house full of girls, and he laughed as she described waking up to find the

Christmas tree surrounded in pinks and lavenders, and everything Barbie.

She soon found out that Paul's childhood had not been much better than his adult years. He described how his illegal immigrant parents had come to America when his mother was less than four months pregnant. They'd taken the arduous journey from mountainous Brazil to Los Angeles with the express purpose of having Paul born on American soil.

Shortly after his sixth birthday, following an argument with neighbors, his parents were reported to the immigration authorities and deported. Paul had been left to be raised by an elderly uncle who died while Paul was in the military. What surprised Amber most was the feeling of intense patriotism his parents had instilled in Paul. Even with everything that had happened to them, they still thought America was a great country.

"Do you visit them often?" she asked, taking a bite of one of the small sandwiches.

"Not as often as I would like," he admitted. "They live in the remote village where my mother was born. It's kind of hard to get to. I want to take Joachim to see them, but I'll wait until he's older."

"Do you have any siblings?"

"I have two little brothers, Carlos is twelve and Petie is sixteen, and a little sister, Maria, she's almost ten." He smiled. "That one's going to be trouble."

"I'm sure she takes after her big brother."

His eyes slid to hers, and his sexy grin made her heart flutter. "Maybe."

His grin became a frown.

"What's wrong?" Amber asked.

"I send money to help, but my father just sends it back. I've told him I can well afford it, but he says they don't need much. When I visit, I'm greeted with lots of hugs and kisses, but I always feel like a visiting friend of the family, not a member. Does that sound strange?"

"Not when you consider that you weren't raised with them. And the fact that you were raised in a completely different culture. I guess it would be natural to feel a bit distant."

"When Petie turns eighteen, I'm going to try to get him a student visa and bring him here to go to school. If he wants to come, of course."

Amber studied his face as he spoke, wondering if he knew how much of himself he had revealed with that last statement. The hope and joy she could hear in his voice at the possibility of having one of his siblings with him. She had always taken family for granted, having grown up in a house full of sisters. She could not imagine the loneliness of a boy growing up alone, with only an old man for companionship, knowing that hundreds of miles away he had brothers, a sister, a mother and a father, and they wanted to be with him as much as he wanted to be with them.

"I'm surprised you never tried to go back."

He smiled. "I did when I was eleven, right after I received a letter from my parents saying Petie had been born. My uncle insisted he couldn't afford the trip, but I was determined to see my little brother. I ran away in the middle of the night. Unfortunately, it was a rainy night. By the time my uncle found me the next morning, I had gotten no more than eight blocks away. I was soaked, scared, lost, hungry and more than willing to accept my punishment for running away."

She laughed. "You poor thing."

"My uncle didn't think so." He shook his head. "I couldn't sit down for a week."

She laughed harder.

"Do you know how beautiful you are?" he said.

That sobered her. She lowered her eyes. "Don't say things like that."

"It's nothing more than the truth."

Feeling his intense eyes burning into her, she searched her scrambled mind for a different topic, but kept coming up with a blank. All she could think about was, would he move closer? Would he touch her?

Instead, he turned toward the tree, focusing his attention on the flashing lights.

The pair sat in silence for several minutes, before Paul's deep tenor voice cut through the quiet. *"No he soñado siempre para encontrar a alguien como usted, no más de noches solas que nunca lo haré no, a través usted opinión usted satisfará esta parte vacía, he estado buscando para cuál falta en mi corazón..."*

Amber lay her head against the sofa, listening to the softly sung lyrics, and finding herself lost in the sweet melody. "That's pretty. What does it mean?"

He lay his head back. "Nothing. It's just a Spanish lullaby." He listened tensely as she yawned and stretched, but relaxed when she made no attempt to get up. Somehow, just being in her presence was enough.

"It's lovely." Her words slurred, and Paul knew she was falling asleep.

He turned his head to look at her. "Yes, it is."

She faded off to sleep and Paul sat for a long time, just watching her before he felt his own tiredness coming down on him. The lyrics of the popular Spanish song just kept playing over and over again in his mind.

He knew when the morning came, he would do what he planned. He would take her to the airport and put her on an airplane, and never see her again. It would hurt like hell, and he would always wonder what if. But Paul knew the pain of losing her now was nothing compared to the devastation of losing her later.

He'd sung the verses in Spanish, hoping she would not understand the lyrics. But now, looking at her sleeping form, he whispered a few verses in English.

"I have always dreamed to find someone like you, no more lonely nights, I'll never make it through, won't you say you will fulfill this empty part, I've been searching for what's missing in my heart."

He had only one conscious thought before falling off to sleep. How could this happen so fast?

Chapter 14

Paul was awakened by feather-soft kisses across his lean midsection. Realizing the tinkling sensation was caused by someone's lips flickering over his stomach was one thing. Understanding whose lips was another.

Paul took in his surroundings and realized he was on the couch, and given the sunlight streaming in through the bay windows, apparently he'd slept there all night. A warm tongue tracing the outside of his belly button was all he could stand before he sat straight up and found himself looking into Amber's golden eyes. He knew she'd been at this seduction long enough to work herself into quite an arousal.

With two quick moves, she was straddling his lap. Her slender arms came around his neck, and her lips came down on his. He put his hands on her waist, with every intention of setting her away, but she felt too good beneath his palms. Instead his arms closed around her waist and pulled her closer. He slanted his head to take her tongue into his mouth. No one should taste this good so early in the morning, he thought, enjoying her sweet flavor.

He felt her fingers winding their way through his thick curls until she was massaging his scalp and holding his face to hers. Her soft breasts pressed against his chest were too good to resist. Paul felt himself swelling beneath her.

Her body was perfectly positioned over his. If not for their clothes, it would've been so easy to just slip inside her. She felt it, too, and her whole body reacted, grinding against his crotch until he thought he would die if he did not get inside her. Using more force than he intended, he flipped her over on the couch and came over her.

His fingers unsnapped her jeans and dove inside seeking her heat. He skimmed over her tight curls and moaned when he felt her hot moisture on his hand. She was so ready for him, and he was certainly ready for her. Her legs parted, and Paul didn't think he could stand it another moment.

He sat back and pulled his T-shirt over his head. Before he could remove more, she reached for him pulling him back down on top of her. He couldn't have denied her anything she wanted, and she made it clear what she wanted. She wrapped her hands around his bottom and pulled him tight against her center, while gyrating her hips.

Reaching between their bodies, Paul worked to get her pants down her legs, and she twisted her body this way and that trying to help.

Her hands slipped inside the back of his jeans and she squeezed his tight flesh.

They were almost there, almost naked. Her jeans were

down to her knees. She continued to kiss his neck, his chest, any flesh she could reach. They were so close…and then it happened.

A strong and powerful cry came through the baby monitor. That scream was followed by another angry howl. Then another, and another, and Paul roared in frustration.

He pressed his forehead to Amber's, feeling the smooth sheen of moisture on her face. She was as desperate for him as he was for her.

But his son needed him. He pulled away, and she held onto him with more strength than he would've imagined.

"Paul!" Her eyes pleaded her case, and he almost caved.

"I have to," he whispered with a soft kiss on her cheek. He lifted his heavy body off of her.

He stared down at the beautiful, half-naked woman on his couch…once again. The small, dark bush of hair between her legs was singing a siren song to him.

As if to remind him of his responsibility, another soulful cry came through the monitor.

"I'm sorry," he said, then turned to leave. He made it as far as the door.

Paul returned to the sofa, and before Amber realized what he was doing, her jeans and panties lay in a small pile on the floor. He knelt beside the couch and whispered in her ear, "Open your legs for me."

She did, and felt a trembling finger slide inside her body. He slid his finger back and forth, building momentum, and then two fingers working with equal skill.

Amber reached for him, but it was awkward with him kneeling beside her. "Come inside me, Paul," she begged, having never wanted anything as badly as she wanted to feel him at that moment.

"Shh," he whispered and covered her mouth with his. His clever fingers continued to work their magic.

Amber felt her body lifting from the sofa. The tension was becoming too unbearable, the pleasure too intense. He took her tiny nub between his thumb and index finger, rubbed once and she exploded, crying out, but the sound was lost in Paul's mouth.

She was still floating back down to earth when another irate bawling noise came through the monitor.

Within seconds, Paul was on his feet again, staring down at her prone form. Amber smiled at him in satisfaction. He frowned in response, and disappeared up the stairs.

Bothered by that frown, as soon as she'd righted her clothes, Amber followed Paul to the nursery and found him sitting in the rocking chair with Joachim on his lap. The baby was cradled in his arm, sucking on a pacifier and playing with his own fingers.

Paul's eyes were trained on the wall on the other side of the room, but she knew his thoughts were elsewhere.

"Is everything okay?" she asked.

His dark eyes shot to her face, and Amber felt the coldness reflected in their inky depths. "One of his feet got caught between the bars. That's why he was crying."

Amber's heart skipped a beat, as she covered her open mouth with both hands. "Oh, my God!" She came to kneel in front of the chair examining the baby. "Is he okay?"

Paul stood. "Yes, no thanks to—" He shifted his son to his other arm. "Yes, he's fine." He stepped around her and headed to the door.

"You blame me, don't you?"

He stopped at the doorway. "No, Amber, I blame myself." He turned to face her. "I blame my insatiable lust for you. I blame Luther for sending me after you. But I don't blame you."

Her eyes narrowed. "Liar."

His mouth twisted in a sneer. "You made me one."

"What's that supposed to mean?"

He walked back until he was toe-to-toe with her. "Do you have to have every man you meet? Why couldn't you have just left me alone? Now what am I supposed to do with this ache in my chest? This need for you? You've had your little holiday fling playing lover to me, and mother to Joachim, and now you'll fly off and forget about both of us in a matter of days!"

"That's not true," she whispered.

"But I won't forget you, Amber." He reached out and cupped her chin. "Now that I've tasted you, felt you, watched you come." His eyes closed, and he took a deep breath. "How the hell am I supposed to forget that?"

He turned and walked away again. As he reached the door he called back over his shoulder, "Be ready to go by noon."

At eleven fifty-nine Paul knocked on the guest room door. "Amber, are you ready?"

Amber sat on the side of the bed glaring at the door. *Punctual bastard.* "Here I come," she called back.

She stood and smoothed out the bedspread, taking her time to make sure the lines were straight. She took one final look around the room, hoping to find something out of place, anything that would delay taking those final few steps to reach the door.

Everything was just as it should be. She picked up the group of shopping bags piled on a chair. Those she'd arrived with, and the ones she obtained when Paul took her shopping. It was all she had. After all, she'd only been here four days.

Four days... How could anyone's life change so much in four days?

She shook her head. Stalling was nothing but self-inflicted torture. Best to get it over with, and get on with her life. She crossed the room and opened the door.

"Ready?" he asked, his chiseled jaw set in a hard line. But even that could not take away from his overall handsomeness. The man truly was beautiful.

She nodded, and he stepped aside for her. As she moved down the hall toward the stairs, Amber felt like a condemned man being led to the gas chamber. Only, she was not exactly sure of her crime.

She could've believed that he was angry about what happened to Joachim while he was making love to her. Lord knows, she had enough guilt about that herself. But somehow she knew that was not all there was to it.

Actually, it started with that frown he gave her before he went upstairs. But what inspired it? As she recalled, at the precise moment he frowned at her, she was feeling good—no, she was feeling great! And even though he had not shared in the experience, anger seemed a bit extreme.

She slipped on the stair, and his hand shot out and caught her. "Watch your step," he said, close to her ear. Very close. So close in fact, his soft breath tickled the hairs on the back of her neck.

She glanced over her shoulder with a confused expression.

"Where's Joachim?" she asked when they were halfway down the stairs.

"I left him in his playpen before I came up to get you."

"Were you expecting a fight?" she asked with a snicker. "Leaving both hands free just in case?"

He didn't say anything in response.

Because she was feeling her own share of anger and disappointment, Amber decided it was time for him to experience a little of the famous Lockhart stubbornness. She stopped on the step and braced herself as Paul ran into the back of her.

"Why did you stop?"

She glanced over her shoulder. "I asked you a question. Did you think I would put up a fight?"

His dark eyes hardened. "Why would you? I'm sure you'll find someone to fill your bed soon enough. A man who'll accept what you give him and ask for nothing more. A man who will use your body and care nothing for your heart. That *is* the kind of man you want, Amber, isn't it?"

Boy, did that backfire! She started down the stairs again, but felt his fingers lock on her upper arm and jerk her back.

"Now you answer my question. That is the kind of man you want, isn't it?"

The tip of his nose was almost touching hers, and instead of being intimidated, all Amber could think about was the sweet, minty smell of his breath and how good his mouth would taste.

"Isn't it?" he demanded with a slight shake of her arm.

How easy it would be to deny the accusation. To tell him the truth. To let him know how much he'd come to mean to her. But she was just not feeling that generous.

She arched a haughty eyebrow. "That's *exactly* the kind of man I want."

Paul stared into her eyes for several longs moments. His full lips twisted in a snarl. "He can have you."

He released her arm and moved around her, hurrying down the remaining stairs and around the corner into the kitchen.

Amber leaned against the wall, trying to get her bearings. Okay, it was official. He was much better at the mean and snappy thing. She felt tears in her eyes but was determined he would not see her cry.

No, she would save her tears for when she boarded the plane. Then she would have a good, long cry on the flight back to Detroit. And when she stepped off the plane in Detroit, she would close the door on Paul Gutierrez forever. But he was wrong about one thing. She would never forget her time with the Gutierrez men.

"Blizzard?" Amber's eyes widened in surprise. "What blizzard?"

"The entire midwest is getting bombarded. They say it's one of the worst storms of the decade," the haggard ticket attendant said. "It's been all over the news. I don't see how you could've missed it ."

Amber glanced at Paul, who was standing beside her. "I've been kinda busy."

The older, white woman peered at Amber over the top of her half glasses, then she looked at Paul and back to Amber. "I'm sure. The most I can do at this point is put you on a standby flight. It might get out of here today, but that's not guaranteed."

"Well…" Amber hesitated, as her mind scrabbled for an answer to her latest dilemma. This was the last thing she'd expected to hear. "Umm, when do they expect it to let up?"

"Not for at least forty-eight hours. That's why they have been telling everyone to stock up on water and candles." She sighed in exasperation. "How could you not know about this? You should always check the weather conditions when you plan to travel."

Amber bit her lip. The last thing she needed was to be scolded like a child by this woman. "Do you know of a hotel in walking distance of here?"

Paul spoke up for the first time. "Why do you need a hotel?"

"Yes," the attendant interrupted. "There's one not half a block—"

"She *doesn't* need a hotel." Paul said, glaring at the woman.

The woman said nothing more.

"Paul, don't give me a hard time about this. I'm just going to check into a hotel and wait the storm out."

"I'm not giving you a hard time. I'm not giving you any time. You're coming home with me."

"If you are not buying a ticket today, could you step aside so someone else can?" the woman asked, making a gesture with her hands.

"Well?" Paul asked tartly, and Amber did her best to ignore him.

"Can you tell me where I can rent a car?" Amber asked the attendant.

"Down the escalator, and to your—"

"She doesn't need a rental car or a hotel!" Paul growled at the ticket attendant.

The woman reared back from the counter. "Fine!" She turned her eyes on Amber. "Just take your caveman and get out of my line."

"Caveman?" Paul leaned across the counter. "Who are you calling—"

"Paul!" Amber took hold of his arm, and was surprised to

feel his muscles tensed beneath his shirt. "Paul, let's just go." She gave his arm a hard jerk, and guided him from the counter.

Paul resisted for a moment, then led the baby's stroller away.

Once they were away from the crowd, Amber swung around to face him. "Just what do you think you are doing?"

"Why would you rent a car, or check into a hotel, when all you have to do is come back to Moreno Valley with me? I promise not to charge you for the room, and you can use one of my cars anytime you need it. So, what's the problem?"

"I think you know what the problem is. It's the reason I'm trying to leave today."

"We can work around that. But there is no reason to check in to a hotel."

"Work around it? Exactly how do you propose we work around it, Paul? You kicked me out, remember?"

Paul looked down at the floor for several seconds, then lifted his eyes to Amber. She could see some decision had been made. "I'm sorry," he said.

"Look, Paul, I appreciate what you're trying to do, but we've said our goodbyes and I think it's best that we leave it at that." She glanced down at the baby in the stroller. Joachim's wide eyes were going in every direction as he tried to take in everything at once. "It was hard enough the first time."

"Amber, have you ever wanted something so bad, and then you find out you can't have it? But still, you want it so bad, it makes you angry that you can't have it?"

She looked at him, afraid to answer.

"That's how bad I want you. So bad that knowing I can't have you makes me angry. And I took that anger out on you."

Her heart swelled with hope. "But you can have me."

He placed a finger over her lips and shook his head. "No, not the way I want you." He chuckled to himself. "Sometimes I forget how young you are. And that's our problem—timing. See, I've lived long enough to know that whatever this is—this magic between us—it's special and rare." He moved his finger from her mouth. "It's okay. We'll go back to Moreno Valley and try to go back to the way things were before we were intimate. And when the storm lets up, I'll bring you back and send you home. And maybe if I'm lucky, one day you'll realize these few days we shared were different than anything you've ever known and you'll come back to me. And if not, that's okay, too. I didn't mean what I said earlier. I don't blame Luther for sending me after you. I thank him with all my heart. Because through you, I've discovered that I still have the ability and desire to love a woman with my whole being. After what Michelle put me through, I wasn't sure I could. But now I know…because I love you."

Amber could almost feel her heart breaking inside her chest. "We've only known each other for four days."

"But I've known your soul forever. Look, I'm sorry for the way I've been treating you. If you come back to Moreno Valley with me, I promise to lock Crazy Paul away in the attic, and you won't have to deal with him anymore. Okay?"

"Crazy Paul, huh?" She smiled, then chuckled. "You nearly gave that poor ticket lady a heart attack, hissing and snarling at her."

He frowned. "I don't hiss and snarl."

She took his hand in hers, and the trio started moving toward the exit. "Oh, I know *you* don't. But Crazy Paul does."

Chapter 15

When they pulled up to Paul's house, a little over an hour later, Amber was still complaining about the fact that none of her sisters had mentioned anything about a blizzard in the past few days.

"I talked to Pearl for over an hour yesterday, and she said nothing."

"Hmm," Paul grunted, only half listening. Most of his attention was directed at the black Mustang parked across the street. He would have to see it from the rear to be certain, but he was pretty sure that was the same car he'd seen a couple of days ago, when they came home from the street fair.

"You know, if this is going to be a long-term arrangement we're going to need more groceries." Amber continued to chat away. "Mind if I take the SUV and go out to the store later?"

Paul continued to watch the Mustang in the rearview mirror. "Maybe that isn't such a good idea."

"Why not?"

He glanced at her pretty face and wondered if he should tell her the truth. Should he share his suspicions that the person in the car was Dashuan Kennedy or someone working for him? No, there was no reason in alarming her until he knew for certain.

"I can take you."

"Why, when I can take myself?"

Paul was beginning to realize there was no legitimate excuse. Especially when he'd just told her she could use the car anytime she wanted. He found the perfect explanation.

"You don't know where the grocery store is."

Her eyebrows crinkled in exasperation. "Fine."

He almost smiled at her disgruntled expression. But he was just too relieved that he would not have to let her go out by herself. Until he found out who was in that black car, Paul had no intention of letting her out of his sight.

He helped her get Joachim out of the backseat and guided them onto the porch. He unlocked the door and went into the house ahead of them, and did a quick but discreet sweep of all the rooms. Once he was satisfied that there were no signs of a break-in, he told Amber he was going out to check the mail.

Instead of going to the mailbox, he headed across the street toward the black car. When the engine came on, he started to run, but the car sped away from the curb and down the street before he could reach it. He stood in the middle of the street trying to read the digits on the license plate, but only got four. Luckily, four was more than enough to run a search.

So his suspicions were correct. Somehow, against the odds, Dashuan Kennedy had found her. Still, he wouldn't say anything to Amber until he decided how to handle it. He looked up and down the street in both directions to be sure there was no one else watching the house, before going back inside.

Paul went straight to his office and with special software searched for the partial plate number, but after almost an hour of searching, he still had not narrowed the list of possible matches enough to identify the vehicle.

He stood and stretched, and was surprised to find Amber standing in the doorway watching him. "There you are." She smiled. "You went out to get the mail an hour ago, and that was the last I saw of you."

Paul sat back down and focused his attention on the computer screen. If they were going to make this friend thing work, he would have to avoid looking at her lovely face.

"I wanted to get some work done." He opened a file on the computer. He wasn't even sure which one it was. "Did you need something?"

He glanced at her and noticed her smile had faded some. "No, just wanted to know what you wanted for dinner."

He sat back in his chair. "Look, Amber, you shouldn't feel obligated to cook every night."

"I don't. I enjoy it."

"Okay." He looked through a stack of files on the desk, pretending to look for something. "Anything else?"

She was quiet for so long, he was forced to glance at her again.

She was leaning against the doorway, her hazel eyes narrowed on his face. "Is this the way it's going to be now, Paul?"

"What do you mean?"

"This stiffness. Like we're strangers."

"According to you, we're not much more than that," he muttered, and regretted it.

She sighed. "You know what? I don't need this." She turned and walked away.

Paul started to breathe a sigh of relief, and then suddenly she was there again.

"Is this why you brought me back here? So you could continue to give me the cold shoulder?" Her eyes were practically glowing. "You said if I came back here with you, things could be the way they were before. Instead, you've just picked up where you left off this morning."

Paul stood and walked around the desk, heading toward her. He watched as she took a defensive stance. But instead of stopping, he walked right around her and into the kitchen. Amber tilted her head curiously and fell into step behind him.

He bypassed the playpen where Joachim was sleeping, and walked over to the freezer. He opened the door, and stood there for a moment before pulling out a frozen pack of steak. He tossed the meat on the counter, and it sounded like a brick hitting concrete. "Steak. I want steak for dinner. Happy now?"

Amber threw up her hands and groaned. She turned and headed out of the kitchen. "I knew I should've just checked in to a hotel!" A moment later, he heard her stomping up the stairs.

Paul leaned against the kitchen sink and hung his head. He had so many conflicting feelings racing through his tortured brain.

He took several deep breaths to get control of his

temper. He knew Amber was right about the way he was treating her, but it wasn't a conscious action.

He felt like a starving man who'd been offered a small morsel of food. By rights, he should've never turned it down, because a morsel was more than he'd had in a long time. But at the same time, he knew that morsel would only awaken his hunger for more. Much more.

Instead of taking it in stride as he did everything else in life, he seemed determined to make Amber pay for denying him what he wanted most.

He glanced at his sleeping son, remembering the scene that had awaited him when he arrived in the nursery that morning. He'd stopped by the bathroom to clean up, thinking that Joachim's cry was just for attention. But nothing could describe the guilt and fear he'd felt when he walked into the room and saw his son's little foot caught between the bars of the crib, heard Joachim crying as he tried frantically to get it free.

Paul had immediately begun to gently knead his soft flesh, while making cooing noises in an attempt to calm him. After a few minutes, he managed to manipulate the foot enough to slide it back between the bars.

He hugged his baby close to his chest. Memories of the day he'd found him in the hotel with his mother's body flooded Paul's mind. Only this time, it had not been Michelle's irresponsible behavior that left him vulnerable; it had been Paul's.

He'd allowed a temptress to seduce him into ignoring his son's needs. The worst part was in knowing how much he'd enjoyed stroking her soft flesh, feeling her liquid warmth on his hand, how tempted he'd been to climb on top of her and take his own satisfaction. He'd blocked out

Joachim's cries for the sake of sexual gratification. And yes, she was right, some part of him even blamed Amber, for being so damn desirable.

Even now she continued to taunt him with her presence. He'd wanted her back under his roof, back within his grasp, and he'd lied to get her there. He told her they could go back to the way things were before, knowing full well that they never could.

He glanced once at the package of steaks sitting on the counter, before picking up the telephone and dialing the number of his favorite local restaurant.

Barney Roberts glanced around the small, crowded café in Studio City. He spotted the man he was meeting. After all, Dashuan Kennedy was not the kind of man to blend into a crowd. His sheer size assured that.

Barney was not surprised to see that Dashuan sat alone and unbothered. Since celebrity sightings were a common occurrence in this trendy L.A, suburb, the local residents were unilaterally unimpressed.

He maneuvered his way through the tables and held out his hand. "Mr. Kennedy, I'm Barney Roberts. What a pleasure it is to meet you, sir. I'm a big fan."

Dashuan gave his best camera smile. "The pleasure is all mine." He gestured to the chair across from him. "Have a seat. I understand you're interested in becoming a part of my security team."

Barney undid the button on his suit jacket, and sat down. "Yes, sir, I am."

Barney had thought it was nothing more than pure luck that put him and a member of Dashuan Kennedy's security detail at that car wash at the same time.

The man had commented on Barney's sports car, and Barney had taken note of the late model Mustang the man was washing. When the guy mentioned that the car belonged to Dashuan Kennedy, Barney had recognized the name.

Through conversation the two men had discovered they shared the same line of work, and the bodyguard mentioned that Dashuan was looking to increase the size of his security team by one man. After being fired by Paul Gutierrez almost a week ago, Barney had barely been able to contain his enthusiasm.

"I don't stand on formality, so please call me Dashuan." Dashuan smiled his winning smile again. "Can I call you Barney?"

"Absolutely."

"Did you bring a résumé?"

Barney handed over the manila folder he was carrying, feeling like an idiot for not thinking of it first.

Dashuan opened the folder and skimmed the information on the resume. "According to this, your last employer was a company called G-Force?"

There was not the slightest note of recognition in his voice. "Yes, we provide security protection for celebrities such as yourself. My last assignment was part of the detail for Lacy Hill." He took a long swallow from the water glass on the table.

Dashuan smiled. "Is she as hot in person as she is in her pictures?"

"Hotter."

"Not a bad job to have. So, why did you give it up?"

Barney took another sip of water. He'd practiced this lie for two days now, trying to make it sound smooth and natural. "Well, I'm from Detroit, and my family has been bugging me to move back there." He took another sip, thinking of the wonderful beaches he'd played along as a child…in Newport News, Virginia.

Barney had chosen that particular lie because he did indeed have family in Detroit, and thus it would be an easy lie to support if there ever became a need.

Dashuan glanced back at the file. "I see."

While there were no eyes on him, Barney tugged at his silk tie. He felt like it was choking him. He wondered what kind of employer Dashuan Kennedy would make. He was a pretty boy, and probably spent most of his off-court time chasing women. Not that it mattered. All Barney wanted was a chance to start over. He couldn't afford to be particular.

After a while, Dashuan put the folder down on the table. He intertwined his fingers and leaned forward. "Well, just from your résumé, I believe you could be the perfect addition to my security team, Barney."

Barney's face spread in a wide grin. "Thank you. You won't reg—"

Dashuan put up a hand to still the feverent thanks. "But…"

Barney's smile fell off his face as if it had never been there. He knew it was too easy.

"But," Dashuan continued, "there is only so much you can learn about a man on paper. See, Barney, for me, loyalty is not only a desirable quality, it's crucial."

Barney frowned, wondering if he was being toyed with. Seeing how the reason Paul let him go was betrayal, he was beginning to think that maybe this was all some elaborate hoax. But just in case it wasn't, he answered, "I completely agree."

Dashuan tilted his head to the side, studying the other

man, and Barney struggled not to squirm under the scrutiny. "Are you willing to prove your loyalty to me, Barney?"

There was something hard and flinty in Dashuan Kennedy's eyes, and Barney was wondering why he had not seen it before now. "What do I have to do?" he asked hesitantly.

"I tell you what…" He dug in his jacket pocket for a pen and scribbled something on a napkin. "This is my offer." He pushed the paper across the table to Barney.

Barney's eyes widened at the figure written there. He turned surprised eyes on Dashuan, knowing that this test of loyalty was no longer a barrier. There was little he was not willing to do for that amount of money.

"You see, Barney, I treat my employees well, because I demand a lot from them. I know I can depend on them. I need to know I can depend on *you,* Barney." He tapped the paper, drawing Barney's attention back to the figure there. "Can I depend on you, Barney?"

Barney knew a hustle when he saw one. Whatever this man was about to ask him would cost him his soul. He glanced back at the paper, realizing that he probably would've sold it for a lot less. He looked into Dashuan's hard eyes, and all illusions of new beginnings fell away.

He licked his lips. "I'm listening."

Dashuan nodded in satisfaction. "Tell me what you know about Paul Gutierrez."

Barney's eyes narrowed on his new employer's face as everything began to click into place. The coincidence of running into the bodyguard at the car wash, the miraculous job opening on Dashuan's security team. Everything had led to this moment.

When he considered what lengths Dashuan went to get him, Barney realized he was almost flattered.

Once he accepted reality for what it was, he opened his mouth and proceeded to tell Dashuan everything he knew about his former employer and friend.

Chapter 16

Amber had resigned herself to waiting out the snowstorm in her borrowed bedroom. That way she would not have to deal with Paul at all. Of course, it only took her about thirty minutes to see the ludicrousness of trying to hide from a man in his own house.

Still, she could at least give herself one evening of reprieve. She was curled up in the middle of the bed going into her fourth consecutive hour of the Weather Channel forecast when the wonderful smells drifted under the bedroom door and across the room. She fought with every ounce of strength not to go downstairs, but her empty belly won the battle against her will.

She crept down the stairs, trying to make as little noise as possible. She just wanted to see what smelled so good, and then she would return upstairs, or so she tried to convince herself.

As she turned the corner to go into the kitchen, she stopped and caught her breath. The kitchen table was covered in a shiny red tablecloth, and sitting in the middle of the table was a small bouquet of mixed flowers. On each side of the bouquet, glowed a single white candle. Although she did not see the CD player, she could hear soft jazz music playing.

There were two plate settings on opposite sides of the table, and even from a distance Amber could see the intricate design of the china. She approached, and the high-pitched murmuring sounds coming from the other side of the table made her tilt her head to see past the bouquet.

Between the two settings was Joachim in his high chair, which was pushed back from the table. She smiled to see he was all dressed up in a dapper little powder-blue onesie, which his father had been smart enough to cover with a bib.

As soon as he spotted her, his quiet play turned into loud screeches and he stretched his little arms toward her. Amber picked him up, and having gotten what he wanted he settled down once more. Amber continued to circle the table, taking in the different foil-covered dishes.

Everything smelled wonderful, the table setting was beautiful, and little Joachim was adorable…. Her eyes widened as she realized what she was looking at.

A seduction!

Still holding the baby she turned to leave, knowing the only thing that could make this seduction a coup d'état would be adding Paul to the mix. She was almost out of the room, when she heard his soft voice behind her.

"Hungry?"

God, yes! And she was not thinking of food. Amber took a deep breath and turned to see him standing just outside the pantry, holding a bottle of wine in each hand.

"What is all this?"

"Dinner." He held up both bottles. "Red or white?"

Her eyes ran over his long form, noting his usual jeans and T-shirt had been replaced by a pair of black slacks and a cream-colored silk shirt. The top two buttons of the shirt were open, exposing a small patch of curly black hair. Her mind flashed back to the couch when he pulled his shirt over his head, his muscles rippling. *This is such a bad idea.*

He walked over and placed both bottles on the table.

"Did you do all this?" She gestured to the table.

Paul arched an eyebrow. "I only do chili, remember? No, I ordered from a restaurant in town." His dark eyes took in her close proximity to the door. "You won't stay and have dinner with me?"

"Um, no." She glanced over her shoulder. "I'm not hungry," she lied, and turned to leave.

"You were right earlier." Paul's softly spoken words stopped her in her tracks. " I have been a real jerk. I'm sorry." He stuffed his hands in his pockets. "Seems like I've been saying that to you a lot. Give me a chance to make it up to you."

There was such sincerity in his voice, Amber thought she would melt where she was standing. "Apology accepted." She glanced back at the welcoming table. "But I'm not that hungry."

He studied her face for a moment, before nodding in understanding. "Amber, it's just dinner." He held out his hand.

Amber glanced down at his strong hand, and sighed in resignation before putting Joachim back in his high chair. "What have we got here?"

Paul began opening the containers. Amber looked down

at plump juicy steaks and laughed. "Wow, I guess you did want steak for dinner."

Because of conversation, they were still eating almost an hour later. Paul was telling Amber about some of his influential clients. His roster boasted everyone from foreign dignitaries temporarily on assignment in Los Angeles, to famous actors and actresses.

Amber was duly impressed. "What's she like in person?" She was asking about her favorite box-office actress.

Paul shrugged. "She's actually a nice lady."

Her expression turned playful, as she nudged his arm. "She ever hit on you?"

The blush that ran up his face was a dead giveaway.

"She did, didn't she?"

He shrugged. "A gentleman doesn't kiss and tell."

She stabbed at another broccoli stalk, and tried to ignore the slight tinge of jealousy she was feeling.

"What's your major?" he asked, wiping his mouth with his napkin, before lifting the glass of red wine to his lips.

Amber looked up, a bit surprised by the question. "What?"

"You said you were in school, so what's your major?"

She looked away guiltily. "Um, I don't have one yet."

He titled his head to look at her. "What year are you in?"

"Sophomore," she muttered.

"I'm sorry. Did you say sophomore?"

She hesitated, and then deciding it made little difference, she nodded.

"Oh, I thought you were a full-time student. Do you go part-time?"

Amber shifted in her chair. The conversation was becoming uncomfortable. "Um, no. I'm a full-time student."

Paul frowned. "How long have you been in school?"

She sighed, hoping this would be the last intrusive question. She almost refused to answer, but she had learned enough about Paul to know that would only make him that much more curious. "Three years and four months."

"And you've only earned enough credits to qualify as a sophomore?"

"Yes!" she snapped. "What's it to you?"

"Nothing." He shook his head and turned his attention back to his food.

Amber put her fork on her plate. "Look, I just can't make up my mind what I want to do."

His dark eyes narrowed on her face. "Yeah, I've noticed that about you. But eventually you have to make a choice. Follow your instincts."

Her mouth twisted derisively. "You don't understand. My instincts stink."

He smiled. "No, you just think they do."

Something about his smug assurance grated on her nerves. "Oh, yeah?" she asked with heavy sarcasm. "What else do you know, Paul?"

He took a bite of steak and leaned back in his chair. Once he was finished chewing, he began. "Well, I know you are impulsive, optimistic, loyal and proud. You're funny, and intelligent and beautiful…." He paused. "Inside and out."

The intensity of his feelings was there, written in his eyes, in every line of his face, in his words, even the tone of his voice. Amber wanted to believe he could know her so well, but it was hard to accept that anyone could in so short a time.

As if sensing her train of thought, Paul continued. "I

know you're impulsive because you came out here with a man you barely know. But I was wrong before when I called you a gold digger."

"You called me a gold digger?"

"The point is…" He pushed on, hoping to avoid a confrontation. "You came out here with Kennedy because you believed you had a chance at a relationship." He pointed his fork at her. "That's what I call optimistic."

Amber found herself intrigued by his analysis. She folded her arms across her chest. "Go on."

"You're extremely loyal, even when you shouldn't be. I hear how you talk about your sisters, and even Kennedy. After the way he treated you, we both know all it would take is a phone call to a tabloid to ruin him. Yet, you've never said a single word about getting even."

She smirked. "Maybe I just never thought about it."

"Oh, you've thought about it, I'm sure. But it's not something you would ever do, because you're—"

"Loyal."

"And proud." He reached across the table and took her hand in his. "But I don't mind your pride, because it's kept you here with me this long." He lifted her hand and brought it to his lips. "And beautiful," he said seductively, "so beautiful. More beautiful than you know. Because all you see is your physical beauty. You don't even recognize your own inner beauty."

She frowned in confusion.

Paul placed her hand back on the table and let it go. He cut another piece of steak. "You are so much more than what you give yourself credit for being."

Amber fought to tap down the wonderful swelling in her heart. He meant everything he was saying, and she wanted to believe him. But for everything he thought he knew, he still did not know her.

"I'm flattered but you're wrong, Paul. What you see is what you get. There is no deeper, hidden meaning behind most of what I do. I'm classically indecisive."

Paul released a heavy, long-suffering sigh. "Unfortunately, I know that, too."

"What's that supposed to mean?" she asked, pulling a tiny piece of meat off the tip of her steak and mashing it between her thumb and index finger.

Paul watched the strange behavior, but said nothing until she reached over and put it between his son's lips. "What are you doing?"

By the time he'd got the question out, the tiny piece of meat had already disappeared. Joachim's brown eyes lit up in excitement as he smacked his lips.

"What are you doing feeding him table food?" he asked again.

Amber's eyes widened. "Table food? You make it sound like he's a puppy."

"No, he's a baby. And babies don't eat steak, any more than puppies should."

Amber titled her head, perplexed by Paul's angry response. "What's the big deal?"

"I just told you, he's a baby!"

"An *eight-month-old* baby!"

"So what?"

Amber reached over and pulled down Joachim's lower lip, to expose a tiny rice-grain-size whitening on the top of his bottom gums. "He's starting to teethe, Paul." She placed the meat in his mouth before his father could object. "When do you plan to start him on baby food?"

Paul frowned, realizing he'd never noticed the tiny tooth coming in. Nor had he considered the timetable for solid foods. But he wasn't about to admit that to a childless, single woman who apparently had more natural instinct than he had actual experience.

"When his pediatrician recommends it."

She made a strange expression, and for once, Paul had no idea what she was thinking. "You may want to consider a different pediatrician."

Paul glanced back at his son, whose attention was trained on Amber. Why hadn't he thought of any of this?

Amber mashed up another piece of meat and lifted it to Joachim's mouth. She looked at Paul. "Can I?"

Before Paul could answer, Joachim grabbed her arm with both hands pulling the meat toward his mouth.

Paul smiled. "Doesn't look like my opinion matters." They both chuckled as Joachim smacked his lips.

Later that night, despite the bits of meat and vegetables he'd consumed, Joachim still took his whole bottle of formula before falling off to sleep.

When Paul returned from the nursery he found Amber sitting on the couch staring at the lit tree. Hearing him enter the room, she looked over her shoulder. "I think we did a great job, don't you?"

He smiled, taking in the festive tree that would not even be there if not for her. "Not bad at all." He sat next to her on the couch, frowning. " I can't believe I didn't notice that tooth."

She yawned. "It's no wonder. Most babies cry when they're teething. But Joachim is such a happy baby, he rarely cries at all."

Paul noted the touch of pride in her voice, but said nothing about it. *That's it, son. Win her over for us.* He settled back on the couch. "About what we were discussing earlier…what do you enjoy doing?"

"What do you mean?"

"Just what I said. What do you like to do?"

Amber thought for a moment. "Decorate. I love decorating *anything*." She glanced around the living room. "For instance, this house is beautiful, but let me tell you, Paul, it's begging for some TLC."

Not just the house. He kept the comment to himself. "You think my house needs some help?"

She chuckled. "Are you kidding? All these white walls are leaving me snow-blind."

His eyes slanted away, as a stroke of genius came to him. He got up off the couch and went out of the room. "Be right back," he called.

A couple of minutes later, he returned with his checkbook. He sat back down and took a pen from his pocket. "Give me an amount."

Amber glanced from him to the checkbook and back. "What?"

"If I were to hire you to decorate my house, how much would it cost?"

"You're kidding?"

He faced her. "Look, you said yourself that you're indecisive. You like decorating, but you're not sure if interior design should be your major. I'm just trying to help you decide and get my house decorated at the same time. So…name your price."

Amber felt her heart racing. The challenge of one room would've been enough to excite her, but he was offering her carte blanche on his whole house. Just to be certain, she asked, "The *whole* house?"

"The whole house—although there is one catch."

Her eyes narrowed. "I knew it!"

"You have to stay here until you're finished."

"How long?"

"How long do you need?"

Her eyes took on a faraway expression, as she tried to imagine each room and what it entailed. It was too much to answer on the spur of the moment. "Can I have some time to come up with a quote?"

Paul smiled at the professional tone in her voice. "By all means. Take as long as you need." *Take forever if you like.*

She smiled, and it became a grin. She hopped up off the couch, and hurried toward the door.

"Where are you going?"

"To get started," she answered, as if it were the obvious answer.

"Can't you start tomorrow?"

"Are you kidding me? I have to come up with color schemes and take measurements, and— By the way, can I hire contractors?"

"For what?" Paul's eyes widened, as he was beginning to wonder what he'd gotten himself in to. All he'd envisioned were maybe some curtains and a couple coats of paint.

"Never mind. I can make it work without them." And then she was gone.

Paul sat back and crossed his legs at the ankles, feeling quite pleased with himself.

Chapter 17

One week later, Paul was in the kitchen pouring cereal into a bowl when the phone rang. He grabbed the cordless off the counter. "Hello?"

"Hey, man, what's up?"

"Hey, Luther, how's it going?"

"That's kind of why I'm calling."

Paul turned and opened the refrigerator door. "Oh?"

"Yeah, it's been two weeks since you brought Amber back to your house, and we were all wondering when she planned to come home?"

"You have to ask her." Paul opened the milk and poured it over his breakfast.

"She talked to Pearl yesterday, and said something about some project you have her working on?"

"She's redecorating my house," Paul said with a smile.

There was such a long pause, Paul was beginning to

wonder if the call had dropped. Finally Luther said, "Come again?"

"It's more like a test."

"A test?"

"An aptitude test. We're trying to find what she's good at. As far as I can tell, her special skill seems to be spending my money."

"Paul, what the hell are you talking about?"

Paul laughed. He could afford to laugh. He was winning. At the rate things were going Amber would not be able to deny her feelings for him much longer.

"Like I said, talk to Amber, she can tell you all about it. She has big plans for this place." He frowned. "Big plans."

He was remembering the additional two thousand he'd shelled out yesterday for something called a secretary. Apparently, he needed it for one of the guest bedrooms. He was more than a little disappointed when the deliverymen carried in a small desk.

"Paul, what's going on? The blizzard passed over almost three days ago, and Christmas is less than two weeks away. Do you think she'll be finished with your project in time enough to be home for Christmas?"

I hope not. "Not sure. Like I said, you'd have to ask her."

After another long pause Luther spoke again, a sympathetic tone to his voice. "Paul, is something going on between you two?"

Paul stopped stirring the milk into his cereal. "What makes you say that?"

"Come on, man, I know you better than most. That Latin blood of yours makes you…"

Paul's eyes narrowed. "Makes me what, Luther?"

"Hell, man, I was there when you met Michelle,

remember? You fell for her like a rock, even though the rest of us kept telling you she was no good." His tone softened even more. "And look how that turned out. All I'm saying, man, is that you tend to fall in love too quickly."

Paul started stirring his milk again. "Amber's not Michelle."

"I know, I know. Believe me, I love Amber like a little sister. I know how special she is, and I can understand why you would fall for her." He huffed. "If I hadn't been in such a panic, you're probably the last person I would've sent after her, knowing you like I do."

"Too late for regrets. You gave her to me, and I'm keeping her."

"See! See, that's exactly what I mean! You can't say stuff like that about some woman you've only known two weeks."

At that moment, "some woman" appeared in the doorway with Joachim in one arm and a notebook in the other. Both she and Joachim were dressed for outside.

Paul put up a finger to ask her to wait.

"Well, thanks for your concern, but I've got to hang up now. I'm going rug shopping." With that he hung up the phone.

He was halfway across the room when the phone started ringing again.

"Don't you want to get that?" Amber asked.

"No." He grabbed his jacket off the back of a kitchen chair.

"What about your breakfast?" she asked, as he scooped up his keys and guided her out.

"I'm not hungry anymore."

"Paul, can you come here a moment?" Amber called.

Paul was standing by the storefront window watching

the pedestrians and cars outside. He hadn't seen the black Mustang since that day he chased it away. But he wasn't foolish enough to believe that would be the end of it.

So, whenever Amber insisted on going out to buy something more for the house, he insisted on accompanying her. He used his position as the customer as an excuse when she became particularly obstinate about driving herself, when in truth, he couldn't have cared less about what she did with the house.

Unfortunately, using the privilege of buyer's rights gave Amber the impression that he actually cared about fabric swatches and rug textures.

He walked back toward where she was standing in the middle of the showroom with an older salesman, surrounded by carpet pieces.

Paul groaned inwardly.

She had two carpet squares resting on top of the stroller where Joachim was sleeping. He was no more interested in carpet samples than his father.

"What do you think?" she asked when Paul came closer.

He frowned down at the two squares. "About what?"

"The living room." She sighed in exasperation.

He looked closer at the two carpets. "Pink? You want to put pink carpet in the living room?"

"Pink? What are you talking about? This is rose." She pointed at the first one. "And that's mauve."

What the hell is mauve? "I see." He glanced at the salesman, who wore an expression that looked suspiciously like repressed laughter. "What do *you* think?" he asked Amber.

She dug down in her purse and pulled out a small piece of fabric. "Well, here's the sofa." She laid it against the first piece of carpet.

Paul could not hide his confusion. "Huh?"

"The sofa. This is the color and fabric of the new sofa."

"Oh." Paul sighed. He considered himself intelligent, but this was too much to ask of any man. He wanted to ask which was cheaper, but given what he knew about Amber, he figured she probably wouldn't know. She never asked for the price until she'd already made her decision.

He watched her bite her bottom lip in concentration.

"The mauve," she said, nodding. "Definitely, the mauve." She held up the sofa fabric against it. "See, it goes perfectly."

If you say so. "I agree completely," Paul said, and glanced back toward the front of the store. He hated the vulnerability of the place, but doubted Dashuan Kennedy would try anything in so public a place.

Amber was grinning up at him, beaming with pride. "I do have a knack for this, don't I?"

He smiled, unable to do anything else in the face of her joy. "A knack? I was thinking it was more like a gift."

She nudged him with her elbow. "Very funny."

After picking out an unusual shade of blue for the master bedroom, Amber collected her samples and they returned home.

They spent the afternoon as they had for the past week. They shared a light lunch, and then Amber took Joachim with her and returned to her decorating project, and Paul went into his study to work.

Later that day, deciding he needed a break, Paul went in search of Amber. He found her sitting cross-legged in the middle of the floor in one of the guestrooms. She was staring at the blank wall before her, but Paul could almost believe she was seeing something there. Then she bent her head and started writing on a large notepad that rested on her knees.

Paul moved closer and saw Joachim laying on a blanket in front of her. He was on his back trying to wrap a chew ring around his toes. Amber's attention was centered on whatever she was scribbling.

Where he was standing, Paul could see she was drawing what looked like a bookcase. The object in the drawing was not as impressive as the drawing itself.

"Wow, I didn't know you could draw like that," he said with true awe, noting the intricate details, the defined lines. The image was so vivid it was almost three-dimensional.

Amber started, not having heard him enter. She lifted the sketchbook against her chest to hide her drawing. "It just helps me visualize what I want to do. It's no big deal."

Paul could sense her insecurity, and marveled at this beautiful, complex woman who just continued to unfold, revealing layer after layer of unique and fascinating facets of her personality. He sat down beside her, and tugged at the sketchbook. "No big deal? It's amazing."

Looking into his eyes to see if he were just being polite, Amber was surprised to realize he meant it. She released the book.

"How long have you been doing this?" He looked back through the pages, and realized every new piece of furniture that had been brought into his home in the last week had been outlined in the book. What he'd thought was random selection was actually well thought out. And looking at the pictures of full rooms she'd created, he was pleased to see an elegant home coming together.

"Okay, all joking aside," he stated, remembering their playful banter at the carpet store earlier. "You really do have a talent for this."

"You think so?" she asked hesitantly, and Paul turned

to look into her eyes. He understood that anyone who didn't know Amber would take one look at her and assume she had the self-confidence of a lion. She possessed a rare physical beauty, a natural charm and a manner of carrying herself that radiated supreme self-assurance.

But the woman he was looking at now had nothing to do with that pretense. This was the real Amber, a woman who felt she'd lived in the shadow of her sisters most of her life and was in fact insecure about her own value as a human being. There was such a plea for validation in her eyes it reached inside and touched the center of his being.

Without considering the consequence, Paul leaned forward and touched his lips to hers. The banked embers of passion between them roared into a blazing flame.

Wrapping his arm around her, he leaned into her pushing her back onto the carpet, and instead of pushing him away, Amber wrapped her arms around his neck and surrendered to his heavier weight.

Her mouth opened beneath his, welcoming him into the warm haven, and Paul drank her in with ravenous eagerness. He devoured her mouth, toying with her tongue, nipping at her bottom lip.

It had only been a few days since he'd held her in his arms, but it felt like a year. Unable to stop his roaming hands, they traced every inch of her body, refamiliarizing himself with her.

Amber's welcoming response fueled his lust, and soon his trembling hand was beneath her shirt, lifting it to caress the soft mounds of flesh that taunted his dreams.

Her small hands digging into his shoulders told him that her need was as great as his own. And when she lifted her body to his, opening her legs to allow him to settle between her thighs, Paul was almost certain he would explode on the spot.

He looked down at her, with her head thrown back in abandon, her whole body straining toward his. The image was at once erotic and sobering. *No! Not like this!*

Summoning strength of will he didn't know he possessed, Paul pushed himself up.

"What's wrong?" Amber asked with bated breath, her lust-filled eyes tracing every line of his face.

Paul swallowed hard, and said a quick prayer for strength. "No, angel, not like this."

Her lust turned to frustration. "Why not?"

He almost laughed at the disgruntled expression on her face. "No, Amber, I won't take you in the heat of passion when you're so vulnerable." He pushed himself off of her and rolled into a sitting position.

Amber stroked his arm seductively. She was clearly a woman who knew how to get what she wanted. "I'm not vulnerable, Paul. I know what I'm doing. I want you."

Paul closed his eyes against the effect of those three simple words. He understood what Amber would not admit. If they made love like this, she would label it a fling, nothing more than a pleasant interlude in the overall scheme of her life.

But Paul had no intention of being an interlude. He planned to be something much more. And in order to have that, Amber would have to first admit to more than just a physical attraction between them.

Amber was like a wild thing, used to living for the moment and answering to no man. But he planned to change all that.

He intended to tame her.

And if that meant biding his time, waiting until she surrendered, then that was what he would do. Even if it killed him.

"Not like this."

Her angry golden eyes narrowed on his face for several tense moments. She sat up and snatched up her pad. "Fine, then go away. I have work to do," she muttered and turned her back on him. Paul knew that she was turning away from him in more than just the physical sense.

He stood and stared down at her, and she continued to draw, pretending not to notice him standing beside her.

Joachim was lying quietly, his eyelids drooping in an attempt to hold off sleep. His infant son accepted Amber's presence so naturally, as if she had always been a part of his life, even preferring her touch to that of his father's. And Amber so obviously adored his son. He himself was head over heels in love with her, and was almost certain she felt the same, even if she didn't admit it.

Everything had fallen into place so perfectly for them, it was completely obvious to Paul that the three of them belonged together. So why was she having such a hard time accepting it?

Chapter 18

As soon as Paul was out of sight, Amber breathed a sigh of relief. The man's fortitude was unbelievable! And he was beginning to make Amber question the one certainty in her life. Her power over men.

Paul Gutierrez defied everything she thought she knew about men. The first discrepency being that any man will take sex with no strings if it were offered. But during the past two weeks, she'd dangled that prospect beneath his nose any number of ways, and each and every time he'd walked away leaving her aggravated and unsatisfied. She found that she was beginning to agree with him. Love was indeed a nuisance.

And there was no more denying. She was indeed in love with Paul.

The *why* was no great mystery. Combine drop-dead gorgeous Brazilian with loving, dedicated single father, sprinkle in a dash of wealthy entrepreneur and you couldn't help but have a winning recipe.

The *how* was just as simple to explain. Two intense, sexually attracted and unattached people of the opposite sex living in close proximity, sharing the stories of their lives and discovering with every passing day that they have more and more in common. What else could've happened?

For Amber the how and why were understandable. The only question left was *what now?* According to Paul, they should just surrender to what they were feeling and ride off into the sunset together. But Amber was a little more pragmatic—not to mention selfish.

At twenty-one years old, Amber was not anywhere near ready to become a wife and instant mother. How was she supposed to be a good mother to Joachim, when she couldn't even figure out how to support herself? Not to mention the kind of rigid life she could expect with a man as possessive and overbearing as Paul could sometimes be.

Looking at it objectively, it was easy to say no. But it wasn't always easy to be objective. Not when Paul was giving her that sultry look that spoke of decadent promises, or that mischievous smile that showed a crystal clear image of the boy he once was. And when he touched her…the world felt as if it were spinning at a million miles an hour. The man's hands should be declared lethal weapons. No, it was not always easy to be objective about her feelings for him.

And then, of course, there was the added fear that she would never feel for another man the way she felt for Paul. And in truth, she knew in her heart that even if she walked away from what he was offering her, he would always be the measuring rod for any future lovers.

She stood and lifted the sleeping baby, and Joachim

curled against her body as if it was the most natural thing in the world. Amber felt the now familiar stirring in her heart whenever she held his little sleeping body. She kissed the top of his silky curls and carried him into the nursery.

As she tucked the infant into his crib, Amber realized that it was Saturday night and she had no desire to be anywhere other than where she was at that moment. That fact alone was proof that she'd changed. Until she came to live with Paul, she hadn't spent two consecutive Saturday nights at home in the past three years.

Home… Why did this place feel so much like home? She was even decorating it like home.

Instead of making detached purchases based on the personality of her client, Amber was aware that she was choosing items she would have in her own home if she could. The color schemes she was choosing were her favorites, the furniture to her taste. Instead of creating a home for just Paul and Joachim, she was creating a home for herself.

It was so easy, given that Paul had shown little interest in any of it. Except for insisting on going with her to all the stores, he'd left all the decisions in her hands. Did he know what he'd given her with this spontaneous proposition? Could he have any idea how important it had become to her in the past week? The kind of fulfillment she was finding in the project?

She stretched, and picked up the baby monitor as she left the room. Glancing at the hall clock, she saw it was almost six o'clock. She'd planned to make a casserole for dinner, so she headed downstairs toward the kitchen to get started.

Amber chuckled to herself, musing on what her girl-friends back in Detroit would think if they could see party girl Amber Lockhart playing the role of wife and mother. She smirked to herself. They would laugh, of course, and refuse to believe it. How could she blame them? She couldn't believe it herself.

Everyone knew she was too irresponsible, too high-stung, too selfish, too Amber to ever be Mrs. Paul Gutierrez. She hoped Paul would realize it long before he broke down her defenses and caused her to want an impossible dream.

As she turned into the kitchen, she paused in the door, seeing signs of herself everywhere. The furniture catalogs she'd been collecting over the week were stacked on the large dining table. The game she and Paul had started the night before was sitting on top of it. The jacket Paul had lent her was thrown over the back of one of the chairs. She glanced toward the stove where she'd spent yesterday morning reorganizing the area to better suit her cooking style. A stranger would know right away that this was the favorite room in the house.

There were little touches everywhere, small, insignificant signs that revealed the personalities of the tenants. She could see Paul's loafers sitting right outside the door, where he always kicked them off when he came into the house. Joachim's playpen sat almost in the middle of the room, giving him a bird's-eye view of all the goings-on.

Amber wrapped her arms around herself, feeling a chill run down her spine as a terrifying thought occurred to her. No wonder this place felt like home.

It had become home.

Close to midnight, Dashuan Kennedy pulled to the curb and stopped. He turned off the lights and the engine of the rented Mustang and sat watching the dark house across the street. Thanks to the talkative cop that drove him to the police station the night Amber left him, Dashuan had learned a lot about the mystery man who'd confronted him in the hotel lobby. His name, the name of his security company and where he lived.

The police officer hadn't seen Dashuan as a threat. After all, he was a famous athlete. As far as the rookie was concerned, the brawl in the hotel lobby had been nothing more than a little scuffle over a woman.

He hadn't even bothered to process him. Just locked him and his bodyguards in a cell for a few hours—to cool off, he'd said—then the next morning, they were released without any charges being filed against them.

The embarrassment of being detained increased Dashuan's animosity toward the stranger. That, added to the ever growing anxiety that Amber was going to tell someone what she saw, had him wired like a bomb those first forty-eight hours.

But after two days of hearing nothing from the press, Dashuan started to think maybe Amber had decided to take her time and sell her story to the highest bidder. That was good. That would give him time to shut her up once and for all.

He accepted that she had almost certainly told her new lover. And he did not doubt for a minute that Paul Gutierrez was her new lover. Amber was as hot as they came.

He still wasn't sure what he would do about the man, but after an eye-opening conversation with his new bodyguard, direct confrontation was no longer an option.

From what Barney Roberts told him, Amber Lockhart could not have found a better protector. *Paul Gutierrez is a former Navy SEAL with the heart of a Boy Scout.* Those were the exact words Barney had used to sum up his former employer, which meant he couldn't be beaten or bribed.

Dashuan tapped the steering wheel with his index finger as he considered the plan he'd settled on. It was dangerous, no doubt about it. But it had been over two weeks, and he had no idea who Amber might have talked to in that time. Every day he picked up the local tabloids, terrified of seeing his face on the cover.

He knew what people would think if she told them what she'd seen. It wasn't like he was gay, or anything, but that's what everyone would think. He and Kelvin only hooked up occasionally, usually when they'd been drinking.

His hands tightened on the steering wheel, as he kicked himself for the thousandth time about bringing the little bitch with him to L.A. He'd done it to piss off D'marcus Armstrong, the Chargers team owner and his personal adversary. He was also Amber's future brother-in-law.

At the time, Amber's wild nature and fascination with his celebrity status had seemed like the perfect weapon of embarrassment against uptight D'marcus. Instead, Amber's poor timing had caused the plan to go awry and he was now the one in peril.

His eyes ran over the house, examining it in detail and committing it to memory. Yes, it was a dangerous plan, but if it worked he could get rid of both Amber Lockhart and Paul Gutierrez in one cunning move.

The following morning, Amber stood in the kitchen doorway confused by the scene that greeted her. *Who is this woman in my kitchen?*

"Hello?" she said, to the older Hispanic woman breaking eggs over a skillet.

The woman looked up and smiled. "Hello, you must be Amber. I'm Rosalie." She placed a hand on her chest. "I take care of Joachim. It's nice to meet you."

No, I take care of Joachim, she almost said, but held her tongue. There was time enough for that later. For now she needed to know more.

She entered the kitchen and forced a smile. "Nice to meet you." She looked around the room. "Where's Paul?"

"Still upstairs. I always make his breakfast when I first arrive, so he has a hot meal in the mornings before going off to work." She turned and flipped the fried eggs onto a plate with professional skill.

Amber thought about the many mornings she'd watched Paul fix a bowl of cereal for breakfast. She'd just assumed he liked cereal. Why hadn't he said he liked eggs in the morning? She could've made them.

"Would you like some?" Rosalie asked, still holding the skillet in her hand.

Amber shook her head and turned away. "Where's Joachim? He's usually up by seven."

Rosalie smiled. "That's my fault. I've missed him so much, that I woke him when I first arrived to catch up on all my hugs and kisses." She laughed, and it was such a genuine, full-bodied laugh, Amber couldn't help but like it. "I'm afraid I wore the little soul out. As soon as I put him down he fell right back off to sleep."

Rosalie placed the skillet in the sink and started wiping down the counter.

"Good morning," Paul called, entering the kitchen just then. He was dressed today in a powder-blue silk shirt and tie that looked wonderful against his olive skin, and dark navy wool slacks. His casual loafers had been replaced by a pair of Allen-Edmonds, and Amber realized it was only the second time she'd seen him dressed this way. The night he'd rescued her was the first.

He crossed the room and gave Amber a quick peck on the cheek as he had every morning for the past five mornings. Then he headed toward Rosalie and hugged the older woman. "It's good to have you back, Rosalie. We've missed you."

Amber watched the interaction, trying to suppress the envy she felt building in her heart.

She watched as Paul took the plate from the counter as if knowing it was for him, and sat down at the table. "Hmm, I've missed your fried eggs." He winked at Rosalie and began to eat.

Amber did not realize she was glaring at him until he asked, "Why are you glaring at me?"

She shook the expression off her face and made a hand gesture. "Sorry, my mind was a million miles away."

Paul didn't look convinced, but he continued to eat anyway. "I assume you ladies have been introduced."

Rosalie chuckled. "If we waited for you to do it, we'd be standing around all day, just two strangers looking at each other."

Amber wanted to mention that even after being introduced she still didn't know the woman. She realized the remark was coming from spite and she held her tongue.

"Good," Paul continued. "Amber, can I talk to you for a minute?"

Amber crossed the room and took a chair across from him.

Rosalie started to leave the room. "I'm going to put a load in the washer. Be right back."

"I did the laundry yesterday," Amber said smugly.

Rosalie smiled. "Okay then, I guess I'll go check on Joachim." She paused. "Unless, you would like to do that, Amber?"

Amber felt like crawling under the table, realizing how ridiculous she was behaving. "No, that's okay," she said, trying to recover a little of her former dignity.

Rosalie nodded, and left the room.

When Amber turned back to Paul, he was giving her a strange look. There was something in his expression she could not quite identify.

"Look, I'm sorry I didn't tell you about Rosalie coming back today. I only talked to her late last night. Her husband recently had surgery and she's been taking care of him, but now that he's feeling better she was going stir-crazy and wanted to get back to work."

Amber shrugged. "It's your house, Paul. You don't owe me any explanation."

"What's with you this morning?" he asked, reaching over and lifting her chin until he was looking into her eyes. "You feel okay?"

"How am I supposed to feel? I wake up and find some strange woman roaming through the house."

"She's not some strange woman. She's Joachim's caregiver."

"Then what am I?" Amber blurted out the words before she could stop them.

Paul's eyes narrowed on her face. Amber swallowed hard, realizing her big mouth had backed her into a corner.

He ran his thumb over her cheek. "The job is yours whenever you want it, angel. Just say the word."

She turned her head to the side, and Paul's hand fell away. He returned his attention to his breakfast. "I have to go in to the office today, but I should be home no later than five. Rosalie typically leaves about six."

Amber knew how crazy it was to be jealous of Rosalie, but she couldn't seem to get rid of the feeling of resentment. "Fine, I'll see you this evening."

"What's for dinner?" Paul asked, when she turned to walk away.

Amber turned and glowered at him. "Why don't you ask Rosalie?"

With that, she turned and stomped out of the kitchen, never looking back, and never seeing the wide grin on Paul's face.

Chapter 19

It only took two hours for Paul to start missing Amber's constant presence. He knew it would happen, but thought he could at least make it through the first half of the day. She had become a part of him, and he knew she was missing him, too, although, of course, being Amber she would never admit it.

The emptiness was understandable considering they'd practically been joined at the hip for the past two weeks. But still, if it weren't for his monthly staff meeting scheduled for that afternoon…

He stood looking out the window of his executive corner office. It was a prime piece of Los Angeles realty, and less than a year ago he could never have afforded it. But everything had changed last March, when the Kodak Theatre needed additional security personnel for the upcoming Academy Awards at the last moment. An industry friend had recommended Paul's agency, and Paul, recognizing the hand of fate when he saw it, pulled together the necessary manpower in a matter of days. He managed to get his new team bonded and trained within a week, and G-Force made an excellent showing at the ceremony.

The following Monday morning, the phone lines in his small one-room Westwood office began ringing off the hook. At the time, he and Vanessa were the only office staff he had, but they'd managed.

It was this same boom in business that kept him away from home almost day and night for the following months. And the reason Michelle was able to slip away with Joachim long before he found them in the hotel room.

It had only been a few months since all that happened, but it felt like a lifetime ago. Now, G-Force's administrative staff of twenty-three, and field staff of one hundred and fifty-one men and women, provided personal protection to the L.A. elite, did security consulting for Fortune 500 companies and were soon adding a new retail line of security products.

With his newfound success, Paul moved his staff into the elegant suites they now occupied, and bought a new home far away from the hustle and bustle of Hollywood.

G-Force was growing at a phenomenal rate, and Paul was determined to make sure that growth didn't stop anytime soon.

All he needed to complete his new life was a woman to share it with. He smiled to himself, thinking of the angel waiting at home for him. She was as good as gotten.

Just then, his assistant knocked on the door.

"Come in," he called over his shoulder, and turned as the door was opened.

Before Vanessa could introduce the visitor, Keith Montfield circled around her and came into the room. "Well, look who decided to return to the world of the living."

Vanessa just shook her head and closed the door.

Paul started toward his friend with a smile and an outstretched hand. "Hey, Keith, how are you?"

Keith accepted the handshake before flopping down in his favorite chair. "Good. Although, I was starting to worry about you."

"What do you mean?"

"I know you have a home office, but you rarely work completely from home. Were you sick?"

Paul's mouth twisted. "No."

Keith's sharp eyes narrowed on his face. "Glad to hear it. Family okay?"

Paul chuckled and propped himself against the desk. "For a detective you stink at interrogation. Just ask me what you want to know."

"Who's the girl?"

Paul stood and circled the desk trying to decide how to answer. Amber had left the hotel lobby before Keith and his officers arrived, so how did he know about her?

As if reading his mind, a slow smile came across Keith's face. "Oh, I see, you didn't realize I knew about her."

Without revealing anything in his expression, Paul sat down behind the desk. "She's a friend of a friend."

Keith shrugged. "Must be some friend to cause such a fuss. That Kennedy guy couldn't shut up about her."

Paul relaxed. "Did you let him go?"

He nodded. "As the sun was rising, just as you asked. Although I still don't understand why you didn't want us to charge the guy."

"If he'd been arrested, the press would've been all over

it. And then there would've been questions about what caused it—"

"And then they would've wanted to know who was the mystery woman." Keith nodded in understanding.

"Exactly."

"Well, we let him go, although he was none too happy."

Paul rested his elbows on the desk and leaned forward. "What about that other thing?" When his friend dropped his head, he had his answer.

"Sorry, Paul, you were right. When I questioned my men, I found out one of our rookies has a big mouth. The kid was impressed having a big-time celebrity athlete in the back of his patrol car, and he blabbered all the way back to the station." He shook his head. "Freaking idiot. Anyway, you can be sure he won't be making that mistake again."

Paul searched his brain, trying to remember when he first spotted the black Mustang in his neighborhood.

Keith frowned. "You've seen him, haven't you?"

"I hate it when you do that."

"You shouldn't be so easy to read. But if this guy is giving you a hard time, just let me know."

"No, I've just seen a strange car in the neighborhood, but it could be anyone."

"I'd trust my life to your instincts." He stood. "If you think it's him, it's him. So what do you want to do about it?"

Paul shook his head. "Nothing I can do until he makes his move."

"Well, I know you can take care of yourself, old friend, but if you need anything just let me know."

Paul smiled, looking at Keith's stoic expression. When he made that fierce expression, Paul could easily see vestiges of the scrawny kid he'd rescued from the neighborhood bullies all those years ago.

He'd found the boy, bloodied and cornered by a group of neighborhood kids, his thin, little fist balled and preparing to defend himself to the bitter end.

Paul knew the bigger boys wouldn't have hurt the little guy too bad. They just wanted him to prove himself, to prove he could hold his own. But one runt against a dozen just wasn't a fair fight and so he'd intervened…and won a friend for life.

"Want to get some lunch?" Keith asked.

Paul glanced at his watch. "No, we're having our monthly staff meeting later, and I've arranged to have food brought in."

"Okay, well, about the Kennedy thing, just give me a ring if you need anything."

After saying farewell to his friend, Paul returned to his place of contemplation by the window. It was funny how fate had always intervened on his behalf.

By rescuing a skinny little boy all those years ago, he now had a close ally in the LAPD. And for a security specialist that was definitely a good connection. If someone had not recommended him to the head of security at the Kodak Theatre, G-Force would've never had the boom in business that followed. And if Luther had not called him that night asking him to find Amber, he would've never met her. Rosalie had always said he was favored by God. At times like this, he was inclined to believe her.

All morning Rosalie had been torn between amusement and exasperation with Paul's houseguest, but by noon the scale had tipped toward exasperation.

Paul had not told her much about the girl when she'd shown up that morning, only that she was a friend who would be staying with him indefinitely.

Rosalie had thought no more of it, especially when she realized the girl was sleeping in one of the guestrooms, not in the master bedroom with Paul. But now, she realized that sleeping arrangement was more than a little deceptive.

Over the course of the morning, the beautiful young woman had proved to be as territorial as a lioness, and she was guarding her den with an unsettling fierceness. Right then she was sitting in the chair, feeding Joachim his bottle.

It had been like this all day. Amber had not left his side.

Realizing Joachim would not be needing her anytime soon, she decided to pick up around the house a little, but whenever she touched anything, the girl would appear and explain why it could not be moved.

Rosalie had been a wife a long time, and a woman even longer, and she knew what was going on. She was being sent a message, and it wasn't easy to mistake the meaning. She was being told in no uncertain terms that she was not welcome.

After finishing the few breakfast dishes, Rosalie opened the freezer looking for something to prepare for dinner. She always cooked for Paul and left the dinner in the oven before leaving for the evening.

"What are you doing?" she heard the young woman ask.

"I was taking out something for dinner."

"That's okay. I'm planning to fix a roast for dinner. Paul loves my roast."

Rosalie was back to amused. Did this twenty-some-thing beauty see her—a sixty-year-old married woman—as competition for Paul's affection?

In good grace, Rosalie shut the freezer. She turned toward the other woman and felt herself soften a little. There was so much love in her eyes when she looked at that baby. Whatever was going on between her and Paul may not have been resolved yet, but there was no doubt about her feelings for Joachim.

Maybe she could clear things up with a simple statement. "You know," Rosalie said, trying to sound casual, "me and my Enrique have been married for thirty-seven years now."

Amber glanced up at the older woman with a confused expression on her face. "Congratulations." She turned her attention back to the baby.

Rosalie's eyes took on a faraway expression. "He was such a handsome young man, so strong and strapping. Our families worked together in the orange orchards." She sighed dreamily. "Oh, how I enjoyed watching him work. When he would reach up—" she imitated the gesture "—the muscles in his arms would flex and ripple like waves on water."

The girl smiled. "You really love him, don't you?"

Rosalie smiled in return. "Yes, I do."

Amber looked away and her long lashes concealed her eyes. "You're lucky to find the kind of love that lasts a lifetime."

Rosalie shook her head, and frowned. "No, no, not luck. Destiny."

Amber arched an eyebrow. "Destiny?"

"You don't believe in destiny?"

"I guess a little, but not in picking a husband. That decision is too important to leave to destiny."

Rosalie's eyes widened, wondering if maybe she'd misjudged the situation. "You and Paul…"

Amber's eyes widened. "Oh, no! I mean—not that there's anything wrong with Paul…absolutely nothing." She sighed. "He's so not wrong, he's right, know what I mean?"

The look on Rosalie's face said she did not.

"Never mind. Suffice it to say there is no me and Paul." Joachim finished the last of his bottle, so Amber positioned him over her shoulder for burping. She stood and walked over to Rosalie, patting the baby on the back. "Have you ever met a man so perfect in every way, you ask yourself, 'okay, what's wrong with him?' I mean, a guy this perfect should've been snatched up a long time ago, right?"

Rosalie nodded in understanding. "Did it ever occur to you that maybe that guy is asking himself the same questions about you?"

Amber smiled, and it turned into a laugh. "Good point. No, I hadn't thought about it from his point of view."

"When a squirrel is running across an open field, and in his path he discovers a perfect, untouched acorn, do you think the squirrel stops and examines the acorn for flaws or looks around wondering why no one else had taken the acorn? Do you think he drops the acorn back on the ground and leaves it, just in case something is wrong with it?"

Amber quirked an eyebrow at the strange analogy, but said nothing.

"No, he snatches up the acorn as fast as he can, and scurries it away to his home before another squirrel tries to steal it from him. When God blesses you, you don't question the origins of that blessing. You should just thank God, and enjoy the blessing."

"But how do you know a real blessing from a trap of lust?"

Rosalie tilted her head to the side, studying the girl. "You know, I would have to wonder about anyone that nervous about receiving a blessing. Maybe the problem is not the blessing, but that person's sense of worthiness."

Amber's eyes shot back up to meet hers, and Rosalie was amazed at the doubt and fear she saw reflected there.

Seeing that Joachim was falling asleep, she smiled and reached for him, glad for the distraction. "Here, I'll put the little one to bed."

Amber's hands closed around the baby. "No, that's okay, I got him." She turned and walked out of the kitchen.

Rosalie sighed. One step forward and two steps back. With a shake of her head, she continued to clean the kitchen.

Later that afternoon, while Joachim was napping, Amber returned to the guestroom to finish drawing her plans, but after fifteen minutes she realized she was not going to get anything done.

Rosalie had already beat her to the ironing, so there was nothing to do until Joachim rose from his nap. She wandered from room to room, trying to come to grips with the strange longing she'd been feeling all morning. It was almost a sadness, and for the life of her, she could not understand what it was about.

She wandered into Paul's empty office, and as soon as she crossed the threshold and smelled his familiar scent in the air, she had a name for the yearning she'd been experiencing all day. It was not a pleasant realization.

She sat in one of the guest chairs, trying to understand how could she miss someone so much when he'd only been gone a few hours. And it wasn't as if he wasn't coming back. She glanced at the clock. He would be back in three hours—not that she'd been watching the time, or anything.

Laying her head back against the chair, she decided to

stay there for a while. Right or wrong, good or bad, there was no denying the sense of comfort she gained from being among his things. She would deal with the implications of the emotion later.

When Rosalie passed by the door a few minutes later, she saw the girl sleeping in the wing-back chair, and she was more certain than ever of what she'd suspected.

The young lady may not think she knows what she wants, but her heart has already decided. *Poor thing*, she thought, *it's such hard work guarding a den*.

With a chuckle, she continued carrying the basket of freshly ironed clothes upstairs to Paul's bedroom.

Chapter 20

Rosalie was the first to notice Paul when he appeared in the entrance to the kitchen. Hearing the noise, Amber looked up from basting her roast when he came in.

Their eyes locked across the room, and the sudden increase in tension in the room seemed almost palpable. Rosalie had the feeling of standing on a track between two oncoming trains. All she wanted to do was get out of the way before she got ran over.

But there was no collision.

"Hi," Paul said with a smile. His dark eyes roamed over Amber like fingers.

"Hi," Amber said with an answering shy smile.

And that was the end of the lovers' greeting.

Mío Dios! Rosalie picked Joachim up out of his playpen. For the first time all day, Amber did not make a move to stop her. How could they be honest with each other when they couldn't even be honest with themselves? she thought with a shake of her head. She carried the baby out of the room, not even offering up an explanation for leaving.

Paul crossed the room until he was standing beside Amber, and she felt as if the air had disappeared from her lungs as she waited to see what he would do.

"I missed you," he said, rubbing the back of his hand along her cheekbone. He smiled when he felt Amber tremble beneath his touch.

He waited, hoping for some sign that she'd missed him, but none was forthcoming. *What did I expect? That eight hours apart would make her realize that we belong together?*

"Hmm, is that a roast I smell?" Paul turned his attention toward the pan sitting on the lowered oven door.

"Yes." His interest in the roast seemed to break the spell. "It's almost ready if you want to go get washed up."

He turned to walk away, and then turned back. Eight hours may not have seemed like much to her, but for him it had been a lifetime.

Grabbing Amber around the waist, he pulled her close to his body. "Oh, I missed you." His husky words spoken so close to her lips felt like a slight breeze, and then he was kissing her, pressing his lips against hers, applying pressure until she opened her mouth beneath his and his tongue plunged in, seeking her warmth. And in that moment he knew the truth. Despite her calm facade and show of indifference, the same storm was raging inside her. Paul slowed the assault, savoring the taste of her while his hands made small, circular tracings on her back.

It wasn't until he lifted his head that he realized Amber's arms were around his neck clutching the back of his collar. Even after he pulled back, her arms remained locked around him. Looking deep into her golden eyes, Paul grinned in satisfaction. She felt the same way he did, even if she would not say the words.

Feeling more inspired and validated than he had in a long time, he reached behind his neck, unlocking her arms, before placing one last soft kiss on her lips and heading for the downstairs bathroom.

After he was out of sight, Amber returned to preparing dinner and tried to block out the silent message Paul had delivered with his lips. It was much easier to pretend she did not understand what she read in his eyes. She didn't want to think about the wonderful sensations she was experiencing at that moment. Nor did she want to concentrate on the happiness she felt in just knowing he was in the house with her again. She would not think about his warm and tender lips, and how good they always felt.

No, she would not think about any of those things. Because in her heart, in some small corner in the back of her heart, she still did not believe it was real. Men didn't look at Amber Lockhart and see a wife and the mother of their child.

They saw a quick hit, a temporary thrill. One former lover had gone so far as to tell her that he could never have a serious relationship with her because she was too beautiful. He could never trust his friends around her. Amber had always thought that was the most ridiculous excuse for avoiding a relationship that she'd ever heard.

But now she'd topped that with her own lame excuse that Paul was too perfect. How ridiculous, as if that overbearing, uptight man could ever be perfect. She smiled to herself, humming a soft song while she finished preparing dinner. She'd just buttered the baked potatoes when it occurred to her that she was humming the melody to the Spanish lullaby Paul had sung to her the other night. One day, she was going to have to ask him to tell her the words.

Rosalie and Joachim were coming back down the stairs at the same time Paul was coming out of the bathroom. He stopped her at the bottom step.

"Did everything go okay today?" he asked, taking his son from her arms and giving him a soft kiss on the cheek.

Before he'd left that morning, Paul had given Rosalie a warning to keep watch for anything out of the ordinary.

Rosalie had not so much as blinked an eye when the instructions had been given. Because he was in the security business, she probably assumed it had something to do with his work.

"Everything was fine," she said, and hesitated before adding. "Nothing I would not have expected."

Paul frowned. "What do you mean?"

Rosalie just shook her head. "You led me to believe your relationship with the young lady was, um…platonic."

Paul's eyes sharpened on her face. "Did she say something to make you think otherwise?"

"Say?" Rosalie chuckled. "No, there was no need to *say* anything. Her actions spoke for themselves."

Paul was struggling to hold on to his patience with this woman who'd become a dear friend. But if Amber had given some indication of her feelings for him, he wanted to hear it. "Rosalie, what happened today?"

Rosalie gave a soft smile. "Nothing to be concerned about."

"I wish you would not speak in code."

She moved around him. "I have to get going. Enrique will be looking for me."

"How is he?" Paul asked, balancing his son on his hip.

"Much better." Her mouth twisted in a smirk. "Well enough to flirt with his nurses."

Paul smiled and, using his one free arm, helped her into her coat. "I'll see you tomorrow."

She tilted her head to the side as she considered something. "No. I do not think that is a good idea."

"Why not?" Paul was more confused than ever. She was the one who'd asked to come back earlier than expected.

As if reading his thoughts, she answered, "I ask to come back because I thought you were here alone with Joachim. But now I see you are in good hands. I think I will just wait until Enrique is fully recovered—if that is okay with you?"

Paul studied her face. There was something she knew but refused to tell him. "Of course, that's fine. I told you in the beginning to take as much time as you need."

"I know." She reached up and touched his face. "But I think you need this time more."

Paul groaned in frustration. "Rosalie, what's going on? I feel like I'm having a conversation with the Mad Hatter."

Her eyes widened in indignation. "Are you calling me crazy?"

Paul laughed, and hugged her. "Not crazy, just wise beyond my understanding."

Feeling appeased, Rosalie collected her things and turned to leave. "Tell Amber goodbye for me." She glanced at the baby, who was watching her with a half smile.

She leaned over and kissed the tip of his tiny nose. "I'm leaving these two in your hands, little one," she whispered.

Paul watched her until her sedan pulled out of the

driveway. He walked into the kitchen, more certain than ever that Amber had revealed something to Rosalie. But what? Could it have anything to do with that wonderful display of jealousy he'd seen that morning?

Whatever it was, Rosalie obviously felt it was something Amber would have to reveal on her own. But after almost two weeks of living together with no results, he wasn't expecting any sudden confessions or surprises.

But a surprise was what he received. Whether it was a conscious decision or not, Amber seemed to have renewed her determination to seduce him. Paul realized he'd only grown weaker and more susceptible to her advances with every passing day.

Paul had taken Joachim to the nursery to change a dirty diaper, and by the time he returned to the kitchen Amber had turned the tables on him. Literally.

The dining table was once again set for lovers, everything from the emerald-green tablecloth to the lit candles. This time, the dinner was not catered, but made by her own hands.

When he entered the kitchen, she turned her brilliant smile on him, and Paul knew the battle was already half-lost. What man could resist an angel bent on seduction?

"This is nice," he said, taking a seat at the table.

"I remembered how much you enjoyed my roast last week."

He watched as she mashed sliced carrots with the back of her fork, and Joachim watched with equal fascination from his high chair, as if sensing it was for him.

Paul glanced at her face, before cutting into the roast. "How did everything go today?" The way she avoided his eyes revealed more than she knew.

"Fine. Why? Did Rosalie say something?"

There was such nervous tension in her voice. *What the hell happened here today?* Paul wondered for the tenth time. He decided to test the water a little more. "She just said no more than she should've expected. What do you think she meant by that?"

Amber shrugged, and lifted a spoonful of mashed carrots to Joachim's lips. "I have no idea."

"Hmm," Paul muttered around a fork full of roast. He was looking at his plate when he felt a soft finger graze over his bottom lip. When he looked up, Amber was leaning toward him, so close he could feel her soft breath on him.

"You have a little gravy right there," she whispered, and again that finger stroked his bottom lip.

Without thought, Paul's tongue came out and ran over her finger, and then her lips were being pressed to his. Paul was never sure who moved first. All he would later remember was the feel of her soft bottom across his lap.

He could not have stopped his exploring hands if he'd tried. They ran over the outline of her slender form. Along the rounded curve of her thigh, over her abdomen and up to her full breast. It had been so long since he'd touched her, so long since he'd felt the awakening of desire in response to his own passion.

Paul felt his head being tugged back as her fingers wound their way through his curls. Tightening her hold, she pulled his head back to reveal his strong neck. A chill went through his whole body when he felt her warm tongue tracing his vein there. She lapped at a pulsing artery like a vampire preparing to strike. Paul knew that if she were a bloodsucker, he would've been a willing victim.

Cupping a full breast in one hand, he manipulated the flesh, running his thumb over the small nub, feeling the bumpy texture of the surrounding crest. Holding her slight weight in his hand, he imagined the taste of her, the feel of her silky skin beneath his tongue.

Her arms locked around his neck, and she pulled him closer. She undid three buttons, just enough to get her hand inside his shirt, to feel his warm flesh against hers.

Paul was considering carrying her upstairs to his bedroom when the primary reason he could not sounded an alarm. Joachim made a playful noise as he banged his rubber toy against the tray of his high chair.

The loud noise startled them both. Amber sat bolt upright, and would've stood if Paul's arm didn't tighten around her waist at that moment.

They both looked toward the baby, who returned their stare with a wide grin.

Amber gave Paul a guilty look that turned into a shy smile. "You can let me up now."

But instead of smiling in return, Paul stared soberly into her eyes. "You enjoy doing this, don't you?"

"What?" she asked, trying to ignore the wonderful feeling of his full erection pressing against the crease in her jeans. How easy it would be to just shift a little to the left and let him sink into the groove of her body.

"This." He did it for her, moving her until she was sitting right on top of the throbbing organ. Even through their clothing, there was no denying his state. "You like this teasing and taunting me."

Her eyes widened as she realized what she was being accused of. "I'm not a tease."

"No? Then what do you call this?" He gestured to the fact that she was sitting on his lap.

"Hey! Now wait a minute! You put me here!"

His arms released her, and he shifted his weight in a way that almost tossed her to the floor. "Well, now I'm putting you off. Go!"

Amber stood, furious. "Why do you get so angry with me? You're the one who keeps stopping this. I've offered myself to you in more ways than I can remember, and you're the one who keeps rejecting me. Rejecting *us!*"

Paul stood and his face was inches from her. "*I'm* rejecting *us?*" His eyes narrowed as he shook his head. "No, angel, I'm fighting *for* us."

His hungry gaze took in her still aroused form, lingering over the outline of her nipples pressed against the tight T-shirt. He cupped her face between his hands. "Why do you insist on selling yourself so cheaply? Why won't you allow me to give you all that you're worth?" He gestured to the room around them. "Why can't you understand that you're right where you belong? Here with us!"

Amber had to blink back the tears she felt forming in her eyes. "No! I don't belong here! I could never belong here!" With that, she turned and rushed out of the room.

Paul started to go after her, until Joachim began to wail his little heart out as if in sympathy for Amber. Paul decided it was easier to console his son than the woman he loved. He picked him up and bounced him, making cooing noises until he settled down again.

There in the kitchen, Paul acknowledged what he had always known on some level. Amber's deep insecurities were the wall standing between them. And after a lifetime of reinforcement, he had no idea how to even begin to tear it down.

Chapter 21

Amber was unsure when she'd fallen asleep, but she still had a wad of tissue balled in her fist when she was awakened later that night by the sound of her bedroom door opening.

Her heart sped up. She lay still, hoping against hope that he was there for the reason she suspected, but until she could be certain, she lay as frozen as a statue.

Just as quietly as it opened, the door closed again. There was a light scratching noise on the carpet, so light, she had to strain to hear where he was. Amber realized if she had not heard him enter she would never know someone was in the room. How could a man move with such stealth?

Then, he was there, standing by the bed. She could feel his presence as if he'd reached out and touched her. Her eyes darted left and right, and she held her breath waiting to see what he would do next.

There was another light shuffling noise, and then the undeniable sound of a zipper. It took everything in her not to
leap up into his arms. But there was something delicious
in the anticipation of not knowing when he would reach
for her. She'd waited so long for this, she had no intention
of hurrying him.

Amber bit her lip, recognizing the sound of a condom
wrapper being torn. Even in sex, he was protective. She
pulled the covers closer around her as she felt a chill so
intense it raised goose bumps on her body.

The movement revealed that she was awake, because all
the subtle noises stopped. Then the cover was being lifted,
and a slight breeze rushed up her back.

The bed sunk beneath his weight, and he scooted close
behind her. For the first time she felt the whole of his lean,
naked body against hers. Amber couldn't stop the slight
moan that escaped her lips at the incredible feeling.

He chuckled. "That's a good sign." The warm, familiar
voice came out of the darkness, and she felt teeth nipping
at her collarbone.

She couldn't take any more. Amber flipped over until
she was facing him, although all she could see in the dark
room was the outline of his chiseled jaw. She reached up
and pulled his head to hers, needing to taste his lips.
Somehow she knew a kiss would reveal his intentions
better than words ever could.

Her heart almost broke at his warm caress of her lips.
He hadn't changed his mind even a little, and the realization was both comforting and terrifying.

Calling herself an idiot the whole while, she still did
what must be done. "Paul, you know I haven't changed my
mind—"

"Shh, shhh." He covered her mouth with his, plunging his tongue into her warmth and lifting her body against his beneath the cover.

At that moment, Amber knew she would've agreed to anything he wanted if he would only continue down that road. But false promises proved to be unnecessary.

He lifted enough to look into her eyes. "It's okay. I'll take what you're offering for now, and we'll worry about the rest later."

Amber wanted to believe, but she knew enough about Paul to understand what such a concession would cost him. "Are you sure?"

He bent his head and placed a soft kiss on her shoulder. "If this is the only way I can have you, then so be it." His somber expression turned to a playful grin. "Now, let's get rid of these ugly pajamas." He unbuttoned the pajama top and pulled it off her shoulders, revealing her breasts.

Paul took one of the soft mounds into his mouth. She was even sweeter than he remembered. Unable to bear the thought of letting her go, he reached between their bodies and began to push the pajama bottoms down her legs. The elastic waistband made quick work of it.

In a matter of seconds, they lay together naked. Shifting his weight, Paul ran his hand along her inner thigh, seeking to touch that which had tormented his nights from the moment he laid eyes on this woman. Feeling the telltale moisture on his fingers, he knew she was ready. More than ready.

His mouth continued its ravenousness assault, even as he positioned himself over her. "Sorry, angel, next time, I'll go slower, I promise." With that oath, he plunged into her welcoming body.

Amber had no complaints, even when all she could do

was hold on to his muscular arms while he took her on the wildest, most passionate ride of her young life. When he wrapped his large hands around her bottom, squeezing her against him with uncompromising strength, Amber wrapped her legs around his waist.

Watching the changing emotions on his face as he hovered above her was an education in eroticism. The man was beautiful, even with the veins straining in his neck as he fought back the rising tide. But it was no use. In short time, he exploded inside her. The arching of his back, combined with the animalistic sound of satisfaction that came from his throat, was enough to send Amber over the edge. Her climax came on the end of his, but even in his exhausted state Paul held her trembling body against his until she fell limp in his arms.

When the climax subsided, Amber laughed to realize Paul was still holding her up off the bed. He'd held her suspended like that the whole time. She laughed out loud, feeling a unique joy from the top of her head to the bottom of her feet. It was such a supreme feeling of intense happiness, and so unlike anything she'd ever known.

Paul let her body down and rolled over onto his back. "I hope that's not in response to my performance."

She laughed again and rolled over onto his chest. "Not at all." Her tongue darted out to tease his nipple. "Your performance was stellar."

He twisted his mouth. "Stellar, huh? I guess that's pretty good. So, why were you laughing?"

"It's just I've never made love in the air."

"In the air?" he asked in confusion, before remembering. "Oh, that. You felt so good, I was afraid you might disappear if I didn't hold on to you."

Propping her chin on his chest, she gave him a sleepy, lopsided grin. "I'm not going anywhere."

Paul's expression sobered, as he reached out and rubbed her cheek. "I wish I could believe that."

Amber's own grin disappeared. She scooted back, preparing to sit up, but he caught her around the waist and pulled her back down on top of him.

"Sorry, I keep forgetting I'm not supposed to be in love with you."

She pulled away enough to turn on her side. "I wish you wouldn't say things like that."

"I'm an honest man. What can I say?"

Amber felt him tugging at the hair scarf she wore to sleep in. "What are you doing?"

"Looking for your hair," he said, in complete seriousness. The tugging stopped. "It is *your* hair?"

Amber flipped over and punched him lightly on the arm. "Of course, it's my hair!"

Paul laughed. "Just checking."

With another punch, she turned over and snuggled down in his arms. She didn't complain when she felt the scarf come off and her hair tumble down. Paul slid his fingers through the mass, and when he began massaging her scalp she felt like purring.

"Oh, angel," he sighed, "you've got me all twisted in knots."

Amber lay in the dark room. She could've told him he did the same to her, but she knew where that would lead. Somewhere she was not prepared to go.

The following morning, Paul found himself frustrated with Amber's amorous play. He was trying to teach her how to set the alarm system before he left for work, but it was hard to concentrate with her tongue in his ear, or her hand wrapped around his…

"Stop it!" He yanked her hand away. "Amber, this is serious. Now, you have to listen to me."

Feeling her own brand of frustration, she pouted. "Why? It's broad daylight in the middle of suburban land, and every other house has a housewife in it. Who's going to try to break in here?"

A basketball player with a secret to hide, he thought. But of course, he could not tell her that without explaining his suspicions, and the last thing he wanted to do was terrify her.

And she did have a point. Kennedy would be a fool to attack in broad daylight in such a busy neighborhood. But since he knew so little about the man, he didn't want to take any chances.

"Just pay attention," he said, clearing the keypad to begin again. "Now, what you have to remember—" *Oh, God.* She'd managed to work her hands down into his slacks, and this time, he had no desire to break her hold. He leaned against her, savoring the feel of her deft fingers awakening his flesh. "Where's Joachim?" he whispered.

"Sleeping in his playpen," she said, with the confidence of a winner.

Without another thought, Paul switched their position, sliding his hands into her pajamas to find her ready for him. He looked around for a handy chair, and even considered the wall before remembering that he did not have any condoms on him.

Lifting her in his arms, he carried her up the stairs and into his bedroom, where a rapidly diminishing box of condoms sat on the nightstand.

When Paul left for work almost two hours later, Amber stood in the doorway and waved goodbye. Then she locked the door and went about her day, never giving another thought to the security code Paul had made her promise to memorize.

Chapter 22

The attack came around noon. Amber was right in the middle of feeding Joachim.

On their last shopping expedition, Amber had convinced Paul to buy some baby food for Joachim. So far, the infant had refused almost all of the strained food. Amber was beginning to question the wisdom of beginning with table food.

Hearing the doorbell ring, she wiped his mouth. "I'll be right back, and when I do, you're eating those string beans whether you like it or not." She tried to sound stern, but the rude gurgling noise he made, followed by a playful giggle, told her she'd not had the effect she wanted.

The doorbell rang again. "Coming!" She was in such a rush, she swung the door open without looking through the glass, and found herself confronted with four pairs of curious eyes.

"Hi, remember me?" the ringleader said.

Four women stood on the front porch, but Amber only recognized one. The woman she and Paul had run into at the street fair.

"Brenda Michelson," the bright-eyed woman said. "Amber, right?"

Amber was still looking at each woman trying to understand what they were all doing there.

"This is Jennifer Tennyson, Karen Wilson and Carrie Henderson. We're your neighbors!" The woman made the announcement as if Amber had won some sort of lottery.

"Nice to meet you," Amber said, not knowing what else to say.

The four women seemed to come to a stalemate as they waited to be invited in, while the fifth had no intention of extending any such offer.

Brenda decided to take matters into her own hands. "Can we come in?"

"Why?" Amber blurted the question before she could stop herself.

The four looked at each other as if seeking an answer from one another. Brenda stepped up to bat once again. "Just wanted to sit and talk, get to know each other, you know—neighbor to neighbor."

This time when the *why* came to her lips, Amber was able to stop it. "Um, I don't live here, I'm just visiting."

Once again the four women looked at each other, but this time if was as if Amber's statement confirmed something they already believed.

Amber recognized what was going on. She was meeting the gossip patrol. Every community had one, and apparently Paul's had been lying in wait for him to leave her there alone.

After her failure with Joachim and the strained string beans, and now the nosy neighbors, Amber was beginning to wonder if she'd been too hasty in chasing Rosalie away. *Be careful what you wish for.*

As if on cue, Joachim began to make a loud, banging noise. Amber recognized it as him playing with his favorite toy, which happened to be a loud rattler, but to the untrained ear it sounded as if he was having a full-out tantrum.

"Oh, my!" The woman named Carrie tried to look around Amber. "Sounds like someone is pretty cranky."

"Sounds like he's going to regurgitate," Karen added with a slight look of disgust.

The only woman who did not look perturbed was the woman named Jennifer. "Oh, hell, Karen, not every baby noise means they're going to throw up."

"Well, you would know with your *seven* kids," Karen snarled at Jennifer.

Amber's eyes widened, surprised by the number. The woman didn't look a day over thirty.

"And it's *vomit,* not regurgitate. Good Lord! Who uses words like that?" Jennifer rolled her eyes to the sky.

"Someone with six degrees and no job," Carrie said, and the three women laughed. Needless to say, Karen did not laugh.

Instead she said, "Well, excuse me if I prefer to do something productive with my life instead of spending it on my back having babies!"

At that point, the catty remarks turned into a vicious game of name calling. After a while, the argument became embarrassing to Amber.

Meanwhile, in the background Joachim continued his

loud play, and Amber used it as the excuse to escape. "Sorry, ladies, I have to go. It was nice meeting you." With that she slammed the door shut.

The last thing she heard was Brenda calling out to her.

She leaned against the door, shaking her head, stunned by the weirdness of it all. She decided to chalk up the whole strange experience to one more reminder that she was not cut out for the suburban housewife life.

Over dinner that evening, she recounted the whole incident to Paul. Instead of being amused, as she assumed he would be, he was appalled.

"Who the hell do they think they are?"

Seeing his anger, Amber realized she'd made the wrong choice by telling him. "It was no big deal. I thought the whole thing was funny."

"Well, I don't. How dare they come to my house and try to push their way in!" He stabbed at his food. "That's okay, I'll put a stop to that tomorrow."

She reached over and grabbed his arm. "Paul, please don't."

"It's about time someone put a stop to that bunch of busybodies."

"Well, it won't be us, and it won't be now." She made a hand gesture. "Hey, I grew up in the heart of D-town. You think I can't handle a bunch of housewives? Please! And besides, like it or not, Joachim is going to end up going to school with their kids. It's just better to get along with them if we can." She went back to eating, but Paul was frozen in place.

He sat studying her face, wondering if she realized the implications of what she'd just said. *Well, it won't be us...get along with them if we can.*" She sounded like a woman planning a future.

Paul forced himself to return his attention to his dinner before she noticed his staring. The last thing he wanted to do was have her realize her unintentional revelation. He had to fight back the smile he felt forming on his lips.

The next day, Amber came out of the fabric store, pushing the receipts from her purchases down into her purse. She tucked her bags into the back of the stroller, and at the same time, she glanced back over her shoulder and confirmed her suspicions.

The men-in-black wannabes were indeed following her.

She'd noticed them as she was entering the first store on her list. At two o'clock on a Tuesday afternoon in a suburban mall, the two burly men dressed in dark suits and ties stood out like two giant sore thumbs among the throngs of women, strollers and preschool-aged children.

At the time, she'd recognized them as being some sort of security detail. She just had not imagined that they were *her* security detail.

Pushing the stroller with one hand, she dug around in the bottom of her purse until she found her cell phone. She punched in the number she was looking for, and listened to the ringing.

"G-Force Security, the only name you need to know for all your personal protection needs. Vanessa speaking, how may I help you?"

As she asked to speak to Paul, she glanced back over her shoulder. Her escort was following at a discreet distance.

"Paul Gutierrez speaking."

"Do Bert and Ernie belong to you?"

The line went silent for several seconds before he confessed. "Yes."

"Why?"

"Just a precautionary measure."

"Precaution against what?"

"Amber, you're a woman alone in an unfamiliar city."

"I'm in a mall in Orange County. It's not exactly a dark alley in Shanghai."

"Still—"

"What are you not telling me, Paul? First you had that meltdown when you came home last night and found the security system was not activated, and now this." She paused, then asked, "Paul, is someone making threats against you?"

"What do you mean?"

"I know what you do for a living. I'm sure you have your fair share of enemies. If someone was threatening you, I would understand. It would explain this strange behavior."

There was another long silence before he answered. "Yes, someone is threatening me. I didn't want to have to burden you with this. But, if you would just allow me to provide some additional protection for you—at least, until I know this threat is gone."

Amber sighed. "Why didn't you just tell me that to begin with?"

"I didn't want to worry you."

"Well, that was your mistake. You would've found me much more cooperative if you would've just told me the truth."

After a few seconds of silence, Paul said, "Let's have a long talk when I get home, okay?"

"Sure. Is there something more you're not telling me?"

"We'll talk later. Wait, I just remembered I have to work late tonight. Don't wait up for me."

"Okay, I'll leave your dinner in the oven." She lowered her voice. "Feel free to wake me up if you want some dessert."

"Umm, I always want dessert."

Amber sighed, remembering how nicely they'd resolved their differences the night before. *There is nothing like make-up sex.* "Well, I have to go now, Bert and Ernie are starting to draw too much attention."

Paul chuckled. "Actually, they're trained to stay out of sight. You're just too damn smart."

"It's about time you figured that out."

"Please put the alarm on when you get home."

She gave an exaggerated sigh. "Yes, sir."

True to her word, Amber put the alarm on when she got back to the house. She noticed that once the system was activated, and the small blinking red light appeared, Bert and Ernie drove away.

Later that afternoon, the new sofa and love seat arrived. They were even prettier than the pictures in the catalog.

She was so excited with the newest arrivals, that after she saw the deliverymen out of the house, she ran back into the living room to give the furniture a closer inspection… and completely forgot to reset the alarm.

Chapter 23

Amber heard the door to her bedroom opening, and she smiled to herself but didn't turn over to greet him. She'd tried to wait up for Paul, but dozed off and on throughout the night. Glancing at the clock on the nightstand, she could see it was after midnight.

Feeling his presence near the bed, she snuggled under the covers, waiting to feel his warmth against her. "It's about time you got home," she said.

The reprimand was met with silence. An eerie silence. Like an animal sensing danger, Amber tried to sniff the air for Paul's familiar cologne, but the scent, though familiar, was not Paul's.

Something was wrong, something was terribly wrong. She turned over on the bed just in time to see Dashuan Kennedy standing beside the bed, raising a small pistol and aiming it at her head.

Driven by pure instinct, Amber rolled away just as he fired the weapon. She rolled onto the floor and came up on her knees. "Dashuan! What are you doing?"

When he missed his target, he let loose a string of curses and tossed the gun away.

He started across the room toward Amber, and she jumped up on the bed. Straddling the middle, she continued to move opposite Dashuan, even as she calculated the distance to the door. "Why are you doing this?"

"As if you don't know," he snarled and leaped across the bed trying to catch her ankles.

Amber scrambled back up against the headboard.

"Who have you talked to?" He came around the side of the bed, and Amber moved to the far side, trying to remain out of his reach.

"What are you talking about? I haven't talked to anyone!"

"Come here, you lying bitch!" He dived for her again, and Amber jumped off the bed, and took off around the end toward the door.

Dashuan threw a lamp in her direction and Amber ducked. Although, there was no need. His pitch was as bad as his aim. Amber managed to reach the door, but just as she tried to open it, Dashuan was on her. The last thing Amber remembered was being shoved hard against the door.

As soon as Amber's limp body fell to the ground, Dashuan crossed the room and recovered the weapon. Feeling the effects of the struggle, he walked back over to where she was lying, lifted the gun and aimed it at her head.

Somewhere in the distance he could hear the sound of a baby crying. He frowned to himself. He'd forgotten about the baby.

He looked around the room trying to remember everything he'd touched. In the scuffle, his carefully thought out plan had gotten out of hand. He'd been waiting almost two weeks for this opportunity.

He thought he had it three days ago when Gutierrez left the house, until he realized some old lady was in the house with Amber. And then yesterday, just when he started to move in, that group of cackling hens showed up and blew his chance. And today, he'd waited and waited, after she returned from her shopping, after the furniture delivery truck left, and still he waited, and when night fell with no sign of Gutierrez around, Dashuan knew it was now or never.

Getting into the house had been much easier than Barney said it would be. The alarm wasn't even activated. And finding Amber asleep in bed had been perfect. All he had to do was put a bullet in her, and then after wiping his prints off of it, he would use the piece of tape in his pocket to put Gutierrez's fingerprints on it. Barney had told him how to do it. If she had not heard him enter, and reacted so quickly, it would've happened just as it was supposed to.

He held the weapon pointing down at Amber's head. He swallowed hard and tried not to think of her beautiful eyes looking up at him, or her pretty smile when she would laugh at something he'd said. Under different circumstances things might have been good between them. But that was not the way it was going to be.

He took a deep breath. *Don't think about it. Just do it. Don't think about it. Just do it.* He tried to focus his mind on what this woman could do to his life, his career, his reputation, if she had told anyone what she'd seen. Hell, for all he knew, it might already be too late.

He realized his hand was trembling. *Damn. Barney made it sound like it would be so easy.* His palm was sweating, so he rubbed it against his pants leg. *Just do it. Just do it.*

He raised the weapon again and tried to focus it. Amber made a moaning sound and began to roll over. *Do it now! Do it now!*

She turned on her back and looked up at him. Her eyes widened as her memory reminded her of all that had occurred.

"Dashuan, why are you doing this? I never told anyone what I saw. I swear! No one!"

"Shut up! Just shut up!"

He looked around the room trying to think of an alternative solution to pulling the trigger. *The window!*

"Get up!"

Amber scrambled to her feet. "Please, Dashuan, don't do this."

Dashuan grabbed her by the arm and hauled her over to the window. Throwing someone out a window wasn't the same as shooting them, his twisted conscience tried to convince him.

When Amber realized his intent, she dug in her feet, refusing to get any closer to the large window. Being twice her size, Dashuan dragged her across the carpet.

"What the hell is taking so long, man?" An angry male voice came from the hallway.

Amber spun around surprised to realize that Dashuan was not alone. A large burly man appeared in the doorway.

One look in Dashuan's eyes told Barney everything he needed to know. "Just go wait in the car, I'll take care of this."

For an instant, Dashuan almost refused the escape. Then he let go of Amber and crossed the room. As he closed in on Barney, he stopped beside the other man and glanced back at Amber.

"Sorry, but you brought this on yourself." He glanced at Barney. "Just do it quick." And then he was gone.

As soon as Dashuan was through the door, Barney closed it behind him and leaned against it. Only then did Amber notice the gun in his right hand.

His cold, brown eyes stared through her. "Turn around and get on your knees."

"Why are you doing this?" Even in the face of all that was happening, she needed answers.

"Look, I don't want to do this. But you're the only thing standing between me and more money than I've ever seen in my life. Now, don't make this any harder than it has to be. Just turn around and get on your knees."

"No." Amber took a deep breath. "If you're going to kill me, then you look me in the eyes while you do it."

Amber saw the hesitancy flash across his face before he lifted the gun and pointed it at her.

"I don't even know you. Why are you doing this?" Amber refused to go to her grave without knowing the answer.

Barney frowned, and the gun wavered. "Damn, you don't know, do you?"

Fighting the trembling she felt throughout her body, Amber shook her head.

Barney's eyes darted to the side, as he made a decision. "Apparently, you saw something you weren't supposed to. Something Dashuan thinks you will use against him." He glanced over his shoulder, before asking, "What is it? What is this secret that's so important he's willing to kill to keep it?"

Amber glared at the man. "Why would I tell you?"

He shrugged. "Doesn't make a difference one way or the other. I was just curious." He steadied the gun, leveling it at her chest.

He hid it better, but Amber could see that this man was no more a natural killer than Dashuan. Something occurred to her. "Why you?"

"What?"

"Why did Dashuan pick you to help him?"

His eyes narrowed. "You ask too many questions, you know that? Now, shut up and turn around."

Amber knew that turning her back to him would be the biggest mistake she could make. Her mind raced in a thousand different directions as she grasped for a way out. She fought back tears as she considered little Joachim a few doors away.

She could still hear him crying, which meant no one had harmed him—yet. "Just please don't hurt the baby," she blurted out, unable to stop the plea. If there was any chance this man had an ounce of compassion in him, she needed to tap into it.

His eyes widened. "What kind of monster do you think I am?"

If the situation had not been so horrific, Amber thought, it would be laughable. In the dead of night two would-be killers stealing into Paul's home, on the one night he had to work late. Paul…her sisters…would she ever see any of them again?

Sitting in the Mustang in front of the house, Dashuan chewed on his fingernails. He listened in tense silence for the sound of a gunshot to ring out. Glancing into the rearview mirror, he saw a flash of chrome as the large, unmistakable silhouette of Gutierrez's SUV came into view rounding the corner at the end of the block.

Dashuan had seen that SUV too many times not to recognize it. With his heart racing, he put the car into gear and tore away from the curb.

When Paul recognized the car pulling away from in front of his house, he slammed his foot on the gas pedal and shot halfway down the street like a bullet, intending to follow. But, suddenly, as he thought of Amber and Joachim in the house alone, he put on the brakes.

He spun into his drive, shifted to Park and jumped out of the SUV, leaving the door open and the engine running. He found the front door unlocked and crept in. Paul froze in his tracks in the foyer, hearing muffled voices coming from upstairs.

He reached beneath his jacket and pulled his Magnum from its holster. He had no idea how many people were in the house, or even who was in the car that pulled away. His back against the wall, his dark eyes darting in every direction, he maneuvered his way around the room. He removed the safety so as not to make a sound, before checking both the living room and kitchen.

He could hear Joachim's mournful cry coming from upstairs, and he forced himself to take several deeps breaths to rein in the raging impulse to fly up the stairs. The fact that his son was alive to cry was a good sign. This was not the time to let his volatile emotions take over.

As silent as a cat, he climbed the stairs one by one. The long, steel barrel of his Magnum was cold against his muscular thigh. As he came closer to the top of the stairs, the voices he'd heard earlier became more distinctive, and Paul could make out most of the words.

Reaching the top landing, he saw the hall was empty. Paul had never been more thankful for the SEAL training that now gave him the ability to be nothing more than a shadow on the wall. It also gave him the element of surprise.

He considered going to Joachim, but thought better of it when he recognized the noise the baby was making. It was the same cry he gave when he was frustrated or annoyed—not in pain. Paul relaxed, and decided to hold his position just outside Amber's bedroom door. If whoever was in there heard the baby stop crying, they would become suspicious.

Pressing his head against the door, Paul's eyes widened in shock when he recognized Barney's voice. *What is he doing here?*

Paul's mind worked rapidly, as he tried to reevaluate what he knew. All this time, he'd thought the threat to Amber was Dashuan Kennedy. But could he have been wrong? Could the person stalking them have been Barney, wanting some sort of revenge for being fired? And if so, then who was in the black Mustang?

He shook his head in silent dismissal of the many questions. Nothing was making sense anymore. And why Barney was here didn't matter, not now, not when Amber's life hung in the balance. He concentrated on formulating a plan of attack.

"Move over there," he heard Barney say from the far side of the room, and then there was a scuffling noise. He almost burst into the room, until he heard Amber's calm voice respond.

"Look out the window. He left you." Amber chuckled.

"No. Something must've happened. He'll be back." Paul could hear the uncertainty underlining the words.

"Face it, he abandoned you. Left you to take the fall."

"Shut up!"

Paul could tell Barney was getting nervous, which could be good or bad, depending on his stability.

"Just go," Amber said persuasively. "Leave now, and no one will be the wiser."

Barney gave a hard laugh. "I'm supposed to trust you not to say anything? You forget, your big mouth is why we're here in the first place."

"I don't even know who you are!"

There was a lengthy silence, and Paul knew Barney was considering what she said. *That's it, angel, work on whatever is left of his conscience.*

"You don't want to kill me. We both know that." There was courage in her voice even as she pleaded for her life, and Paul had never been more impressed with her. Another woman would have been a hysterical, sobbing wreck. But instead, his beautiful girl was bargaining with her captor.

"Just go," she whispered.

"I can't!" he snapped.

"Why not?"

Barney chuckled, and Paul could almost hear the sneer in his voice. He knew in that moment, Barney had made up his mind to go through with it.

"I have my own reasons for being here. Did I mention I used to work for Paul until he fired me a few weeks ago?"

"What does that have to do with me?" Amber asked.

"Nothing—except that Dashuan Kennedy has promised me more money than I ever dreamed of seeing in my lifetime, if I help him with this." He huffed in disgust. "All

I was supposed to do was drive the car and keep a lookout. I never expected him to punk out this way, but since he did, I guess it's up to me to finish it."

"Don't you see? He didn't punk out, he set you up."

"What are you talking about?"

"You think this is a coincidence? When the police find me, they're going to ask Paul about his enemies, and guess whose name is going to come up? Not Dashuan. Paul doesn't even know Dashuan. And even if you name him, it won't stick, because he'll have a better alibi than you—since he's nowhere around! That's probably why he left, to go create an alibi. Face it—he's setting you up to take the fall!"

So, Dashuan was here. Paul glanced back down the stairs, listening to make sure the Mustang had not returned, and then slowly leaned forward to try the door handle. Amber was doing a good job of confusing Barney, but he couldn't take the chance she'd talk him out of it.

"I'm going to frame Paul."

Paul's hand froze on the chrome knob. He stood still, waiting to see if his presence had been detected.

Barney chuckled, but it was not a pleasant sound. "Well, well, well, I finally found a way to shut you up. Yeah, that's right. This isn't just about you and Dashuan. See, when I'm finished here I'm going to use tape to put someone else's fingerprints on the gun. Wanna take a guess whose fingerprints I'm going to use?"

"Just because he fired you?" Amber asked in sorrowful amazement.

"He didn't just fire me—he stripped me of my professional reputation! He knew what would happen once word got out about why he fired me. But that's okay. Dashuan

Kennedy is going to pay me a king's ransom—and all I have to do is get rid of you."

"You're no murderer," she said. "If you were, I would be dead by now."

"I told you to shut up! You don't know anything about me!"

Paul knew Amber was losing the battle, he could hear the desperation in Barney's voice.

With precise movements Paul began to turn the door handle. He managed to get the door cracked wide enough to see the scene inside.

Barney was standing with his back to the door, and Amber stood between him and the window. The moment his eyes found her frightened face, he regretted opening the door. Up until then, he'd been able to keep a certain professional cool, but seeing Amber standing at the other end of a gun barrel, knowing how quickly it could be over, trembling started in the heels of his feet and worked its way up to the top of his head.

God, please don't take her away from me—not like this! He took a deep breath to try and gain control of himself. He even forced his mind to block out his son's cries. In a matter of seconds Amber could be dead. He had to act fast.

"Turn around and get on your knees," Barney growled.

Paul knew it was now or never. He opened the door farther. For one split second Amber's eyes flashed to his face, but she looked away.

"Like I said before—" she lifted her chin and looked Barney directly in the eyes "—if you're going to do it, you will have to look me in the face."

"Fine, have it your way."

Paul heard the pistol cocking, as a bullet slid into the chamber and prepared to be fired. He had two choices, and a split second to make his decision. He tucked his Magnum in its holster, threw open the door and dived across the room landing on Barney's back. He heard the weapon fire, but was too involved in staying on top of the assailant to verify where the round went.

Barney's large, beefy hands tried to grip his neck and roll Paul beneath him. He was the bigger and stronger of the two men, but Paul's sleeker body made his movements more precise, allowing him to maneuver better.

He flipped with Barney and found himself straddling the other man. He reared back and punched him in the face. The image of the gun being pointed at Amber, the sound of his son crying, the realization of what he would've come home to if he'd arrived an hour later, all those images and more were planted in his mind as he hit the man again and again. He was so consumed with fury, he had not even noticed that Barney had stopped fighting back.

Small, warm hands came down on his shoulders. In a distant recess of his mind, he heard Amber calling to him. "Paul! Paul! It's over!"

He was pulling back for another blow when he noticed the blood that covered his hand and the other man's face.

He looked up in relief to see Amber, unharmed, standing beside him. "It's over." She took his face between her hands, forcing him to look at her, trying to break through his haze of madness.

"It's over."

Paul scrambled up off the limp, unconscious body, and staggered across the room. His head was spinning and he stopped in the doorway. He felt Amber's soft body beside him as she braced his weight against her side and guided him into Joachim's room.

Together they approached the crib and found a red, tear-stained face staring back at them in outrage. Joachim was angry at having been ignored for so long, but as Paul lifted him from the crib he saw that his son was in no way harmed. Apparently, neither Barney nor his accomplice had time to come into the nursery.

Amber took the baby from his arms. "Sit down before you fall down," she said, guiding him toward the rocking chair. "You rest. I'll go call the police."

Paul slumped down in the chair, but before Amber could turn away he grabbed her hand and pulled her closer. "That can wait," he said, tugging her down onto his lap. "Right now I just need to hold you."

Amber surrendered easily. Sitting on his lap, she lifted her legs over the arm of the chair to accommodate Joachim, who was still whimpering. Paul grabbed a pacifier that was within reach, and the baby accepted the peace offering. Taking a couple of deep breaths, he settled into Amber's arms.

Chapter 24

Tucking her head beneath Paul's chin, Amber took her own series of deep, fortifying breaths. She had never been so terrified in her life. She was certain she was going to die. Listening to Joachim's cries was the only thing that kept her focused. As fearful as she was of her own fate, she was even more afraid of what they would do to him once she was dead.

So, instead of doing something stupid like attacking that bear of a man and getting herself killed even faster, or falling to her knees and begging for her life, she'd tried to talk to him, to reason with him, especially when she realized he was hesitant about what he felt he had to do. Although, she had no doubt that he would've done it, she knew he did not *want* to kill her. As soon as she realized that, she played on it, trying to reason with him. And when she was certain it wouldn't work, when she knew that she was about to die, suddenly there was Paul. Like an avenging angel sent by God, standing in plain sight right behind the man, with a terrifying intensity burning in his dark eyes.

One look in those eyes, and Amber knew she would be fine. She knew that Paul would never let anyone hurt her. She knew he spoke the truth when he told her he loved her. And she knew she would never be satisfied with anything less than that love.

Snuggling deeper into his arms, Amber fought off the deep exhaustion that was beckoning her to close her eyes and sleep. There was still a potential murderer in the next room.

"What now?" she asked Paul. When she received no answer, she looked up at his face, wondering if he had fallen asleep himself. "Paul?"

"Marry me."

Amber twisted her body to look at him. The two words were unexpected, to say the least, but more intriguing was that they were not spoken as a question, just a statement.

"What?" Her thin brows crinkled in confusion.

"I want you to marry me."

"Paul, you don't know what you're saying. Let's call the police before this man wakes up." She moved to stand up.

Paul wrapped his arms around her shoulders and held her to him. "Don't you see? It could've all been over so quickly. I could've lost you, Joachim, everything. We keep messing around like we have all the time in the world. I thought if I let you go back to Detroit, in time, you would realize that you love me and come back to me. But what if you never made it to Detroit? What if your plane went down? Or I'm killed in a car accident? What if we never get that second chance? Now is all we're promised. We can't waste it. Right now is all we've got. I love you, and

I believe you love me. We have to make the most of that love now, while we can."

Amber tilted her head, wondering where this was coming from. Agreeing with him would have been the easiest thing in the world. After all, she *did* agree with him. Looking down the barrel of a gun had a way of bringing things into perspective. But she was also concerned that this soulful affirmation was stress induced, and once the dust settled he would regret rushing into marriage with a woman he barely knew.

"We'll talk about this later," she said.

His grip on her shoulders tightened. "Don't you get it? There is no later!"

Looking into his troubled eyes, Amber sighed in disappointment. She was right. This was the stress talking. "I know." She decided to appease him. It was the easiest way to move on to what came next. The killer wouldn't be unconscious all night. They needed to call the police.

Paul's eyes narrowed on her face. "No, you don't. But you will. Say yes."

"Paul, we're—"

"Say yes, just to shut me up."

She felt the corner of her mouth lift. "Okay. Yes—just to shut you up."

"When this is all over, we'll fly to Vegas and get married."

Amber studied his eyes, and the determination she saw there caused her to hesitate. She was almost certain once the adrenaline slowed, once their assailant was taken into custody, once everything returned to normal, Paul would reconsider his hasty proposal. There was a huge difference between saying you love someone and making a lifetime commitment.

In the morning, all this would be forgotten. But for the moment, it was fun to consider flying down to Vegas for the quickie wedding that would make her his wife and Joachim's mother. The fantasy was too good to resist. For now, she would allow herself to believe in the impossible.

"A Vegas wedding it is. Of course, we'll have to renew our vows in front of my family."

He smiled. "If you insist."

That gentle smile was a welcome sight after all they'd been through. It was like sun shining through the clouds after a long, hard rain.

She reached over to hug him, but Joachim decided he'd had enough of being squeezed between the couple, and he began to squirm and whimper once more.

Paul seemed content to leave the matter where it stood. He patted her thigh. "He's probably hungry. You go feed him, and I'll take care of our guest."

Amber stood with the baby. "Just be careful," she said, before turning to head for the door.

"Wait," he called, coming to his feet. Paul moved around her and into the hall. One glance into her bedroom, and he nodded for her to come out. "He's still out cold."

"He said he used to work for you, and you fired him, is that true?" She glanced down at the bloodied man and looked away. Some part of her did not want to remember that Paul was the one who'd done that.

"Yes."

She avoided looking at Paul's bloodstained clothes. Concentrating on Joachim in her arms she asked, "Why did you fire him?"

Paul's head turned, and his dark eyes focused on her

face. "He betrayed me. Betrayal is the only thing I cannot forgive, Amber."

Her eyes narrowed, as she tried to grab on to the hidden meaning she felt was flying over her head at that moment. Was that a warning?

Before she could decide, he gave her a light pat on her bottom. "Go on downstairs. I don't want you here when he wakes up."

She didn't want to be there, either. She started down the stairs, and then remembered something. "Paul, Dashuan was here earlier. He tried to kill me first, and couldn't, so this guy took over."

Paul titled his head in consideration. "When I pulled up there was a black Mustang speeding away from the house."

"That had to be Dashuan. I tried to convince him—" she nodded toward Barney "—that Dashuan was letting him take the fall."

"I know. I heard. You did great, by the way."

"Not great enough. He was about to shoot me, anyway."

Paul closed his eyes in painful remembrance. "I know. Let's not talk about it."

With that dismissal, Amber carried Joachim downstairs to the kitchen, saying a silent prayer that Paul would call the police and they would arrive, and this monster would be out of their lives for good. They could decide what to do about the *other* monster, later.

The police arrived ten minutes later. That must be one of the perks of having cop friends, Amber thought. Sitting on the living room couch, she watched Paul talking to a detective near the front door.

Dazed and rumpled, Barney Roberts had been led out

of the house in cuffs several minutes ago, and one of the uniformed officers had already taken her statement.

She could tell by the way they kept their heads together that whatever Paul was telling the detective now was probably off the record. Paul was calling in a favor. But for what?

She stood and wrapped her arms around her body to hold off the cool chill she couldn't shake. Needing something to do, she walked over to the large bay window that looked out on the street. Her eyes scanned the houses across the street, and she could see more than one curtain moving.

She shook her head. Paul's nosy neighbors. Our nosy neighbors. She bit her bottom lip, knowing she should deny herself such unrealistic fantasies. But at that moment, she needed that fantasy. After the night she'd had, she deserved a little indulgence.

She heard the front door shut, and a few minutes later Paul came up behind her. He wrapped his arms around her waist as they watched the police cruisers pull away from the house.

"What were you and that detective talking about?" she asked, letting the curtain fall back in place.

"Just tying up some loose ends."

"Is one of those loose ends named Dashuan Kennedy?"

He turned her around in his arms, and placed a kiss on her lips. "Maybe."

"Paul, please don't—"

"Shh." He covered her lips with one finger. "Not now. I don't want to think of Dashuan Kennedy, or Barney Roberts, or anything other than taking you upstairs to my bed right now."

She smiled. "How can I argue with that?"

He smiled in return, but his smile was much more sensuous. "You can't."

Taking her hand, he led her out of the living room and toward the stairs. Just as he placed his foot on the bottom stair, he paused. "Hang on."

He walked over to the alarm key pad and punched in the numbers to activate it. His thoughtful expression turned to a frown, and Amber recognized the instant he discovered the truth.

His head turned toward her. "Amber, if you had the alarm on, how did they get in the house?"

Damn. Things were going so well, too. Now, their night of lovemaking was about to be overridden by Paul's anger when she told him that she had forgotten to set the alarm.

Instead of answering, she reached up and unbuttoned her pajama top, letting it slide off her bronze shoulders. She let her eyes convey her thoughts even as she began backing up the stairs. Her smile returned when Paul began to follow.

She knew Paul well enough to know the subject would not be closed forever, but it was closed for the night, and that was enough. Because tonight she needed the feel of his hands on her body, she needed the throbbing inside her quenched, she needed him.

With seductive eyes and unspoken invitation Amber guided him into the bedroom. But before she could initiate anything more, Paul sat down on the bed and pulled her onto his lap.

He fell back, and she was forced to go over with him. His large hands wrapped around her bottom and pulled her up on his waist. "Make love to me, Amber," he said, burying his face between her breasts.

The words were almost a plea, and Amber knew that what Paul needed from her went beyond the physical. He needed her comfort in the most basic sense of the word.

She wasn't sure how to give him what he needed, but she would find a way. Somehow, she would make him understand.

She leaned forward and kissed him, a gentle touching of the lips. When he began to respond she applied more pressure, forcing him to part his lips beneath hers. Paul moaned in pleasure, and Amber felt a sort of feminine power swelling inside her.

She kissed him harder, holding his face between her hands so she could devour his wonderful-tasting mouth. Relaxing in her hold, he let her guide and direct their interaction with complete submission.

The feeling of control was drugging, erotic, and soon she was working his shirt off his body, and then his slacks and underwear, as her mouth explored every inch of his hard body.

Her tongue slid across his taut abdomen, up and over his nipple, and when he arched his back, Amber felt the excitement in her own body reaching a pinnacle.

She removed her pajamas and Paul didn't move. She took a condom from his drawer and ripped it open. With concentration and gentleness, she slid it down his erection. Lying prone, Paul watched her through lowered lashes, with his hands fisted at his side. He bit his bottom lip as she climbed on top of his body, sitting low on his thighs.

The patch of hair at her center rubbed against his muscled leg, and Paul grabbed her hips, trying to bring her down on his throbbing organ. Amber resisted, enjoying her newfound power too much to have it end.

She took him in her hand and stroked him, watching the tortured expressions play across his handsome face.

Amber licked her dry lips, unsure how much longer she

herself could hold out. Then his head fell back, and the rod in her fingers tightened even more. She felt the pressure building relentlessly, and knew that if she did not move now it would soon be too late.

She lifted her hips and lowered herself down on him even as he began to climax inside her. Heated and dripping wet with anticipation, Amber felt her own body explode even before he was all the way inside her.

Paul wrapped his arms around her waist to hold her pressed against him as his body bucked beneath her. All Amber could do was try to not be unseated as the man she loved went wild beneath her.

All remnants of gentleness disappeared and he turned, flipping her beneath him and holding her down by the shoulders, pushing into her body in long, steady strokes. Amber felt her legs fall open, needing to take as much of him as possible inside her. The pressure was soon building once again, and then she was falling…falling…falling.

Chapter 25

Amber rolled over and was surprised to find no solid wall of flesh blocking her path. She reached out her hand and felt around, only to feel the cool, empty sheets beneath her fingers. Opening her eyes, she sat up and looked around. She was alone in the bedroom.

She dressed in her pajamas and went in search of Paul, hoping to coerce him into returning to bed. Just as she opened the door, she heard a loud scraping sound followed by voices.

"Vanessa, please lift that chair before you wake Amber."

Amber recognized Paul's deep voice, even though he was attempting to whisper. The Vanessa he spoke of had to be his secretary.

Amber could hear movement back and forth across the hardwood floor of the foyer, and she realized there were several people in the house.

"When will you be back?" A woman spoke, and Amber recognized that voice as Rosalie.

What is going on? Amber peeked out the door and saw that the upstairs hall was empty. She crept across the carpet to the railing that overlooked the foyer. Below, she saw Paul standing at the small side table writing out a check. Rosalie was standing beside him, watching what he was doing.

"Paul, I told you that is not necessary. Me and Enrique will take care of Joachim, you don't have to do this."

Paul ripped the check from the book and handed it to her. "Of course I do. We'll be gone one, maybe two weeks. You'll have to buy more formula and baby food."

Amber watched as a petite, chubby blonde came into view. She was cradling a stack of papers in her arm, and her head was bent forward as she concentrated on the top paper. "Paul, what about the licenses for your systems? Weren't you suppose to take care of that this week?"

Paul shook his head, as he tucked his checkbook back in the drawer of the table. "The prototypes are faulty, remember?"

"Oh, yeah, okay, I'll reschedule your appointment with the committee."

Amber watched the busy scene below in fascination. Joachim's caregiver, Paul's secretary—they all seemed to be rushing to get things done. Was Paul going somewhere? He seemed to be preparing for some kind of trip. But wouldn't he have told her if he were leaving?

"You wanted to see me, boss?" Just then, a young man opened the front door and came into the house, talking in his regular speaking voice. When Paul spun around to face him, the man stopped dead in his tracks.

Vanessa put a finger to her lips and used her other hand to point up. "Matt, you'll wake his fiancée."

Matt lifted his eyes and his mouth fell open in surprise. "You mean the fiancée who's standing at the railing, watching us?"

Everyone turned and looked up.

Paul smiled and headed toward the staircase. "Morning, angel, I thought you were still sleeping." He took the stairs two at a time until he was standing beside her.

"What's going on?" Amber asked, even as he took her arm and guided her back to his bedroom.

"Just trying to tie up some loose ends before we leave." He placed a gentle kiss just behind her ear.

"Hey, boss, what did you need?" Matt called from downstairs.

"Vanessa knows what needs to be done," Paul called back as he entered his bedroom and closed the door.

"Where are you going?" Amber asked, still confused and trying not to be distracted by Paul's busy fingers as they worked to unbutton what she had just buttoned.

"Me? You mean *we,* don't you?" He pulled her against him and took a breast into his mouth.

Amber felt her knees buckle beneath her, but Paul already had her in his arms and was carrying her to the bed. He laid her down and came over the top of her.

"I promised myself that the next time we did this we would be husband and wife, but who the hell am I kidding?"

Amber had a feeling something important was happening and she should be coherent long enough to find out what. But it was hard to concentrate with the wonderful throbbing organ pressed against her thigh.

"Paul, what's going on?"

Paul kissed her, before running his tongue along her bottom lip.

Amber moaned under the warm assault and wrapped her arms around his neck, winding her fingers through his thick curls.

Paul shifted her body, allowing himself to fit her much better. "Feel that?"

His hot breath on her neck was like an aphrodisiac.

"Oh, yes." She sighed, wanting to get rid of the clothes between them.

"That's Joachim's little sister anxiously waiting to be made." Paul slipped his hands into the back of her pajama pants, squeezing the soft mounds of flesh beneath. He began to work the pants down her legs, and Amber wiggled left and right in an attempt to help him.

She wanted nothing more than to feel him deep inside her. To feel him explode with her, to feel—

Joachim's little sister?

She pushed herself up on her elbows. "What did you say?" She used one hand to push some wayward strands of hair out of her face.

"Shhh." His wicked tongue darted across her collarbone. "Just relax, angel, and I'll take you to heaven." His large hand wrapped around her thighs and pulled her legs apart.

Amber found she was not strong enough to resist him. She lay back and felt the rush of cool air as the pajama pants slid down her legs. A few seconds later, she felt the length of Paul's naked body bearing her down into the mattress.

She held on to his muscular arms, and her heartbeat accelerated as Paul's hand came between their bodies, working himself into her. Her eyes opened wide when she realized that it was his natural skin she was feeling.

"Wait!" Amber insisted, pushing herself up on her elbows again. "You're not wearing a condom!"

Paul lifted his head, and Amber could see the fire burning in his dark eyes was being restrained. "We don't need a condom. We're about to be married. So what if you get pregnant?"

"So what?" His casual dismissal of her feelings was enough to cool her off. She pushed back until their bodies were no longer touching. Sitting up against the headboard, she wrapped the sheet around her partially nude body. "Look, Paul, I know what we said last night about getting married, but we were both distraught, and—"

"No way." Paul sat back on his haunches, glaring at her. "I can't believe this." He shook his head in disbelief. "I can't *freaking* believe this." He stood up.

"How can we get married when we know so little about each other?" she pleaded. "I mean, think about it…we've never even talked about whether we want more children."

"Of course, we want more children!"

"No, Paul! *You* want more children. You just assume I do. You've never asked."

"Do you want to have children?" he asked, for the first time sounding hesitant, and Amber realized he was starting to get it.

"I—I don't know. Maybe. I don't know."

"Damn." He huffed. "You're right. I never asked. You're so good with Joachim, I just assumed you'd want more."

"And even if I did, not now. I'm still in school. I would want to get my degree first. Get my career established."

Paul's eyes slid away, guilty, and Amber could almost read his thoughts.

"Did you think I would just be happy being your wife?"

Paul flopped down on the end of the bed, his back to her. "Yes."

She pulled her knees up to her chest to keep from scooting across the bed to him, which was what she wanted to do. He looked so dejected and confused. She wanted to comfort him. But she had to be strong, make him understand things would never be the way he wanted.

"This's what I'm talking about, Paul. I've known you less than a month. How can you think we can have a life together?"

"We can have a life together, Amber, a good one. But you're right. I should've asked you how you felt before now."

She buried her face against her legs. "This is all happening so fast. You just proposed last night, and I wake up this morning and find you making preparations to go to Vegas. I assume that's what's going on here?" She gestured toward the door, and he nodded. "Paul, what's your hurry? We have a lifetime to get married."

"If I wait, I'll lose you."

"What do you mean?"

"It always happens. When I wait too long, things get away from me, things come unraveled. If I wait, I'll lose you."

"No, you won't." Unable to stop herself, she reached out and stroked his arm.

"When my parents went back to Brazil, I waited too long to follow, and then when I tried it was too late. When I went into the military, I waited too long to come out and ended up in a war I wanted no part of. When Michelle left, I waited too long to look for her…and she died."

"Oh, Paul." Amber crawled across the bed, wrapping her arms around his shoulders, pressing her chest to his back. "Michelle's death wasn't your fault."

"If we wait, you'll go back to Detroit and be lost to me forever."

"No, I won't."

His arms came up and covered hers. "Then prove it, prove that no matter whether we wait, we'll be together. Marry me now."

"That's not fair."

"Why not? Because you know I'm right? You say you love me now, but what happens when there are two thousand miles between us? I'm not foolish enough to believe you'll waste your life pining over me. No, my only chance is to hold on to you now, while I have you."

She turned so she could see his face. "Do you want a woman you feel you have to bind to you with a ring?"

"As long as that woman is you, absolutely."

"How secure could you be in a marriage like that, Paul?"

"Very secure. I know once we're married you'll take your vows seriously, but without those vows, you'll think of yourself as a free woman."

She sat up and pushed him hard. "I am a *free* woman, and no marriage license is going to change that."

Paul quirked an eyebrow at her, but said nothing.

She sighed. "This will never work. You're too domineering."

Paul stood, and went around the bed to pick up his jeans. "Okay, fine. No Vegas wedding, but how about a Vegas vacation?"

Amber's eyes narrowed in suspicion. She didn't trust this easy surrender, not for a moment. "What do you mean?"

"We've both been through a lot these last couple of weeks." He slipped on his jeans and began looking for his T-shirt. "I think we deserve a break. I've already booked the hotel and bought tickets online. Even arranged for Rosalie to keep Joachim. Why don't we take this time to get away?"

She bit her lip considering. She'd always wanted to see Las Vegas. And Paul was right. After last night, some time away sounded like a wonderful idea. "Okay, as long as you promise that once we get there, you won't go all heman on me, and try to force me down the aisle."

Paul came around to where she sat on the bed, bent and placed a kiss on her forehead. "Amber, I promise I will never force you to do anything." With that, he walked out of the bedroom, closing the door behind him.

Amber sat on the bed for several minutes just staring at the door. He had said what she wanted to hear, and yet for some reason she found no assurance whatsoever in his promise.

Paul was wonderful in so many ways. There was no denying he was a good, kind, caring man. A warm, loving father. A strong protector and able provider. But he had the determined will of an enraged bull—and all that strength of mind seemed to be focused on making her his wife and the mother of his children.

Any other woman would be flattered by the attention. Any other woman would be eager to accept his offer. But she was not any other woman, she was Amber Lockhart, known only for her beautiful form and empty soul. She smiled and seduced and charmed her way through life, but there was no real substance. She was a trophy, good for show but nothing more. Every man she'd ever dated had confirmed that belief, everyone from Mason the cruise ship guy to the married professor to Dashuan Kennedy.

And just as she was not any other woman, Paul was not any other man. He expected her to be more than a pretty face. He expected her to be worthy of his love. And she could fool him for a time, but she couldn't marry him. A lifetime was too long to hold up the pretense. One morning Paul would wake up and discover he'd married a fraud.

Chapter 26

"Welcome back to the Bellagio, Mr. Gutierrez. I hope you and your guest enjoy your stay." The desk clerk smiled as she handed over the key card. "John will show you to your suite."

Paul wrapped his arm around Amber's waist and guided her toward the elevators as they followed behind the bellhop who carried their two suitcases.

"Welcome back?" Amber whispered in his ear, trying not to look like the country hick she felt. "How often do you stay here?"

The elegance of the beautiful resort was overwhelming, everything from the breathtaking water fountains to the glass ceilings and indoor gardens.

"Not often," he said, with a kiss on her temple. "And it's usually for business."

They followed their bellhop into the elevator, and the guard standing beside the button panel smiled in greeting.

The chrome doors closed behind them. Amber was still reeling from the harmless statement the desk clerk had made. It was not meant as an insult, but for some reason, Amber was still offended. *I hope you and your* guest *enjoy your stay. Guest?*

She was not his guest. She was the woman he loved, his lover, the woman he wanted as his wife, and this knowledge brought her undeniable pride.

The elevator stopped and the doors began to open. Amber moved forward to step out, but Paul stopped her. She glanced up and saw a man standing just outside the doors. Not just any man.

Her mouth fell open when she recognized her favorite action star, Richard Burrow.

She turned stunned eyes on Paul, who nodded.

It occurred to Amber that Paul never treated her like a silly, starstuck groupie, even though she constantly asked him about his celebrity clients and friends.

"Paul?" Richard Burrow stepped forward into the elevator. Recognizing his friend, he held out his hand. "I thought that was you."

Paul shook the other man's hand. "Richard, good to see you."

Richard Burrow's eyes went to Amber.

Amber noticed that Paul seemed hesitant to make the introduction. "Richard, this is my fiancée, Amber Lockhart."

Richard's eyes shot back to Paul's and Amber watched as some kind of silent challenge passed between the two men. "Your fiancée?"

Paul nodded. "That's right."

Although what Paul was saying wasn't exactly the truth, it wasn't really a lie, either, Amber thought.

Their whole relationship was becoming more and more confusing by the second. Still, instinctively, she knew not to contradict what he was saying. There was a reason for it, she was sure of that.

Richard smiled his camera smile, and Amber thought he was as fine in person as in his movies. "Nice to meet you, Amber." He extended his hand.

It was a harmless gesture—but, still she glanced at Paul, and found his full attention still centered on Richard.

She decided it would be rude not to accept the handshake. "The pleasure is mine. I'm a big fan."

His smile turned cunning. "Really? That's nice to know."

"Are you going down, Mr. Burrow?" The guard interrupted the tense interaction.

"Um, yes, I am." Richard glanced over his shoulder, only then realizing they were not alone in the elevator.

"So, Richard, what are you doing in town?" Paul asked, and Amber tried not to flinch when she felt his arm tighten around her waist.

"I've agreed to be a judge for the Miss USA pageant."

"Oh, I didn't realize that was this weekend."

Richard's eyes returned to Amber. "You should be one of the contestants, Amber. You're absolutely breathtaking."

"Thank you." Amber tried not to blush. But the intense scrutiny in his eyes was unsettling.

The bell rang again as the elevator came to a stop on the thirty-fourth floor. John the bellhop gestured to the opening doors. "This way."

"Goodbye, Mr. Burrows, it was nice meeting you," Amber said as she allowed herself to be guided out of the elevator by Paul.

"Call me Richard," he said with an award-winning smile. "Good seeing you again, Paul."

Paul said nothing.

They were almost to their suite when Amber heard Richard call out to them. She turned to see him standing between the chrome doors, holding them open with his hands.

"Paul, I'm having a little get-together in my suite tonight. If you two aren't busy, why don't you stop by? You'll probably know everyone there." He chuckled.

Amber wanted to say yes, imagining all the famous people who'd be there, but Richard didn't ask her, he asked Paul, and once again on some instinctive level, Amber knew there was a reason for it.

"No thanks, we're going to see a show tonight. Maybe next time," Paul answered as they continued down the hall.

"Well, if you reconsider, my suite number is 3180," he called out, and let the doors close.

"Here you are." The bellhop opened the suite door and gestured them ahead of him. He followed them in and headed straight for the bedroom.

"Oh, Paul, this is beautiful." Amber turned in a circle, taking in the luxurious suite. She moved from room to room, amazed at the spaciousness of it all. "What are we going to do with all this room?"

Paul's mouth twisted in a knowing smirk. "I can think of some things."

The bellhop returned from the bedroom. "Will you be needing anything else?"

"No." Paul shook his hand, discreetly placing a pack of bills in the center. "We're fine for now." He ushered the bellhop out, then came toward her where she stood looking out the window at the city below.

He leaned forward and kissed her. "So, what do you want to do first?"

"What do you want to do?"

He tilted his head as if the answer were obvious. "What do I always want to do?"

She chuckled. "Why don't we start with an activity that involves being clothed?"

His mouth twisted in a wicked grin. "That does not present a problem for me."

She gave an exaggerated sigh. "Okay, how about an activity outside the suite?"

His expression turned thoughtful. "That's workable— depending on how much of an exhibitionist you are."

She laughed. "We are not having sex in public!"

He shrugged. "Have it your way for now, as long as we get to do what I want to do later."

She toyed with the top button of his shirt, working up the nerve to ask the question she wanted to ask. "How about we go to Richard Burrow's party tonight?"

He gave her a quick peck on the cheek, before letting his hands fall away from her. "No. I know Richard is handsome and famous, but he's also a son of a bitch." He turned and headed for the bedroom. "We're staying away from him."

"He seemed harmless enough," she called after him.

Paul stopped in the doorway. "I know him, Amber. He's not to be trusted." He disappeared through the bedroom door, and Amber turned back to the view of Vegas. It really was pretty.

"Do you have tickets to a show?"

"I will," he answered.

Her mouth twisted. "You don't have to trust someone to go to their party," she muttered.

"He wants you."

Paul's voice was so close, it startled her. She turned in surprise to see him standing behind her with a small, white box in his hand. "What?"

"He wants you. He thinks he can take you away from me. That's why he invited us tonight. He wants a chance to seduce you."

"Do you think I can be so easily seduced?" When several seconds passed, and he didn't answer, Amber could not hide her disappointment. "Do you, Paul?"

"No, not unless you want to be." He glanced at the small box in his hand.

"Do you think I want to be?" Amber wasn't interested in the box, only in Paul's answers. This conversation was becoming revealing and painful, but she needed to know the truth. She needed to know what Paul really thought of her.

"I don't know what you want. I know you won't commit to me. I know you like the freedom of being with whomever you want, whenever you want. So, if you found Richard attractive, I don't know what you would do."

Amber felt a sharp pain, as if someone had punched her in the stomach. Feeling as if her legs would not hold her much longer, she crossed the room and sat down on the couch.

Paul came and stood in front of her. "Angel, I meant no harm. You asked me if I thought you wanted to be seduced by Richard Burrow, but that's a question only you can answer."

Amber wrapped her arms around her waist and tried to block out the presence of the man standing in front of her. After all, he was only repeating what she'd heard a thousand times. It was impossible to ignore him or the hurtful words.

This was Paul, not Dashuan, not Mason the cruise ship guy, or Mike, Mr. I-can't-trust-you-around-my-friends. This was Paul, the love of her life, her ideal man, and he was repeating what all those other men had said. She was a beautiful shell with nothing inside.

Paul stood for several seconds waiting for her to answer. When she didn't, he placed the box on the table in front of her. "I don't have to tell you what's inside, I'm sure you can guess. I ordered it to be delivered here when I made the hotel reservation, before we had our conversation this morning. It's yours…whether you ever choose to wear it or not. It will always be yours…just like my heart."

Amber glanced down at the box but made no move to pick it up. "Why would you want to marry a woman you don't trust?"

"No, angel, you're twisting what I said." Paul kneeled before her. "I trust you completely. With my heart, with my son, with my future. Trust is not the issue. What you *want* is the problem. You don't know…and until you do, there are no guarantees for us." Using his index finger he lifted her chin. "We are alike in so many ways, Amber. And this is one of them. You and me, we don't do things in half measures."

He sat down beside her. "You won't commit to me, because you know if you do, it will be for a lifetime, and you're not sure you're ready for that. And you're right. Once I know you're mine, I'll never let you go. It's the same reason you date the kind of guys you do, guys who won't expect you to commit. You can play with them for a while and move on."

She picked up the white box, but instead of opening it, she just twirled it between her fingers, needing some activity to keep her shaky hands occupied. "But not you?"

"No. Not me. I know a diamond when I see one."

Amber considered what he was saying and realized his words were hitting too close to home. "So, what am I doing here with you?" She smirked. "Since you're obviously not my type."

He smiled. "You love me. You don't want to love me, but you do. If you had your way, you would go on being a party girl. No strings, no responsibility, no expectations from anyone. It's one of the reasons you did not want to face your sisters. They expect things of you, they believe in you, and you are terrified of disappointing them."

She turned her head and glared at him. "Who made you such an Amber expert?"

"You did." He leaned forward and kissed her cheek. "With every word, and every action. You wanted me to understand you. Whether it was conscious or not, you reached out to me, and I accepted the invitation."

She put the box down and stood. She didn't want to hear anything else he had to say. Her thoughts were getting scrambled.

"Amber, everything you want is yours for the taking." He lifted the box and wrapped her fingers around it. "But, first, you have to acknowledge that you want it. I can't do that part for you."

She tossed the box onto his lap, circled around the glass coffee table and headed toward the door. "What a lousy holiday this is turning out to be."

She opened the door and paused. "We've tried this in every way possible, Paul, and it is becoming obvious that you and I will never work as a couple. I'm going to enjoy my only night in Vegas, and tomorrow we'll go our separate ways." She walked out of the suite and pulled the door closed behind her.

Chapter 27

Paul lay his head back on the couch and took a deep breath. "Way to go, Paul," he berated himself out loud. He'd learned a long time ago that Amber could only take reality in small doses.

She was not the self-actualizing type. She lived in a pleasant little delusional world, and seemed content to stay there. He knew she'd convinced herself that she was worthless, and that was just fine with her, because it gave her license to behave badly and expect to always be forgiven, because after all, that's just Amber. But Paul knew that was not the real Amber.

He saw the real Amber sitting cross-legged in the middle of the kitchen floor, trying to coerce his son into eating a spoonful of nasty strained peas. He saw the real Amber creating magic on a sketch pad and then finding the materials to bring her visions to life. He saw the real Amber lying in his arms at night, telling him about the pain of losing her parents at such a young age. He knew the real Amber. And for some reason, he'd gotten it into his head to make her see it. But she wasn't interested in the real Amber.

After a lifetime of convincing herself that the world saw her as an empty-headed toy, it would take more than a conversation to convince her that she was the primary instigator behind that misconception.

He picked up the box and opened it. The three-carat diamond solitaire twinkled against the white velvet background. After they'd made love the night before, Amber had fallen fast asleep, but Paul had gotten up and turned on his laptop searching for the perfect stone on the Internet. In fact, between making the arrangements for their trip and tying up his business affairs Paul had not slept at all.

Now, here they were on what should've been their honeymoon, and instead he was sitting alone in the suite, while Amber was who knew where, doing who knew what with who knew who.

Who knew who…? Paul had a pretty good guess about that one. He may not know where she was now, but he was certain of where he could find her later that night. Richard Burrow's suite. He knew she would go to the party, just as sure as he knew everything else about her. She now felt she had something to prove. She needed to reaffirm her belief that she was nothing more than a plaything. Paul felt his jawbone tightening, knowing Richard would be more than willing to accommodate her.

Richard was a dead man.

He stood and crossed the room, planning to go and warn the other man to keep his hands off of her, but halfway to the door, it suddenly hit him.

He couldn't help her with this.

He could go to Richard's suite later and drag her out. But she would only find some other way to prove her point at a later time. Nothing would change, until she did. He could give her his love…but until she was able to accept it, it would mean nothing.

He turned, and with slumped shoulders went into the bedroom. His memories flashed to Michelle. Through Amber, he'd come to understand her wild behavior better. Just like Amber, Michelle had been acting out of her own insecurities. And just like Amber, he could not save her.

He knelt beside the bed and said a quick prayer, asking God to watch over his beloved and to bring her back to him. As a child, his uncle never missed mass and always dragged Paul along with him. As an adult, Paul wasn't much for mass anymore, but he'd never stopped praying.

He stretched across the bed, and the exhaustion of the previous two days came down hard on him. He yawned and closed his eyes. He could only hope that Amber came to understand her true worth before it was too late—for both of them.

What the hell am I doing here? Amber asked herself that question for the twentieth time as she stood outside Suite 3180 waiting for someone to answer her knock.

She could hear the music and the laughter coming from the other side of the door. She raised her hand to knock again, but paused. Maybe this was a sign from God, she thought. Maybe He was giving her a chance to change her mind. She decided she liked that reasoning and turned to walk away.

She was almost to the elevators when the door to the suite opened and Richard rushed out into the hallway. He looked in both directions and quickly spotted her. "Amber! Where are you going?" He hurried toward her down the hall.

She watched the handsome man approaching—he looked like a movie coming to life right before her eyes.

Richard took in her appearance and she realized she was still wearing the jeans and pink cashmere sweater he'd seen her in earlier.

"Sorry, I was in such a hurry, I didn't have time to change. Am I too casual? I'll just pop upstairs and change," she said, deciding her attire was the perfect excuse to leave.

"No, you're fine," he said. "Come on in."

As they entered the suite, the music blasted in her ears. The lights seemed much brighter than those in the hallway, and the room was filled with people dancing and mingling.

Amber looked in every direction, surprised and excited by how many of the guests she recognized. Her eyes noticed a pretty, petite blond woman sitting on the arm of one of the large lounge chairs, talking to a brunette woman sitting in the chair. "Is that Melanie Hartwell?"

Richard looked in the direction she nodded. "In the flesh."

When the brunette turned in her direction, Amber's mouth fell open. "And that's Sanaa Lathan she's talking to! She's one of my favorite actresses."

Richard smiled at her. "I see you know your actresses. Come on, I want to introduce you to some people."

She started to follow him through the crowd, but couldn't stop from looking around in every direction. Which was why she didn't see the large man standing in her way. Bumping hard against his lower back, she stumbled, but felt a hand reach out and catch her before she fell.

"Are you okay?"

Shaking it off, Amber looked up and up, and up. The

farther up she looked, the wider her eyes got. "You're Zeke Henry," she said in utter amazement.

He smiled. "I know."

Richard was beside her again. "Having a good time, Zeke?"

The athlete looked at the other man over her head. "You always know how to throw a party, Richard."

"Have you met Amber Lockhart?" He settled his hands on her shoulders, possessively.

"I guess you could call it a meeting." Zeke winked at Amber, and laughed.

Amber tried to smile through her mortification.

"Can you excuse us?" Richard was already guiding her away. "There are some other people I want her to meet before they leave."

"Not a problem. Nice meeting you, Amber." Zeke smiled again, and turned back to the group he was talking to earlier.

"Likewise." She barely had time to call over her shoulder, before Richard was hustling her through the crowd.

True to his word, Richard introduced her to almost everyone there, and by the end of the evening, Amber thought she had met almost every celebrity she knew and many she did not know. Most were nice people, but there were a few who definitely altered her opinion of them. Especially Lacy Hill, who turned out to be a complete bitch. Although, in truth, Amber knew it wasn't really her fault.

It was because of a conversation she'd overheard coming out of the bathroom. Lacy was with another celeb, telling her about some guy she wanted to bed. Amber had thought nothing of it until Lacy mentioned the name Paul. Amber had stopped dead in her tracks, knowing there was no way Lacy could be talking about *her* Paul. But as Lacy continued talking, using words like *hot Latin lover,* the impossible became possible.

Amber didn't realize she was glaring at the woman, until Lacy said, "Do I know you?"

Amber held onto her temper with both hands, and managed to give a civil answer. "No, it's just you look a lot like my favorite singer."

Lacy smiled. "Yes, it's me." She puffed up her chest, expecting the adoration she was certain was to follow.

Amber put on her best face of awe and innocence. "You mean, you're *really* Christina Aguilera?"

Lacy's eyes narrowed on her face with murderous intent, before she turned her back on Amber.

Amber turned away with a pleased smirk. It was little compensation but it would have to do. Imagine that woman thinking she could have Paul.

Paul is mine—and he's going to stay that way.

As she moved back into the main room, Richard was suddenly at her elbow again, where he'd been most of the night.

He offered her a drink for the hundredth time, and Amber refused for the hundredth time. After Mason, the cruise ship guy, she made a rule never to accept drinks from men at parties.

Richard placed the drink on the tray of a passing waiter. "Are you having a good time?" He spoke loudly to be heard over the music.

Amber smiled and nodded. "A great time! Thanks for inviting me."

He licked his lips. "Thank you for coming."

Something in his expression seemed sinister. "You know, I noticed you haven't asked where Paul is."

He shrugged. "I figured if you showed up it wouldn't be with Paul."

"Why not?"

Richard's lips turned up in an almost boyish grin. "Paul's not exactly my biggest fan."

Amber tilted her head to look at him, becoming more intrigued by the second. "What's the history between you two?"

Richard looked away dismissively. "It's a long, boring story."

"I've got time."

He looked at her again. "Ask Paul. If he wants you to know, he'll tell you."

"Does it involve a woman?"

His expression turned cunning. "Surprisingly, no. At least, not up until now."

Amber looked away, breaking eye contact. She knew Richard thought her appearance tonight meant she was making herself available to him. And in truth, she wasn't sure herself why she'd come, but she knew that was not the reason.

Richard Burrow was handsome, famous and, from what she'd seen tonight, charming...but he was not Paul. In the end, that was all that mattered.

She made a deliberate glance at her wristwatch. "Richard, I've had a great time, but I better be getting back to my suite." She turned to walk away and felt Richard grab her arm.

"So soon?" he asked, with a strange expression in his eyes.

Amber tried to understand that look. It wasn't disappointment, more like a challenge, or more precisely, the acceptance of a challenge.

But she hadn't challenged him—had she? "Yes, it's getting late, and Paul will be expecting me back soon."

He snorted.

She frowned and glanced down to where he was still holding on to her. "Will you let my arm go?"

He stared at her for several long moments. With his tongue pressed against the inside of his cheek, he looked like he was in deep contemplation. Amber feared that after such an enjoyable evening, she was going to have to end it with a bad scene.

Then suddenly, he let her go. "I have to admit, Amber, I'm more than a little disappointed. I'd heard good things about you—really good things."

Her eyes narrowed on his face. Considering they'd only met earlier that afternoon, she didn't understand what he could possibly mean.

He smiled and lifted his hand to her face. "D said you were a lot of fun."

"D?" she asked hesitantly, fearing she already knew who "D" was.

"Oh, didn't I mention that we had a mutual friend?" He leaned forward. "In fact, I was a bit surprised when Paul introduced you as his fiancée earlier. From what Dashuan said, you are not the settling down type." He winked. "If you know what I mean."

Amber felt her heart sink. She knew exactly what he meant. She felt her hands begin to tremble. She had to get out of there. "Dashuan Kennedy doesn't know a damn thing about me," she said between clenched teeth, then turned and began to push her way through the crowd toward the door.

Once she was out in the hallway again, Amber leaned against the wall and took a deep breath. *Will it ever end?*

"What is wrong with me?" She hit her head against the

wall. "What the hell is wrong with me?" she shouted at no one in particular. The only answer was the tears that formed in her eyes and rolled down her cheeks.

Just then she heard the suite door opening. She hurried down the hallway. She could hear a group of people laughing and talking behind her, and not wanting anyone to see her crying, she darted past the elevators and into the stairwell. It was the perfect place to have a good cry. So, she sat down on the top stair, buried her face in her hands and did exactly that.

D said you were a lot of fun. How many times had she heard statements like that? And still after all this time, it hurt like hell. To know you'd been reduced to nothing more than a name men tossed around when someone was looking for an easy score.

How do I end up in these situations? Amber replayed the day in her head. It started so good, leaving Moreno Valley with Paul, checking in to their beautiful hotel suite, playfully flirting with him about making love in public.

The memories were enough to bring a smile to her face, and she used her index finger to wipe the tears from her eyes. So, where had it all gone so wrong?

When you left the suite and went looking for trouble.

Sitting alone in the hotel stairwell, Amber forced herself to look at her actions. For the first time, she considered her own behavior and what part it played in her life.

Paul had said more than once that she was to blame for the way men treated her. Could that be true? Did she sell herself short?

If she just took into account the things that had happened today, she would have no choice but to admit that there was some truth to it. After all, she'd left the safe, comforting arms of a man she knew loved her to go in search of a playboy, movie star looking for a quick hit. If that was not self-destructive behavior, what was?

And Paul did love her, almost as much as she loved him. And she did so love him. Only him. In fact, what she felt was so strong, so all-consuming Amber was certain she had fallen in love for the first time. Nothing, no man, no relationship, nothing in her life had ever felt like Paul. But would love be enough to hold them together?

After all, as much as Paul wanted it, she could never be the typical suburban housewife. He wanted to marry her, but she knew he was thinking from his heart, not his head. And what kind of mother would she be to Joachim? Poor little dove had already had one lousy mother, he didn't need another.

But if she mustered the strength to walk away, what kind of life would she have without Paul? Somehow the thought of returning to her soulless existence held no appeal. Back to the Dashuans and Richards of the world. Back to the endless rounds of meaningless parties and meaningless relationships. Back to being Amber, the party girl. The Amber her friends and family knew.

But not Paul.

Paul saw her creative side and encouraged it. Paul saw the tiny ember of her innermost desires and fanned them into flames. Paul saw deep inside her soul and understood her. He'd even said as much. *You wanted me to understand you. Whether it was conscious or not, you reached out to me, and I accepted the invitation.*

But why? Why could Paul see the Amber no one else bothered to look for? Why was he willing to offer her a life she never dared to hope for?

Shamefully, her conscience let her sit there in ignorance for several silent minutes before it finally provided the answer. *Because he loves you, dingbat!*

Chapter 28

Paul was awakened by a warm, feather-light touch gliding across his lower back. He turned on his side to see Amber sitting beside him on the bed.

Once she saw he was awake, she folded her legs beneath her and held up her left ring finger. "It doesn't fit."

He glanced at the slightly oversized diamond and felt his heart skip a beat. Could it be? Was she real or was this all just a dream? Would he wake up and find he was still alone?

Some part of him was content to let the dream continue. Amber sitting beside him wearing his ring was far better than the reality he'd fallen asleep to. But the other part of him needed to know the truth, no matter how painful. So, he reached out and took her hand in his.

She was real.

With a deep sigh of relief, he brought her hand to his

lips and kissed her palm. The motion shook the ring, and it slid from her finger.

Amber scooped it up out of the folds of the bed comforter. "See? It keeps sliding off."

Paul braced himself on his elbows as his eyes narrowed on her face. "Does it matter?"

She huffed. "If you expect me to wear it, it does."

Paul sat up. "Don't play with me, Amber. What are you saying?"

Amber bit her lip, and he could see she was having trouble finding the right words. It would've been so easy to fill in the blanks for her. But he had to hear her say the words herself. She had to tell him, or he would never know for certain if what happened next was her idea or his.

She shrugged. "I'm saying…yes."

Her words were spoken so softly, Paul almost didn't hear her. He wanted to let it be enough, but letting her off easy now would only cost them later. "What did you say?"

She turned glaring amber eyes on his face. "You want me to beg?"

He sat up and pulled her into his arms. "No, angel, never that, but I have to know that this is want *you* want. Amber, I have no idea what brought you back here tonight. I know what I *want* to believe. But how can I be sure, if you don't tell me?"

Amber wrapped her arms around his neck and squeezed him tight against her. "This is what brought me back here." Her soft lips kissed his neck. "I feel so good when you hold me. I don't mean just sexually good. Just…good—if that makes any sense."

Paul buried his head in her hair. It made complete sense to him. It had from the moment those elevator doors opened and she stepped into his life. In his heart he knew they always would make sense.

Paul pulled away from her and took her face between his hands, forcing her to look into his eyes. "Amber, will you marry me?"

She smiled, and it quickly became a grin. "Yes! Yes! Yes!" Amber threw herself against him in excitement, and they both tumbled back onto the bed. The diamond solitaire bounced off her finger and across the bed.

"My ring!" Amber raced after it, breaking free of Paul's hold. She reached over the side of the bed and recovered it from the floor.

She slid it back on her finger, twisting it this way and that. Paul noticed that she seemed fascinated by the way the light reflected off of it. He was more fascinated by the perfect round bottom laying across his midsection.

"You have great taste, by the way," she said, examining her engagement ring.

"I know," he said, running his open palm across her upturned butt.

"It is beautiful." She twisted her mouth thoughtfully. "Three-carat?"

Coming from any other woman, at any other time, Paul might've been offended. But he was so satisfied with life at that moment, he would've provided a full appraisal for her, if she'd asked. Instead, he playfully slapped her. "You are such a gold digger."

Her eyes widened in shock. "I am not. I'm just curious." She pushed him back down and sat up. She twisted her mouth, trying to hide the smirk she felt forming. "What woman doesn't like to feel appreciated?"

Suddenly, Paul was over her, his heavy weight bearing

her back down. Busy fingers worked the buttons of her sweater. "You are appreciated, Amber." His lips traced a line along her cheek until he found her mouth. "More appreciated than you can ever imagine. More valued than all the diamonds in the world. More beautiful than anything I've ever seen. And I will treasure you the rest of my life." He kissed her with gentle persuasion. His warm tongue gliding across her bottom lip, darting in and out until her lips parted beneath his. Then he was inside, tasting, savoring her sweetness.

His mouth traced the path along her collarbone and along the opening of her sweater. His large hand skimmed across her waist.

Paul ran his tongue over every inch of her exposed skin as it came into view. As the sweater slid off one shoulder, then the other, he was there, kissing and tasting her warm flesh. Only then, holding her in his arms again, was he able to silently confess the fear that had held his heart in a tight grip for the past few hours. Only then was he able to release all his doubts, his secret terrifying thoughts. And as her fingers tightened around his neck, only then could he express his silent thanks that his worst fear had not come to fruition. At that moment, he knew, in his bones he knew, that wherever she'd been that evening, no man had tasted what belonged only to him. Wherever she'd been, she'd come back to him the same as she left.

Just before dawn, the couple stood waiting outside the double doors leading into the small wedding chapel. Amber could not stop the trembling in her hands as she stood next to Paul, holding a small bouquet of red roses.

She was looking around the small foyer, trying to

ignore the fear that was threatening to take over every part of her body.

Her attention was brought back to Paul as she felt him tugging the bouquet out of her hands. "Angel, you're about to snap the stems. Let me have them."

She hesitantly released the flowers, and Paul took her hand and guided her to the wood bench a few feet away.

"Come and sit with me." He sat down and tugged on her hand until she sat beside him. He pulled her close against his side.

Amber took a deep breath and snuggled against him and relaxed. What was it about this man that he had this kind of calming effect on her?

He placed a gentle kiss on the top of her head. "Better?"

She smiled against his chest. "Yes."

"I know this is not the kind of wedding you wanted, but I promise we'll have a big ceremony as soon—"

She shook her head, wanting to ease him. "No, that's not it."

He lifted her away from him so he could see her face. "Are you having second thoughts?"

She smiled, seeing the fear and uncertainty in his eyes. Paul always seemed so confident and self-assured, she found it comforting to know he was as nervous as she.

"No second thoughts. I love you with all my heart, and I want to be your wife more than anything in the world."

"Then what is it?"

Amber toyed with the large diamond ring that now fit snug on her finger. The Bellagio had proven their superior service once again, finding a jeweler to size the ring at four in the morning.

She frowned, trying to find the right words. "I've never

had to take care of anyone but myself. I wonder what kind of mother I'll be to Joachim."

He smiled. "You'll be a wonderful mother. Joachim loves you as much as I do. And you won't be alone. We'll be together."

"I know, it's just…" Her frown deepened. "I'm scared."

"Of what?"

She turned her head toward his chest again to hide her face. "Of not being…good enough."

He pulled her away again, and lifted her chin with his index finger. "Angel, how can you not be good enough? You're perfect."

She huffed. "You're biased."

He chuckled. "Yes, I am, but that's okay. I'm supposed to be. Amber, no one knows for certain what the future will hold. All you can do is follow the path your heart leads you down." He leaned forward and kissed her. It was just a soft touch of their lips.

"After Michelle, I thought I couldn't trust another woman. I never imagined someone like you existed. But here we are. Sometimes, you just have to trust the Universal Power."

"But what if—"

"Shhh." He kissed her once more. "Life is full of ifs. We'll just take them as they come. As long as I have you, I can handle whatever life throws at us."

Amber felt her chest swell with all the love and passion she had inside her. Paul's unwavering faith in the rightness of their union was a satisfaction like nothing she'd ever known. He gave her a new confidence, not only in herself, but in her potential as both a woman and a human being. No one had ever believed in her so completely. She knew in that moment, sitting on the little bench in the Chapel of Love Wedding Chapel that with their love, together they could conquer whatever may come their way.

The double doors opened and a young Caucasian couple stepped out. They were both dressed in blue jeans and T-shirts, but despite their casual appearance, something in their faces, in the way they looked at each other, told anyone who saw them that something phenomenal had just happened in their lives.

Paul stood and handed her the bouquet. "Ready?"

She smiled and stood with him. "I've been ready for you a long time."

A middle-aged man, wearing a clergyman's white collar and black robe came to the entrance. He smiled, and gestured to the aisle leading to the front of the chapel. "Right this way."

Paul looked deep into Amber's golden eyes, and she nodded in silent agreement. Taking her hand, he led her down the aisle.

The ceremony was short as they exchanged the traditional vows in the presence of the minister and the organist, who doubled as a witness.

"I, Amber Lockhart, take thee, Paul Gutierrez, to be my husband, and before God and these witnesses, I promise to be a true and faithful wife." With trembling hands Amber placed the plain gold band on Paul's finger.

He lifted her shaky hands to his lips and kissed each palm in reassurance. And somehow, Amber knew he would always be there for her in this way. His strong hands there to steady her when she staggered.

Paul slid the diamond-studded band onto her finger in front of the solitaire. "With this ring, I thee wed, and with all my worldly goods. I thee endow. In sickness, and in health, in poverty and in wealth, 'til death do us part—I love you so much."

Before the minister could complete the ceremony, Paul pulled her into his arms with a powerful intensity that caught Amber off guard. He kissed her, long and lovingly, oblivious to the others in the room. "Say you love me," he whispered against her mouth.

"I do, I do," She returned the kiss with equal passion, needing to make him understand his importance to her, needing him to know that she returned everything he was feeling and more. "I do love you, more than I ever imagined I could love another human being."

She threw her arms around his neck and whispered in his ear, "And thank you for teaching me to love myself."

* * * * *

Watch for the final title in Kimani Romance's
THE LOCKHARTS—THREE WEDDINGS
& A REUNION
For four sassy sisters, romance changes everything!
FORBIDDEN TEMPTATION
By Gwynne Forster
Available in November 2007

Never Without *You...* *Again*

National bestselling author
FRANCINE CRAFT

When Hunter Davis returns to town, high school
principal Theda Coles is torn between the need to
uphold her reputation and the burning passion she still
feels for her onetime love. But her resistance melts in
the face of their all-consuming desire and she can't stop
seeing him—even though their relationship
means risking her career...

"Ms. Craft is a master at storytelling."
—*Romantic Times BOOKreviews*

*Available the first week of October
wherever books are sold.*

KIMANI™
ROMANCE

www.kimanipress.com KPFC0371007

*No commitment, no strings, no promises...
but then love got in the way!*

LET ME Love you

LINDA WALTERS

Skye Thompson's Miami getaway brought more than
sun, sand and warm breezes...it led to steamy passion
with Dr. Terrance Marshall. Their weekend together
was just what a woman on the rebound needed—until
the unwanted complication of love interfered. But with
both living separate, busy lives in different cities, could
Skye and Terrance find a way to be together?

*Available the first week of October
wherever books are sold.*

He looked good enough to eat...and she was hungry!

The Trouble with Luv'

PAMELA YAYE

When feisty, aggressive, sensuous Ebony Garrett
propositions him, Xavier Reed turns her down cold.
He's more interested in demure, classy, marriage-
minded women. But when a church function reveals
Ebony's softer side, Xavier melts like butter.
Only, is he really ready to risk the heat?

"Yaye has written a beautiful romance
with a lot of sensual heat."
—*Imani Book Club Review* on *Other People's Business*

*Available the first week of October
wherever books are sold.*

KIMANI™
ROMANCE

www.kimanipress.com   KPPY0391007

National bestselling author

ROCHELLE ALERS

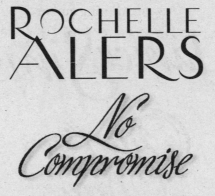

No Compromise

In charge of a program for victimized women,
Jolene Walker has no time or energy for a personal
life...until she meets army captain Michael Kirkland.
This sexy, compelling man is tempting her to trade
her long eighteen-hour workdays for sultry nights
of sizzling passion. But their bliss is shattered when
Jolene takes on a mysterious new client, plunging
her into a world of terrifying danger.

"Alers paints such vivid descriptions that when Jolene
becomes the target of a murderer, you almost feel as
though someone you know is in great danger."
—*Library Journal*

Available the first week of October
wherever books are sold.

ARABESQUE®

www.kimanipress.com

KPRA0181007

Will one secret destroy their love?

Award-winning author

Janice Sims

One fine Day

The Bryant Family trilogy continues with this heartfelt story in which Jason Bryant tries to convince lovely bookstore owner Sara Minton to marry him. Their love is unlike anything Jason has ever felt, and he knows Sara feels the same way...so why does she keep refusing him, saying she'll marry him "one day"? He knows she's hiding something...but what?

Available the first week of October
wherever books are sold.

ARABESQUE®

www.kimanipress.com

KPJS0141007

*I*t happened in an instant.
One stormy December night, two cars collided,
shattering four peoples' lives forever....

Essence Bestselling Author

MONICA MCKAYHAN

The EVENING After

In the aftermath of the accident that took her husband,
Lainey Williams struggles with loss, guilt and regret over her
far-from-perfect union. Nathan Sullivan, on the other hand, is
dealing with a comatose wife, forcing him to reassess his life.

It begins as two grieving people offering comfort and
friendship to one another. But as trust...and passion...
grow, a secret is revealed, risking the newly rebuilt
lives of these two people.

The Evening After is "another wonderful novel
that will leave you satisfied and uplifted."
—Margaret Johnson-Hudge, author of *True Lies*

*Available the first week of October
wherever books are sold.*

www.kimanipress.com   KPMM0371007

GET THE GENUINE LOVE
YOU DESERVE...

NATIONAL BESTSELLING AUTHOR
Vikki Johnson

Addicted to
COUNTERFEIT
LOVE

Many people in today's world are unable to recognize
what a genuine loving partnership should be and
often sabotage one when it does come along. In this
moving volume, Vikki Johnson offers memorable
words that will help readers identify destructive love
patterns and encourage them to demand the love
that they are entitled to.

Available the first week of October wherever books are sold.

www.kimanipress.com   KPVJ0381007